POISON IN THE PEN

Antony and his learned junior Wellesley went up to their rooms soon after eleven. "I'll see you at breakfast, I expect," Wellesley was saying, as they reached the door of Antony's room. "After that . . . I say, it's like a hothouse in here."

Antony crossed to the window. "What you really need," Wellesley said, crossing the room in his turn, "is a breath of fresh air."

Antony stepped aside and watched Wellesley put his hand up to the window catch. Then there was a sharp sound of breaking glass, Wellesley gave a grunt of pain and staggered back with a hand to his shoulder, and something heavy fell to the floor.

It lay on the floor, a piece of jagged stone, with a folded paper encircling it and fastened with a string. The message had been cut from a newspaper:

neither Shall A wicked Woman have LIBERTY to go abroad

"We best phone the police," Antony said.

LET'S CHOOSE EXECUTORS

Sara Woods

AVON
PUBLISHERS OF BARD, CAMELOT, DISCUS AND FLARE BOOKS

AVON BOOKS
A division of
The Hearst Corporation
1790 Broadway
New York, New York 10019

Copyright © 1966 by Sara Woods
Published by arrangement with the author
Library of Congress Catalog Card Number: 67-13706
ISBN: 0-380-69860-9

First Avon Printing, April 1986

AVON TRADEMARK REG. U. S. PAT. OFF. AND IN
OTHER COUNTRIES, MARCA REGISTRADA, HECHO EN
U. S. A.

Printed in the U. S. A.

K-R 10 9 8 7 6 5 4 3 2 1

"Let's choose executors, and talk of wills."
—*King Richard II*, Act III, Scene ii

TUESDAY, 28TH JANUARY

IT HAD been stuffy in the courtroom and it was a relief to come out into the open, even on that raw January day, with the sky leaden above and a chilly wind sweeping across the Market Square. Antony Maitland paused halfway down the stone steps from the Shire Hall to savor the moment, and as he stood there his mind had achieved something as near blankness as is possible to sentient man; for better or worse the case that had brought him to Chedcombe was finished, and already the arguments that had seemed so important during the last few days were fading, leaving his thoughts pleasantly undisciplined. If he was thinking anything at all it was that it would be good to be home tomorrow; and that, while it would certainly be amusing to dine again in the Bar Mess that evening, on the whole he wished he hadn't promised Wellesley he would be there.

He was about to resume his leisurely descent when a voice hailed him breathlessly from the top of the steps, and when he turned he saw a tall woman in a sack-like beige suit hurrying down to join him. It took him a moment to realize that he had seen her that morning in court, in the stuff gown of a junior barrister, and with her wig pulled down in a haphazard way over thick, untidy hair. "Mr. Maitland!" she said again; and paused a moment, panting. "Want a word with you," she added, and fixed him with an accusing eye. "Don't suppose you remember me, though."

"Oh, but I do." He hoped he didn't sound on the defensive, but he was relieved to be able to deny the charge. "Bigamy, wasn't it? Rather tricky. I was glad the Judge took a lenient view."

"So he might. Fool of a man, but meant well." An expressive gesture consigned her client, if not to oblivion, at least to some point beyond their consideration. "That's not what I wanted to talk to you about. Name's Langhorne; Vera Langhorne."

On the whole, it seemed unlikely that she had accosted him merely to identify herself. But it was cold on the steps and, after all, for today at least his time was his own. And she reminded him of someone; the likeness tantalized him, as such things will, so that he was conscious of a desire to pin the memory down. "Walk across to the George with me, Miss Langhorne," he suggested. "It's a bit early, but I expect they'll give us some tea."

"Well . . . very well." For some reason the invitation seemed to disconcert her. "You may not like what I've got to say," she warned as they reached the pavement and she fell into step beside him. "Want your help."

Maitland slackened his pace a little, to meet her shorter stride. Some point of law, he supposed, that she hadn't met before; though why she should choose him to expound it for her, in preference to one of her colleagues on the West Midland Circuit, he couldn't imagine. "Anything I can do," he promised vaguely. "What's the trouble?"

"I'm worried," she said, and something in her tone made him turn his head to look at her; her eyes met his with a sort of angry defiance, difficult to understand. "There's a girl. I don't think she's getting a square deal."

"What sort of girl?" inquired Maitland cautiously; and realized immediately that there were other questions he might have put, with much greater relevance.

"Nice girl, rather stupid. That's not the point," Vera Langhorne told him. "Have you heard about our local murder?"

"I have, indeed." The casual tone persisted, but when she made no attempt to amplify her statement she found him looking down at her again, and this time more intently. "Are we talking about the defendant?" he asked.

"That's right. I've been briefed, you know. Thing is"— she paused as they reached the door of the inn—"I don't think she's guilty."

"Let's go inside, shall we?" For a moment she stood looking at him, rather as though she hadn't heard what he said; then she turned and crossed the threshold into the dark hall. "That ought to put you in a strong position," said Antony, following her. "I expect you know this place better than I do, but the lounge on the right is quite comfortable. I'll just tell them—"

When he rejoined her a moment later she had already established herself in one of the big, chintz-covered chairs near the window, completely ignoring the invitation of the open fire. He crossed the room a little reluctantly, and stood looking out at the square for a moment before he seated himself in his turn. Not for the first time it occurred to him that there were probably more antique shops in Chedcombe than anywhere of comparable size in Britain; and here even dresses, and groceries, and household goods lurked inconveniently behind the leaded panes of original bow windows. The square was cobbled, and once a week the market was held there, though it was banished to a less central spot for the duration of the Assize; on the whole, he thought it would have been better to have found some other place for the court to assemble, for the Shire Hall, looming now on his left, was more picturesque than convenient. But the town prided itself upon its atmosphere, and even reaped considerable benefit from it during the tourist season; where even the interests of commerce were best served by stability, it was hardly to be expected that so long-standing a tradition would be changed. To complete the picture, a little stream meandered in a pleasantly purposeless way alongside the opposite pavement, causing great inconvenience to shoppers because of the infrequency with which it was bridged. All in all, a pleasing prospect, but now, in the early dusk, not so cheering as a place by the fire would have been. But Miss Langhorne had pushed open her jacket, as though she found the room overwarm.

Now that he had time to look at her he realized that the likeness that had puzzled him was to one of his aunts-by-marriage; which was odd, because she had neither Mrs. Watson's looks nor her presence. A heavily built woman, sixty at a guess, with a weather-beaten complexion and darkish hair that was liberally streaked with gray. Rather a severe expression; perhaps that was where the likeness lay, she didn't look as if she altogether approved of him. He grinned at her as he seated himself, and said, "Well, now?" invitingly.

"I find it frustrating," said Miss Langhorne, and it took him a moment to focus his mind on the point in their conversation to which she had returned. She seemed to have recovered her breath in the interval and spoke less jerkily, though the abruptness was evidently part and parcel of her style. She had a deep voice, rather pleasant, so that he thought of the local Choral Society—if there was one—and was completely, if momentarily, distracted by a vision of her in one of those long, white, nightgown-type dresses so popular in musical circles, bringing good tidings to Zion with enough volume to make the walls quiver. But he didn't have long to indulge in this impertinence. "You're not attending," she complained.

"I was just wondering," said Antony meekly, with a sad disregard for the truth, "how you thought I could help you."

"The thing is, you see, not an easy case." She was deliberately evading the question, and it was probably uncharacteristic that she should do so. "Nice girl, local family. First, old Mrs. Randall changes her will in her favor, then she dies. Can't expect the Randalls to sit down under that. They're considering what action to take—"

"I should have thought it was too late for anything but a witch doctor," said Antony, incautiously speaking his thought aloud. For some reason, Miss Langhorne's society seemed to be having a stimulating, not to say intoxicating, effect. She gave him an admonitory look and said with unnecessary emphasis:

"The will. Undue influence, that kind of thing."

"Was the girl nursing the old lady? Or acting as her companion?"

"Nothing like that. Her goddaughter. Worked in a solicitor's office." She paused, but this time Antony suppressed his impulse to comment facetiously. "I was telling you . . . before they could start anything the police moved in, arrested her for murder."

"For killing Mrs.—the old lady who made the will?"

"Mrs. Randall. Yes, of course." She paused, and leaned back in her chair, rather as though she had already said all that was of importance. "Not my kind of case," she said abruptly. "Will you take it on?"

"My dear Miss Langhorne—" The laughter in his voice was self-directed; he was fully aware of the absurdity of a situation so unconventional that it reduced him to protest. But his companion waved the objection aside.

"Know the rules," she told him. "Take care of them later, if you agree."

"But surely, if you feel that way, one of your colleagues on this circuit would be better placed to act."

"Risk of offending you," said Vera Langhorne gruffly, "all too orthodox. Now, I've heard of you."

Perhaps it was as well that their tea arrived at that moment; the elderly waiter evidently knew Miss Langhorne well, and insisted on fetching a plate of thin bread and butter to supplement the order already given. "That's what she likes, sir," he told Antony as he returned with it, and waited with an obviously benevolent intention until the first cups of tea were poured and he felt assured of their comfort.

Miss Langhorne reached out absent-mindedly for the bread and butter, but she was watching her companion as she did so. Not an easy man to assess, she thought; and certainly not at all what she had expected. A tall man, dark, his hair just springing up again into disorder now that it was no longer confined under his wig. Discount the casual manner, which was probably a pose; discount the disarming quality of his smile . . . he wasn't smiling now. You couldn't disregard his intelligence, she'd been sure of that when she observed him in court earlier in the day. For all that, she wondered if she was altogether wise . . .

"Having second thoughts, Miss Langhorne?" he asked her; and for the moment the gray eyes were amused again.

"Nothing like that," she asserted; although the question seemed to her to have all the uncanny quality of an echo.

"Well, I'm not sure what you want, you know. If it's someone to tell a sob story—"

"I told you, didn't I? I think the girl's innocent." She sounded angry now. "Can't offer any facts to back up that opinion; that's why, when I knew you were here, it seemed too good a chance to miss."

"Er—when does the case come on?"

"From the rate Halford's getting through the list, on Thursday or Friday of this week." She was sure now he was making fun of her.

"If you haven't been able to make anything of it, what do you think I can do in two days?"

She looked at him helplessly. Not the sort of man she liked, even though she had been able to admire his dexterity in court; she didn't want to plead with him, she didn't want to work with him, for that matter. She said stiffly: "Will you try?"

Maitland was frowning again as he looked at her; not exactly aware of her dislike, but knowing at least the effort it took to make the appeal. "I'm going back to town tomorrow," he said.

"Do you have to go?"

He was tempted to say he'd a case coming on immediately, and so finish the question once and for all; he wasn't even sure what scruple prevented the lie. "I suppose not," he said grudgingly.

Her unwillingness matched his own. "Always thought I knew a fact when I saw one. First time in my life, facts don't seem enough."

If she had pressed her point more eloquently, he would certainly have refused her then; instead, he hesitated. She didn't want his help, but she needed it, and not for herself. And unconsciously she added what was perhaps the one thing that could have moved him. "This girl—Fran Gifford—she's frightened; and she has no friends . . . now."

He made no immediate reply, but got up with a sudden movement and went to stand near the window again, looking out into the darkening square. It was all so long ago, but there had been a time just after the war when even to hear a key turn in a lock had been a torment. (Even in his thoughts he conceded that the word had an extravagant ring; the trouble was, it was more apt than any other.) He'd got over that, of course, he should have forgotten it too; but he wasn't a man who carried his memories lightly. So now he could think only that the girl was shut away from her fellows, with nobody to care what happened except this unlikely champion of hers, and perhaps . . . he didn't think it was very likely . . . but perhaps she had done nothing to deserve it. All he knew of the case was some idle gossip, you couldn't judge by that. But . . . "I'm bound by facts, too," he said, and managed to sound indifferent.

"I wasn't implying—" She broke off, and looked up at him resentfully. Now, what had possessed the man to shy off like that, as though she'd been trying to offend him. But it was the sense of mental withdrawal that was worrying her; she didn't realize that his mind was nearer her own now than at any time since this rather odd conversation began. She started again, carefully: "When I see a fact, I—I dragoon it. I suppose I mean, I've no imagination."

He swung round then to face her, and she was surprised to see that he was smiling. "You feel I might give the poor thing more sympathetic treatment? I think that's a fault, you know, not a virture."

Privately, she agreed with him. "Sometimes it may be necessary . . . we all have the virtues of our defects," she said.

He laughed aloud at that, and came back to fling himself down in the chair again. "At the moment, we're both being impulsive," he observed. "I'd have to see your client, you know, before I could decide."

"Yes, of course. We can arrange that when we see Mr. Davenant." She began to feel down the side of her chair, looking for her gloves, and Antony drank the rest of his tea hurriedly and passed his cup.

"Wait a bit!" he said. "You'll have to tell me—"

"I'm not trying to involve you in any irregularity. Byron and Davenant are Miss Gifford's solicitors; I've already spoken to Tommy Davenant, he'd like you to act."

"Then why—? Oh, dear!" he said; and grinned at her again, ruefully.

"Why didn't he brief someone more distinguished in the first place?"

"I only meant . . . well, you said yourself it isn't your kind of case."

"I didn't know that at first; and neither did Tommy, of course. And it was an awkward position for him, you have to admit that." She leaned forward to pass him his cup, and frowned as she noticed that some of the tea had spilled into the saucer.

"What was awkward about it?"

"The firm—Byron and Davenant—were Mrs. Randall's solicitors, and Fran Gifford worked for them."

"So?"

"Fred Byron drew up the will, he'd naturally act for the girl in any proceedings that were taken to upset it. Besides, he's the executor."

"Yes, I see."

"Well, she regards them as her solicitors, very naturally. But Fred Byron is being called for the prosecution—evidence of motive, and all that—so that's why he passed the matter over to Tommy." She paused, and then added slowly, as though doubtful of his understanding: "It might have seemed prejudicial to the public mind if the firm had declined to act altogether. And there's a good deal of hostility in the town already."

Antony was drinking his tea, and did not answer immediately. "Is that what you meant when you said she wasn't getting a square deal?" he asked presently, putting down his cup.

"That was the main reason. And also the will put people against her who should naturally be her friends. She has no family of her own since her mother died a year ago; the Randalls came closest to that, but now—"

"I see," said Maitland again. And, after a pause, "Who's prosecuting?"

"Appleton. Do you know him?"

"Only by name."

"Q.C. Capable." Antony made a mental note to pump his friend Wellesley that evening. Vera Langhorne's thoughts were clearly concentrated on one point only, the problem of getting his agreement. "If you'd walk across the square with me, we could see Tommy Davenant now," she urged. Antony came to his feet, and once more was aware of reluctance.

"You thought at first she was guilty," he said. "What made you change your mind?"

She had found her gloves, and her handbag—an unwieldy object—was standing beside her chair. There was nothing to distract her attention, but she seemed strangely unwilling to answer, and for the first time unready to meet his eye. "I haven't the faintest idea," she said at last. "But after I'd talked to her—"

He could sympathize with her there, and all the more because it was so obvious that the illogicality offended her. "Are you suggesting accident, or suicide?" he asked.

"Neither would hold water as a defense."

"Then . . . an alternative suspect?"

She shook her head, as though the thought bewildered her. "All we can do is try to—to undermine the prosecution's case."

"The equivalent of the Scottish 'not proven'?" He sounded almost angry, and perhaps it was his tone that prompted her to add defensively:

"You don't know anything about the evidence. There's nothing else to be done."

"If you're right about the girl—" He broke off, and then said less heatedly: "You spoke of public opinion. Did they fix on Fran Gifford straightaway?"

"The first story was, Alice Randall had died of a stroke after a quarrel with her grandson, Hugo. But that was before anyone knew it was murder."

"Was there a quarrel?"

"Oh, yes. She cut him out of her will."

"Weren't the police interested in that?"

"I expect so. But everyone thinks it would have been to his advantage to keep her alive, that she'd have been bound to change her mind again and reinstate him."

"I see." He wasn't quite sure what prompted him to add, "What do you think about that?" and her answer took him completely by surprise.

"I wouldn't put it past him to have killed the old lady for nothing but revenge." She paused, watching his expression. "And if you think that's unlikely, just wait till you see him, that's all."

Out in the square, the lamplighter was going his rounds. Antony was silent as they crossed the cobbles toward one of the footbridges, and then turned right, against the flow of the stream. He was thinking gloomily that there were possibilities in this affair that hadn't been immediately apparent, and wondering if his companion was really unaware of them. Not just a matter of deriding the case for the prosecution, of pouncing on the weaknesses and demonstrating them to the jury; but a full-scale defense involving a counterattack . . . the most difficult and (in a court of law) the most unpopular form of maneuver. Unless you could bring it off. But in fairness to the girl . . .

By the time they reached the elegant, gray stone house

which displayed on a neat brass plate the words: BYRON, BYRON & DAVENANT, *Solicitors and Commissioners for Oaths,* he had reached the stage of hoping, uncharitably, that if and when he saw Miss Langhorne's client he would be in no doubt at all about her guilt.

II

Inside, the illusion of elegance vanished. The linoleum was well-waxed, but inappropriate to its setting; the woodwork had a battered air; and some ill-advised person had caused the walls to be painted a hideous shade of chocolate brown to a depth of five or six feet. Above, they were a depressed and indeterminate biscuit, and undeniably grubby.

A door on the right stood open. Miss Langhorne pushed it wide, and went in: a beautifully proportioned room, with a handsome fireplace, three desks, a quantity of filing cabinets, and a large safe that somehow conveyed the impression of incredible antiquity. There were also a number of deed boxes piled up wherever there was room; and on every available surface there were bundles of papers, most of them neatly tied with red tape, others spilling out to add to the general disorder. A red-haired girl with a pleasant, freckled face looked up from her work and smiled. "Why, hallo, Miss Langhorne. We were wondering if you'd be in." Her eyes moved on to take in Maitland's tall figure in the doorway; he thought she looked startled, and nodded at her amiably. Something in the familiar atmosphere had relaxed him again, and he was wondering mainly what the sun did to her, if she contrived to be as freckled as this in midwinter.

Vera Langhorne was decisive now. "Is Mr. Davenant free? This is Mr. Maitland . . . Miss Barber," she added, looking at him over her shoulder. "Well?"

"You can go straight in, Miss Langhorne. He's expecting you."

Down the dreary hall, past a staircase that could have been a showpiece, to a smaller room at the back of the house. It was too dark now to see what lay beyond the window, but the room itself was cozy enough. A wide desk with a green-shaded lamp, comfortable leather chairs (even for clients, thought Antony, amused), and a glass-fronted bookcase whose contents any lawyer could probably have guessed at, without even glancing in its direction.

Thomas Davenant was sitting at his desk sorting cigarette cards into groups of three; he came to his feet as Miss Langhorne burst into the room, but he did not seem at all put out at being caught in this unprofessional activity. He was a youngish, plumpish man with a bristling mustache and a manner as exuberant as his figure; when he had time to look about him more closely, Antony recognized the solicitor as the one grown-up figure in several photographic groups of Scouts that hung on the walls. It couldn't be said that the uniform suited him.

The introduction was sketchily performed. Davenant looked surprised, and then—as an afterthought—gratified, and said, "Well, well, so you managed it?" as he seated himself again and pushed a cigarette box invitingly across the desk. His eyes strayed back to the cards spread out in front of him, and he picked one up from the unsorted pile and placed it beside two others. "That's a leopard," he remarked, pleased.

"Really, Tommy!" Vera Langhorne sounded revolted.

"Yes. Yes, of course. Educational, though," he added regretfully.

"Childish," she told him, not mincing matters.

"Perhaps you're right." He leaned back, and put the tips of his fingers together and coughed dryly; but his eyes were twinkling as he turned to look at Maitland. "What do you make of it?" he said.

"Precisely nothing." For some reason he had been expecting a contemporary of Miss Langhorne, and felt unaccountably put out by the discovery that he'd been about twenty years out of his reckoning.

"Hasn't Vera been telling you—?" Davenant asked indignantly. Then he smiled. "You'd like to go over the papers yourself," he suggested.

"A verbal résumé will do very nicely," said Antony, not without malice.

Davenant sighed. "I suppose there's no way out of it." He looked at Miss Langhorne. "Wouldn't you like—?"

"Leave it to you," she said, and settled herself back in her chair as though she proposed to take no further part in the proceedings. Davenant turned a hopeful eye on Maitland.

"If you've been in town since yesterday, you must have heard something," he asserted.

"An old lady died on New Year's Eve, and is alleged to have been murdered," said Antony unhelpfully. But he caught Davenant's eye, and grinned in spite of himself.

"Well, doesn't that just show you . . . they can't even get that right," the solicitor grumbled. "She certainly took the poison on New Year's Eve, but she died the following morning."

"You'd better start by telling me about the family." Maitland's tone was just a little too patient.

"That's just what I . . . oh, well!" said Davenant, resigning himself. "They own Ravenscroft, a decentish sort of house about two or three miles out of town, and I forget the exact acreage they farm, but it's quite extensive. Mark Randall died back in 1944, and Alice was his widow."

"The deceased?"

"That's right. They had three children, Allan, and Walter, and Nell. She still lives at Ravenscroft, sort of unpaid housekeeper; Walter went into Frost's Bank, and came back to Chedcombe a few years ago as manager of the local branch. He's married, but they have no family. Allan's dead, but he left three youngsters: Hugo, who took over the farm after his father's death; and Mark and Marian, who are twins and still at school."

Antony turned his head, and found Vera Langhorne's eyes fixed on him somberly. She made no sign that there was anything she wished to add to this rather bald account. "Do they live at Ravenscroft too?" he asked.

"Well, of course. Only thing to do in the circumstances, someone had to look after the twins," said Davenant. His gesture was probably intended to convey a sense of the inevitability of the decision. The leopard's hindquarters fluttered, unnoticed, to the floor.

"Not Walter," Miss Langhorne added. "He has a house in town."

"Yes, I see. So we come to the first will."

"They both had money, you know, Mark senior and Alice. She made her will after he died: the property to Allan, as the eldest son; the rest of the estate divided equally between the three of them, except for some minor bequests, that is.''

Maitland had produced an old envelope from his pocket, and was writing on his knee. "Allan . . . Walter . . . Nell," he murmured. "That made Allan's share a pretty big one, I imagine."

"The farm could be profitable," said Davenant. "At least, that's what Walter says. As for the rest of the estate, it cut up at about two hundred thousand at that time, but the value's increased since then. Alice was careful."

"What's wrong with Hugo's management of the farm?"

"Nothing, so far as I know."

"Get the impression, not doing well," Vera Langhorne put in, in her deep voice. "And that's what he told the police the quarrel was about; long-standing affair, not something that had just blown up."

"Does he—? Well, you'll be coming to that, I expect. When did Allan Randall die?"

"Six years ago, he and his wife both. Car smash," she told him. "Go on, Tommy. About the will."

"Hugo was twenty-two at the time; he'd been working on the farm since he left school, so it was natural that he should take over. Sort of bailiff, really, works on a salary; and not a generous one, if I know Alice. But the twins were—what would you say, Vera?—eleven years old at the time, and they had a home with their grandmother, and she was willing to educate them."

"A very natural arrangement." Miss Langhorne nodded her approval.

"Well, be that as it may," said Antony doubtfully, "what about the old lady's will?"

"She added a codicil to leave Ravenscroft to Hugo; Allan's share of the balance to be divided between his three children."

"If Hugo is—is twenty-eight now, and his brother and sister are seventeen—"

"I should have said, he's their half brother. Allan Randall married twice."

"And where does the girl come in . . . your client?"

"Frances Gifford?"

"I believe that's her name." As neither of his companions seemed to have anything to reply to this, he added with a shade of irritation in his voice: "You must know something about her. She worked for you, didn't she?"

"She's—you'll see her yourself tomorrow—a nice girl," said Davenant. Maitland was getting a little tired of this description. "She's been with us five years, came when she was eighteen."

"Father dead, lived with her mother. Mother died last year," Miss Langhorne put in succinctly. "Had she any money of her own, Tommy?"

"None at all. Annuities!" He produced the word forcefully and then looked deprecating, rather as though he had been using strong language. "Alice had her down for a hundred quid; matter of duty, I'd say, though Fran was friendly enough with the younger Randalls. And then what did she do but change her will—another codicil—leaving the whole of Allan's original share to the girl!"

"Including Ravenscroft?"

"Lock, stock and bl-blooming barrel," said Davenant simply.

"How did that come about?"

"Fred Byron ought to be telling you this—my partner, you know; he looked after Alice's affairs. Did Vera explain to you—?"

"That he's being called by the prosecution? She did." He looked at her again as he spoke, and again found her watching him with an oddly guarded expression.

"Well, let's get the dates right. She came in here the day after Boxing Day—Alice, that is—and gave Fred her instructions. I daresay he protested a bit, as one would. It was a rush job, anyway; that was a Friday, and he had his work cut out persuading her to postpone signing until the Monday."

"Did Miss Gifford know what was being done?"

"Not a word. Miss Barber came in on Saturday morning to type the codicil, and she and I witnessed it on Monday afternoon. At least—"

"You think she did know?"

"There's a set of her fingerprints on the draft, as if she'd put her hand down to flatten it so that she could read what it said. But she says she didn't know anything about it until old Mrs. Randall told her on New Year's Eve.''

"Tell me what happened, then. Just what you *know*. ''

"There's a dance in the old Assembly Rooms that night, everyone goes. Alice stayed home alone, and the cook was in, but she's deaf. Fran cut the dance and went to Ravenscroft instead; she says Alice asked her to keep her company . . . just like that. And one of the maids was still there, and let her in. She stayed about an hour, and her landlady says she was crying when she got back to her lodging. When the family got home the old lady had gone to bed, and they didn't disturb her, but Nell heard a noise during the night and went to her mother's room and found her in a sort of convulsion. She phoned the doctor and let him in when he came. Alice died about five A.M.''

"Didn't Miss Randall call anybody . . . her nephew Hugo, for instance?''

"I don't know." He glanced at Vera Langhorne, and added uncertainly, "It wasn't in her statement.''

"Never mind. What was the poison?''

"Foxglove. *Digitalis purpurea,''* Davenant, with an air of achievement at this difficult feat of memory.

"But—''

"You're thinking it wouldn't have been very easy, but in this instance . . . easiest thing in the world. You don't know young Mark.''

"Of course I don't," Maitland agreed tartly. "What about him?''

It was Miss Langhorne who answered, at her most elliptical. "Mania for chemistry. Brilliant future ahead of him. So they say.''

"You mean, he'd been messing about with the stuff?''

"He has a regular laboratory fixed up, can't seem to keep away from it in his school holidays. And he made this extract, this—this glycocide, whatever they call it, and was carrying it around in a test tube in his pocket, telling everyone how deadly it was.''

"And they believed him?''

"Told you, he's a genius," said Vera gruffly.

"And as it happens, he was right," Davenant pointed out.

"How did they know?''

"Because the old lady confiscated it, that's why. Read him a lecture and took it away for safekeeping. Her idea of that was to put it in her workbox; that's where it was on New Year's Eve."

"And was the workbox in the room where she entertained Miss Gifford?"

"Right beside her."

"How was the poison administered?"

"She had a cold coming on . . . Alice, I mean. Maid left her the makings for hot rum and lemon before she went out. She drank it, too, sometime during the evening, and there was digitalis in the glass. The test tube was back in the workbox, empty."

"Fingerprints?"

"Clean as a whistle."

"I see. Did no one think of suicide?"

"Why? She was seventy-five, and as strong as a horse. And she enjoyed her life."

"There was some reason for the changes she made in her will."

Davenant pursed his lips over that. "I admit, as soon as the news of her death got out it was all over town that she'd had a stroke after a violent quarrel with Hugo. But that was nonsense, of course."

"Is the quarrel, at least, a fact?"

"Vera thinks it can be taken for granted." He glanced at her as he spoke, and she nodded but did not attempt to amplify the statement. "I . . . well, I just don't know. Old ladies get some queer ideas."

"Were her wits wandering?"

"No. No, I can't say that. In any case, she was far too tough for a mere emotional upset to unbalance her."

"What does Hugo Randall say?"

"He doesn't know why she changed her will, and he was on as good terms with her as ever."

"Is he being called by the prosecution?"

"No."

"I don't like that." Maitland was frowning.

"Why not?" demanded Miss Langhorne, and he turned and smiled at her; but she had the strangest impression as he did so that he didn't see her at all.

"If it comes to the point, I should so much prefer to be able to cross-examine him."

"This nonsense of Vera's." Davenant's laugh brought Maitland back to the present.

"You don't think there's anything in it?" he asked.

"No, I don't. Where was his motive, if he didn't know of the change of will? And if he did know, he'd less reason than ever to wish her dead."

"I expect you're right." Miss Langhorne had spoken of revenge, and she didn't strike him as being an imaginative person; besides, if they were looking for an alternative murderer, the family was the obvious place to start. "We've reached New Year's Day, haven't we? Mrs. Randall is dead, and the town is gossiping. What then?"

"The doctor wanted an autopsy; it was a queer business, you can't blame him for that. And somehow he heard about the digitalis, and asked for it to be produced; once he found it was missing he'd know pretty well what to look for, I expect, but still it took a day or two. In the meantime, of course, the police started their inquiries, and the news that the young Randalls had been cut out altogether caused a stir in the family, I can tell you. I understand they consulted Neale and Tupper about contesting the will, but no action had been started when the arrest was made. That was at the weekend, the Saturday or Sunday—"

"Sunday," Vera Langhorne put in.

"Yes, well, of course, if she's found guilty—"

"We seem to have missed a point somewhere. What is the case for the Crown?"

"Motive," said Davenant promptly. "And opportunity, of course."

If any amplification were to be done, it seemed he must do it himself. "They'll say she saw the draft codicil, and knew about her inheritance," said Antony. "And then perhaps the old lady changed her mind again, and *that* was what she was telling her on New Year's Eve."

"All the indications seem to point that way."

"Including the landlady's story that she came home in tears. As for opportunity, we can't deny she was there, and the poison was handy, but—"

"You're quite right," said Davenant suddenly. "What I

didn't tell you, she left fingerprints on the workbox; and not only there, but on the kettle and all over the things on the tray—"

"How does she explain that?"

"She says she didn't stay to drink with Alice, just put things ready for her."

"What time did Mrs. Randall usually go to bed?"

"Ten o'clock, or very soon after."

"So the likelihood is, if she hadn't already drunk her hot rum she did so immediately after the girl left her, and then went straight upstairs?"

"That's the idea."

"What did they talk about?"

"Fran says Alice told her about the codicil, and that was the first she'd heard of it."

"And she went home weeping over her good fortune." His tone was sharply satirical, and Miss Langhorne came back into the conversation with an air of gloomy triumph.

"Knew you'd say that. Jury'll think it, too. Even Tommy—"

"I don't want to think ill of Fran," Davenant protested. "But you know as well as I do, one's feelings aren't a reliable guide."

"What is?" Maitland sounded casual, but his eyes were alert and serious.

"Oh, well, the evidence, I suppose."

"And do you really think I can help your client?"

"Must say, no, I don't. But I want her to have every chance."

"Yes, I see. But Miss Langhorne is quite capable—"

"Heard what he said about evidence," she interrupted without ceremony. "That's what I meant when we were talking about facts; I can't see past them." Antony was frowning again. "At least, you'll see her," she urged.

"Did I promise you that?"

"I think you did. Well, tacitly at least."

"Tomorrow, then. Can you arrange it?" he asked the solicitor.

"Yes, of course. Will you be free, Vera?"

To Maitland's relief, she shook her head. "Got to be in court," she said. "Anyway, better alone."

"Will you meet me for lunch, then?" he asked her. "I

may have some ideas, even if I do decide to take the afternoon train.''

"Very well." She got up and nodded to the solicitor, and began to move towards the door.

"Are you at the George? I'll pick you up there at ten o'clock." Davenant glanced at his watch as he rose. "Awkward journey, out to the prison. But easy enough by car.''

Antony couldn't decide whether these rather disjointed remarks were due to nervousness or whether his interest had already strayed . . . back to the half-sorted cigarette cards, or forward to the signing of his letters and the journey home. Whichever it was, it seemed to be a fairly safe bet that the solicitor was glad to see them go.

It was quite dark when they reached the street again, and the air felt damp as though it might start to rain at any time. Vera Langhorne stopped on the pavement, and gestured. "I'll say good night, Maitland. I go down North Street." He was amused to note that she had dropped the prefix to his name, once their professional relationship was established.

"Shall I see you in the Mess tonight?"

"No." The nearest lamp was some feet away, and he couldn't see her expression; he thought she sounded scornful. "My home town, you see. That's why I joined this circuit."

"Did you know old Mrs. Randall?"

"Not personally. Knew of her, of course. Active on committees . . . old people's home . . . unmarried mothers . . . that sort of thing."

"I see." He contemplated this picture, and wondered why he found it unattractive. "Popular in the town?"

"No reason why she shouldn't be. Anyway, in demand."

"Free with her money?"

"Not exactly. No harm in hoping," she told him; and, after waiting a moment to see if he had any further comment, turned and stumped away with a brief "Good night."

He stood a moment watching her, and as she passed under the light it occurred to him that the sack-like costume wasn't really warm enough for a day like this, but she had shown no signs of discomfort. He wondered what sort of a living she made; a capable woman, but that might not be enough . . .

He shrugged, and turned away, and began to walk towards the nearest footbridge.

III

He telephoned Jenny from his room at the hotel. "I may still be home tomorrow, love, but not on the early train."

"You said it would all be over today." She wasn't complaining, just stating a fact. "Or is this something else?"

"I'm not sure." She'd be sitting at the desk in the corner, he thought, and smiling at the phone as though he could actually see her; and he wondered suddenly what out-of-the-way job she had found for herself during his absence. It might be something quite appallingly complicated . . . "You see," he told her, "there's a girl."

"A nice girl?" asked Jenny; he could hear the amusement in her voice.

"So I'm told. I haven't seen her yet." He explained briefly what had happened, and Jenny said when he had finished:

"You don't sound very keen."

"I'm not. For one thing, Miss Langhorne's a genuine dragon. I don't want to get scorched."

"But you'd be leading," she pointed out.

"Don't you believe it. Nominally, perhaps . . . you know, love, it's the queerest thing, she did her best to persuade me, but all the time I had a feeling she didn't really want me to agree."

"That's just silly."

"Yes, I suppose. What are you doing tonight, Jenny?"

"Uncle Nick's taking me to the theater."

"Then you can tell him—" (Sir Nicholas Harding was not only his uncle, he was the head of chambers.)

"I will!" Jenny promised.

"And you'd better get him to ask Mallory to postpone the conference with Bellerby's client; no, perhaps you'd better ring him yourself in the morning. If I stay on here they'll have to send the papers in that malicious wounding business down to me . . . perhaps it would be best if Willett brought them by train. But I'll phone you tomorrow, as soon as I know."

"All right then. And . . . Antony—"

"What is it, love?"

"I'd like you to come home. But if you think she's *really* a nice girl, you'd better stay."

WEDNESDAY, 29TH JANUARY

IT WAS no warmer the next morning, and it had snowed very slightly overnight. In the town this had done no more than dampen the pavement, adding only a little to the disagreeableness of the day; but as they reached the outskirts the landscape took on an unfamiliar, rather makeshift air. The fields that had been plowed in autumn showed no signs of the fall, but as the road climbed steadily the close-cropped grassland was well sprinkled with white, and for a mile or so as they crossed Daneshill the roadway, too, was covered, and there had even been some drifting.

Davenant had arrived on time, driving a Humber whose heating system seemed to be functioning admirably. There was really no excuse for Maitland's gloom; if called upon to justify it he would most likely have said that his companion was too cheerful, the outlook too depressing. Not altogether an honest reply, as he liked these rolling hills. But this was an errand he always hated; he stared out of the window, and replied as briefly as possible to Davenant's attempts at conversation.

After a while, however, he was moved to comment. "Isn't it rather inconvenient, having the place as far out as this?"

"A modern prison in Chedcombe?" Davenant grinned, but he kept his eyes on the road. "We shouldn't like that at all; think of our image."

"I suppose you get a lot of visitors in summer," said Antony vaguely.

"They come in droves." He left the statement to stand alone for a moment, and then added thoughtfully: "We show them the old lockup, of course, and the stocks and whipping post. But that's different. Hallowed by time. They wouldn't like this place.''

They were running into a village now, not very different from the others they had seen except for a terrace of square, unadorned stone houses standing in seeming isolation on the outskirts; a turn in the road, and they were driving beside the monotonous length of a high wall, and presently—after a wait while the tall gates were opened—came into a courtyard very like its medieval counterpart, except that there was no feeling of life about it. Davenant's tone might have disparaged today's tendency to keep anything unpleasant out of sight, but as Antony got out of the car he felt the attitude had something to recommend it. No feat of imagination could induce the visitors to Chedcombe to take the threat of the stocks seriously; but they might very well be able to visualize themselves as temporary residents of this grim building . . . not at all the sort of idea to encourage the holiday spirit.

For the moment he had nothing to occupy his mind . . . just listen to Davenant explaining their errand, follow where they were led, and wait for the girl to join them. A smallish room with a shiny wood table and several hard chairs. He strolled to the barred window and saw that the land fell away steeply to the river, silver-gray under the sullen sky. To the right he could see the row of warders' houses, and behind them the meadows were in flood. A better prospect than rooftops and chimney pots . . . one saw the mud, the other the stars . . . and did either make any difference when the door was locked, and you hadn't got the key?

He was still standing there when the door opened and the girl came in.

His first thought when he turned to look at her was that Miss Langhorne's appraisal had been right, supposing her to mean ''nice'' in the sense of rather unimaginative respectability. Frances Gifford was small, with mouse-colored hair, thick and nearly straight, a round face, and an almost frightening pallor. The green dress she wore was the wrong shade for her coloring, and gave her a sickly look. Davenant had moved forward, introducing him, explaining his presence; a consultation? . . . well, that was fair enough . . . or could it be that the truth would serve them better? She had a firm chin, and if her lips were clamped together too tightly, that was understandable; but the solicitor, who knew her well, should have a better idea than he of her reserves of strength.

She was seated now, and Davenant had gone back to the chair he had already chosen. So far, she hadn't raised her eyes, except briefly at the first mention of Maitland's name. He stayed where he was, by the window, and said, looking down at her, "You must be heartily sick of answering questions by now."

She had brown eyes, he saw, and they met his with a startled look. Then she said, "Yes . . . oh, yes," and smiled at him. He thought it cost her a considerable effort.

"I was talking to Miss Langhorne yesterday. She asked me to help, if I can."

"She's been very kind." She was back again behind the mask of conventional politeness; he thought he had never heard a more unenthusiastic statement.

"So you see—" He didn't try to make that into a sentence, and after a moment she said gravely:

"I don't, really; but I'm grateful, of course. What do you want to know?"

"Tell me about yourself, first." Was this, after all, the best beginning? "How old are you?"

"I was twenty-three in November. There's nothing to tell," she protested.

"About your parents."

"My father was an accountant, he died just before I left school. Mother died last year; well, it was a year and a month ago, really. At Christmas."

"For someone who doesn't like answering questions," Maitland complained, "you're not making it very easy." She raised her eyes, and again there was the startled look. "If you were a little more forthcoming I shouldn't have to ask so many," he told her.

"But I don't know—" She seemed to think better of the denial. "I suppose you want to know all the same things Miss Langhorne asked me."

"I'm afraid I do."

"She seemed to think it was important, how things were left financially. And the answer is, really, that there wasn't anything to leave. Mother had an annuity, not a big one. But, of course, I was working, and that helped."

"And since last year?"

"I manage very well. My lodgings don't cost too much. I have a bed-sitting room at Mrs. Harlow's, and my meals with the family." She paused, and eyed him doubtfully. "If they ask me in court if I wouldn't have liked a lot of money, I couldn't say no!"

"Don't worry about that." He came and sat down at the table, and gave her his sudden smile. "If you said anything different, no one would believe you."

"I suppose not." Her eyes were frankly appraising now, weighing him up, wondering. He thought she relaxed a little, a very little, but he couldn't be sure. "What else shall I tell you?"

"About your job."

"But Mr. Davenant knows—"

"He's not much better at explaining things than you are," said Antony in a confiding tone.

"I don't think that's true, but all the same . . . it was my first job, you know, and I always thought I got it because of Aunt Alice really—"

"Your aunt?"

"No, I meant . . . Mrs. Randall . . . my godmother . . . I called her that."

"I see."

"Mr. Byron was her solicitor, but you know that, I expect. I felt very stupid at first, there was such a lot to learn. Not just legal things, I mean—" She broke off, and glanced at Davenant, but he was staring up at the window and seemed to have withdrawn his attention altogether from what was happening. Fran seemed to find this reassuring, and added more confidently: "Everything seems strange, when you've just left school. Afterwards, I began to enjoy myself."

"Did you work for Mr. Byron?"

"No, that was Elsie's job. Elsie Barber. I was Mr. Davenant's clerk, but when we were busy it didn't make much difference." The momentary animation died, she looked at Maitland almost with apology. "You can't possibly find that interesting," she said.

"How else do you think I'm going to find out about your background?" He hadn't expected her to try to answer that, and was taken aback when she said, with the first bitterness she had shown:

"I should have thought there'd have been plenty of people in Chedcombe who were only too ready to tell you all about me."

"I expect there are," he said coolly.

"But you prefer to judge for yourself?" The words were thrown at him like a challenge. He heard Davenant shift in his chair and said quickly, to forestall an interruption:

"I *must* judge for myself."

She flushed at that, and he thought how much better she looked with some color in her cheeks. Now, what on earth had possessed Vera Langhorne to tell him the girl was stupid? After a silence, while she seemed to be struggling with the implications of his remark, she said steadily but with unmistakable sadness: "I can't expect anything else, can I?"

Davenant exclaimed, "My dear Fran!" but they both of them ignored him.

"It's the best I can do," Maitland told her; and wondered as he spoke if he'd been right in thinking she could bear the truth. But unless she could he hadn't a hope of getting beneath the surface of her mind. Even now . . .

"I don't like being . . . something under a microscope," she burst out.

"I'm sure you don't." His tone held no trace of sympathy; after a moment she laughed, but he thought until she spoke that she was still angry. There was a hardness in her voice, but no bitterness now.

"Not your problem, Mr. Maitland? All right, go on with your inquisition."

He relaxed then, and gave her a grin. "A badly mixed metaphor, Miss Gifford. Never mind. Tell me about your friends."

"If you mean special friends . . . Elsie, I suppose. I know a lot of people, you do in a small town."

"Are you engaged to be married?"

"No."

"Or likely to be?"

"No." She didn't remind him again of her position, but something in her tone made him add:

"If all this hadn't happened—?"

"There was nobody!"

"These friends of yours, then. Are the Randall family among them?"

"I know them well." The defenses were raised again now; a quiet, reserved girl, with no sparkle about her. Was this how Vera Langhorne had seen her client?

"Were you fond of old Mrs. Randall?"

She hesitated over that. "Sort of," she said, and glanced at Tommy Davenant. He said, as though in answer to a spoken appeal:

"She wasn't an easy person to love. At least, I shouldn't think so." He paused, to think that over; evidently he had decided to accept the position into which Maitland had maneuvered him, however little he liked it. "Strait-laced," he added, at last.

"Well, was she fond of you?" Antony asked the girl.

"I don't know." Clearly, the question had never occurred to Fran Gifford before. "I ought to know that, I suppose, but I always just took her for granted."

"Then tell me about the rest of the family."

"I don't like Walter. I'm always seeing him when I go to the Bank, and he's so nice . . . condescending!"

"There are other members of the family," Antony reminded her.

"Yes, well . . . Nell's a dear," she said, "and rather fun. She was a particular friend of my mother's, that's why I know her so well."

"The others?"

"I've been wondering about Mark. He's clever, you know, and he's always wrapped up in some experiment. But it can't be easy for him, knowing the way Aunt Alice died."

"I doubt if he cares," said Davenant brusquely. "Self-centered little blighter."

"Oh, no!"

"Don't you think so?"

"Well . . . perhaps. But he can be quite kind, when he remembers."

This seemed rather a doubtful recommendation. "What

about his sister, then?'' Maitland asked. ''His twin sister, isn't it?''

''They're seventeen,'' said Fran. ''Aunt Alice said, a difficult age.''

''And is it?''

''It's just that Marian is suddenly very grown up. Not all the time, of course.''

''I thought you liked her, Fran,'' said Davenant, puzzled.

''I do. That's what I'm telling you.'' She turned back to Antony again. ''Aunt Alice was very strict, you see, and not very sensible.''

''I don't see the connection, I'm afraid.''

''She thought Marian was quite *abandoned,*'' she explained. ''And she isn't at all. Just young.''

Maitland had pulled from his pocket the ragged envelope on which he had made notes the day before. He scowled down at this and said, at his vaguest: ''That only leaves Hugo Randall, doesn't it?''

''He's very nice,'' said Fran, in a reserved tone. (That word again; it was surprising how many different things it could be made to mean.) She found his eyes fixed on her and added, as though she realized the baldness of the statement: ''He loves Ravenscroft, you know; but the farm keeps him busy.''

''You're telling me you didn't see much of him?''

''Not exactly. I told you I was often at Ravenscroft. I meant, he doesn't have too much time for making friends.''

''Or inclination,'' said Davenant.

''It's just that he—'' She broke off there with rather a helpless look.

''What, Miss Gifford?''

''I was going to say, he has to think of the twins. They're a—a great responsibility.''

''Well, how did this rather mixed household get along? It was Mrs. Randall's idea, was it, that they should all live together?''

''I don't know. It's just . . . it's always been like that.''

''If you mean, did the role of matriarch appeal to her? . . . it did,'' said Davenant. ''And you know that, Fran, as well as I do.''

She shook her head stubbornly, but why persist, after all?

She was uneasy at the mere mention of Hugo, and that was understandable enough if she felt guilty about having supplanted him. "Did you know the contents of Mrs. Randall's will?" he asked. "I mean, before she made the recent change."

"I never thought about it."

"Not even to wonder if she'd remembered you?"

"Why should she? There were so many in the family."

"Weren't you at all curious when she came to the office so soon after Christmas?"

"She often had business with Mr. Byron."

"She came in twice . . . remember?"

"Why not?"

"Well, when did you learn of the change in your favor?"

"That night . . . the night I went to Ravenscroft . . . New Year's Eve."

Maitland got up, and strolled across to the window. "Mr. Davenant explained to you, I expect, that your fingerprints were found on the draft of the codicil." He was staring out as he spoke, down at the swiftly flowing river.

"That could easily have happened, if it was lying on Elsie's desk."

"Could it? Without your knowing what it was?"

"Don't you believe me?"

"I'm asking you to explain." He turned and smiled at her. "It won't be any good your asking the Crown counsel that, you know."

"Will he ask me . . . about the fingerprints?"

"Among other things."

"Well, you see, if I wanted to find a particular document I'd know what it looked like. It might be among a whole heap of stuff, but I wouldn't have to read anything else to identify it."

"I see." He left the window and came to stand near the table again, his hands resting lightly on the back of one of the wooden chairs. "Lie number one," he said, and watched the color flame in her cheeks again. "I wonder why."

"I don't have to answer your questions," she told him fiercely.

"No," he conceded. "But it will be different in court."

"I may not go into the witness box."

"Is that what Miss Langhorne says?"

"No. She says I must. But—"

"Of course you must, Fran," said Davenant impatiently. "And none of this prevarication either."

"Well, I'm telling the truth," she persisted. "And I don't like being called a liar."

"Then tell me the truth about New Year's Eve," said Maitland. "Why did you go to Ravenscroft?"

"Aunt Alice asked me. When she left the office the day before." She spoke stiffly; he thought she was quite deliberately keeping her anger alive.

"The thirtieth? The day she signed the codicil?" He glanced at Tommy Davenant, who nodded. The solicitor seemed to have an air of indecision now. "What did she say?"

"Just that she'd be alone, and would like my company."

"And you agreed?"

"I went, didn't I?"

"That wasn't what I asked you. Did you tell her you would go?"

"Yes." She met his eyes, and added defiantly: "I said I would if I could."

"What were your own plans for New Year's Eve?"

"I don't see what that has to do with it."

"You're not going to tell me you were planning to spend it at home."

"I meant to go to the dance. We always did."

"We?"

"A party of us."

"Who?"

"Elsie, and Johnny Lawford; and Johnny's sister Margaret and whoever her boy friend happened to be at the time; and Hugo. And this year the twins were going too."

"That seems to leave you pretty well paired with Hugo. Didn't he mind being turned down?"

"Yes, he did mind rather."

"In spite of that, you went to Ravenscroft?"

"You know I did."

"To keep her company. What time did you arrive?"

"Just after nine."

"And left at ten o'clock. Hardly worth spoiling your party, was it?"

"She asked me to go," said Fran desperately.

"Yes, but why did you agree? Would she have been angry?"

"Perhaps. But I wouldn't—"

"You wouldn't have cared about that?"

"Not really. But she was an old lady, I didn't like to refuse."

"Yes, that's a good line," said Maitland admiringly. "I might even have believed it, if you'd thought of it before."

"It's so obvious," she told him. "I didn't think I need."

He grinned at that. "All right, then. How did you get to Ravenscroft?"

"By bus to the corner of the lane. Then I walked."

"Hugo Randall didn't meet you?"

Her chin went up. "Why should he? They were having supper at the Lawfords' before the dance."

"How often do the buses run?"

"Every half hour." She was eyeing him consideringly.

"Don't tell me the one before was full, and that's why you were late."

"Why not?"

"On New Year's Eve? The buses *into* town, perhaps—"

"I don't see why you should think so badly of me."

"Put it down to my rotten taste, Miss Gifford." His tone was negligent, and her eyes glinted angrily. Then she said in a small voice:

"I only meant—"

"Never mind. Did you see anybody in the lane?"

"No one at all."

"And when you got to the house?"

"Sophie let me in. The housemaid. She wasn't in uniform, and she told me she was going out but Bob was working late at the garage. And while we were talking we heard his motorbike, and she went back to the kitchen in a hurry."

"And you joined Mrs. Randall? Did you know where to find her?"

"She was in her sitting room; the room she always used. I went straight in and . . . and—"

"I'm afraid I want the details."

"Yes, of course." But she still hesitated for a moment. "She was looking rather severe, and she said 'you've come after all,' even though I'd told her I would. I stood by the fire a minute, warming my hands, and she said, 'If you want some tea you'll have to go to the kitchen. Cook's the only one at home.' She meant Cook wouldn't have heard the bell; she's very deaf."

"Did you fetch the tea?"

"It didn't seem worth it, just for me."

"So what happened?"

"I sat down, and we talked."

"What about, Miss Gifford?" He leaned forward, gripping the back of the chair. "You told the police—didn't you?—that she talked about the change she'd made in her will."

"Yes. That's true."

"What did she say?"

"She just told me. She said she hoped I wouldn't give her cause to regret what she'd done."

"And she told you why."

"No."

"You weren't curious about that?"

"Of course I was. That doesn't mean she told me."

"I thought perhaps that was why she wanted to see you."

She wasn't looking at him now; she wasn't even angry at his persistence. She said carefully: "I don't think she felt she had to explain her actions; not to me, or to anybody."

"She told you what she'd done then, but not her reasons. What did you have to say to that?"

Her hands were clasped on the table in front of her; she looked down at them now with an odd air of surprise that they were twisted so tightly together, and then she dropped them to her lap where they were hidden and couldn't betray her. "I asked her . . . to put things back as they were before." The words seemed to be difficult to find.

"A hundred pounds, instead of a fortune?"

"But it wasn't fair!" She looked up then, and met what she thought was a skeptical look, and added frantically: "Please, Mr. Maitland. You must see it wasn't fair. Whatever he'd—" She broke off with a gasp, and sat staring at him in a frightened way.

He seemed to have lost all sense of urgency now, and to be content to let the silence lengthen. Fran's eyes followed him as he went back to the window again; and Tommy Davenant watched her, frowning. "Whatever he'd done," said Antony slowly, and turned to look down at her. "Who was to blame? Hugo?"

"She was—she was angry with Mark."

"Why?"

"The digitalis, of course. She showed me—"

"Wait a minute! Is that in your statement?"

"Yes, because she asked me to pass her the workbox, and the police wanted to know why I'd handled it."

"Tell me."

"It was on the table by the window. I fetched it for her. That's all."

"And then?"

"She showed me the glass tube with some white powdery stuff in it." Her voice quivered on the words. "She said Mark had been boasting there was poison enough there to kill everyone in the house. She said she'd had enough of his nonsense, so she took it from him."

"Did she believe him?"

"Oh, yes. Anyone would who knew him. He doesn't make mistakes about things like that."

"And you want me to believe that's why she had disinherited the three of them?"

"I didn't say that."

"But it was the only reason she gave you?"

"She didn't say that was why."

"No, I forgot . . . she wouldn't tell you. Is that all you can remember of a conversation that lasted nearly an hour?"

"We talked of other things first; before she said anything about the will."

"I see. What else happened?"

"Nothing . . . nothing!"

"You know, I'm sure, that there are still more fingerprints of yours to be explained away."

"Yes."

"Tell me, then."

"She never stayed up much after ten. I said I ought to go then, the bus would pass the end of the lane at twenty past, but sometimes it was early. She'd been complaining of a cold coming on, and she asked me to mix her drink for her before I left.''

"Exactly what did that entail?''

"There was some water in the kettle. I picked it up and shook it, as far as I remember, to see how much; and then I plugged it in. There was a glass on the tray. I poured some rum into it, and squeezed half a lemon, and added sugar . . . two spoons, she said; and when the water boiled I poured that in too.''

"How much?''

"Until the tumbler was about three-quarters full.''

"She didn't ask you to share her drink?''

"Oh, no; that would have been leading me astray. She was taking the rum because of her cold.''

"And where was the test tube while all this was going on?''

"Back in the workbox, I suppose. I didn't notice . . . I wasn't very interested . . . then.''

"Did you stay with her while she disposed of this—this medicinal draught?''

"I had to wait for the water to boil; I was afraid I'd miss the bus, so I left as soon as I'd poured it out for her. She said she was going straight to bed as soon as she'd drunk it.''

"Did you see anybody as you left the house? As you walked down the lane?'' She shook her head to both his queries. "Was the bus on time?''

"I only just caught it.''

"And when you got to Chedcombe you went straight home? You didn't think of going to the dance, even though it was still quite early?''

"I couldn't do that!''

He raised an inquiring eyebrow at the vehemence of her tone. "Why not? Because Hugo was angry with you? I'm sure you could have coaxed him out of that. Because you felt guilty and embarrassed at having cut him out? Or because of what the old lady had told you?'' After each question she shook her head again, but in a hopeless way, not as if she were really concerned to deny what he was saying. When he had finished she made no attempt to speak, but raised her eyes to meet his, for the first time with a sort of appeal.

"You were crying when you got back to your lodgings," he said; and still she made no reply.

After a moment he came back to the table, and picked up the envelope he had left lying there and thrust it into his pocket. "I don't think there's any more we can do here, Davenant," he said.

The solicitor came to his feet. "I suppose you're right," he agreed.

The girl had lowered her eyes now and was studying a stain on the tabletop; perhaps someone had spilled ink there. "Mr. Maitland, what did you mean when you said Miss Langhorne had asked you to help?"

"That she wanted me to accept the brief your solicitors have offered me."

"She doesn't want to—to represent me?"

"Nothing like that . . . have you heard of 'going special'? I couldn't appear at all without her, or some other member of the Circuit."

"That's what you wanted to find out . . . if you could believe me. And now you won't be acting for me, of course."

"My dear child—"

"I don't blame you," she said resolutely; and raised her eyes to find him eyeing her with an amused look, which was the last expression she expected to see.

"And I was beginning to think you were quite intelligent," he said.

"You're laughing at me."

"Of course I am." He moved round the table as he spoke, and held out his hand. "I'll see you in court," he assured her.

"But . . . but—" She got up as she spoke and put her hand into his; but her eyes went a little wildly to her solicitor, who shrugged and shook his head, apparently disclaiming all responsibility for what was going on.

"Don't misunderstand me," Maitland told her. "I'm not under any illusions, Fran Gifford, I think you're an unholy little liar." For a moment his grip on her hand tightened; then he released her and stepped back. "Still want my help?" he asked.

He thought she was struggling between tears and anger.

After a moment she said, "I'm afraid," as though somehow this would explain everything to him.

"If you'd trust me—"

"It isn't that. I'd like you to—to act; if you really don't mind."

"Very well then." It wasn't until she was going with the wardress down the long corridor to her cell that it occurred to her that the words had somehow the sound of a threat.

In spite of the bleakness of the day, Davenant took time to mop his brow when they got back into the car again, but he didn't speak until they had turned onto the main road and were running through the village. Then he cast a sidelong glance at his companion. "You were a bit rough on her, weren't you?"

"I meant to be."

"I suppose Vera knows what she's doing."

"I doubt it. It's up to you, really, where we go from here."

"You think you can do something for Fran?"

"I hope you don't want a written guarantee. I think I should like to try."

Davenant seemed to find this unreasonable, and his voice rose a little in protest. "But you didn't believe her!"

"She told us three lies, I think . . . three lies that could convict her, because they make a nonsense of the rest of her story. But that doesn't mean she's a murderess as well."

"I've known Fran for five years," said Davenant, shaking his head. "I'm beginning to wonder if I've ever known her." He drove on in silence until they had left the village behind them, and then added, rather querulously: "I still think you needn't have bullied her so."

"All these fingerprints . . . her own admissions . . . it's a strong case," said Maitland. The tightness in his voice might have been due to anger. "But I don't just want to get an acquittal; what do you think public opinion would do to her in a place like Chedcombe? She's been hurt enough already."

"She might be lucky, at that."

"Do you think so?" But he'd known already that Davenant had no faith in his client's innocence. "Well, the only real defense is to incriminate someone else. And there's the answer to your query . . . that's a game I won't play unless I'm convinced it's justified." He paused, and added thoughtfully: "And even then it's dangerous."

"So that's why you browbeat her like that."

"Oh, for heaven's s-sake!" The tension of the interview dissolved into anger. "If it worried you so much, why didn't you stop it?"

But Tommy Davenant only shook his head.

II

He was inclined to be thoughtful during the rest of the drive back to Chedcombe, a fact which didn't altogether surprise his passenger. He had a luncheon engagement, but promised to be at Maitland's disposal as soon as possible thereafter. Antony went into the George to send a telegram to Jenny, and wait for Vera Langhorne to join him.

She was out of breath again when she arrived, so that he had the impression she must have run all the way from the Shire Hall, though on second thought this seemed unlikely. The bar looked crowded, so he steered her straight into the dining room, where they were early enough to have their choice of tables. He said, as soon as the waiter left them alone: "Have you any idea why that child is lying?"

On being asked her choice of an apéritif, Miss Langhorne had asked for a "gin and It" in rather a dashing way. Now she was eyeing her glass with an air of extreme suspicion, but she transferred her attention to her companion as he spoke. "Thought you understood," she said. "I believe her."

"Every detail of her story?"

"Why not?"

"Because some of it just can't be true."

She sipped her drink, and looked at him somberly over the rim of the glass. "I suppose this means you're catching the afternoon train," she said in a resigned way.

"If you're still of the same mind, I'm staying. Davenant's in despair at the prospect of fixing up the details, but he doesn't know the half of it yet. Mallory will probably take the whole thing as an affront to his dignity, and by the time—"

She ignored this, and interrupted him without ceremony.

"No use at all," she said bluntly, "unless she convinced you."

"I didn't say I thought she killed the old lady," he protested. "I don't. But it would be easier—wouldn't it?—if she told us the truth; or even if I knew why she lied to me."

"Think you're wrong. No reason to disbelieve her. More harm than good if you do."

Antony was silent. He already suspected that the opinion he had formed of Fran Gifford differed a good deal from the one Miss Langhorne held, Fran had probably displayed nothing during her talks with the older woman except the conventional courtesy with which she had first received him that morning. Or perhaps Vera had seen what she preferred to see; he wondered if she would feel so much sympathy for the real Fran Gifford. For himself he preferred the intelligence that had responded to his demands, her spirited reply to his criticisms; and he would have done so even if he had not also sensed under her various defenses the hurt bewilderment of a young mind coming for the first time to grips with life.

"Can see you don't agree with me," said Vera Langhorne, breaking in on his thoughts. "All the same, like you to try."

"I should like that, too."

"Any plans?"

"I'd like a view of Ravenscroft; Davenant's promised to take me out there this afternoon. Had you intended to call Hugo Randall?"

"Can't see what good it would do."

"In view of what you told me . . . what was his relationship with Fran, by the way?"

"Friends seem to have thought they'd make a match of it. Now people say she was leading him on."

"While she made up to the old lady?"

"That's right. Can't see any grounds for attacking him . . . couldn't do it, anyway, on direct examination."

Maitland smiled. "Something might be done," he said. "But I'll have a talk with Randall, if I can, and we'll decide later."

"D'you think it's wise?" She was glowering at him; then

she picked up her glass, and finished what remained of her drink.

"I don't see what else we can do."

"My idea . . . do what I could in cross-examination. Then call the girl, no one else."

"The last word might be useful, but it's a counsel of despair, don't you think?"

Again she capitulated, at least so far as to say: "Well, think it over."

"Are you free this afternoon?"

She shook her head. "Write up some legible notes and leave the papers here for you. Talk them over tomorrow morning."

"Very well." He was still puzzled by her attitude. She seemed both eager and reluctant . . . which didn't make sense.

III

As he had expected, Davenant had not yet returned from lunch when he strolled across the square at about two o'clock, and went into the clerks' office without waiting for an invitation. He circumvented Elsie Barber's attempt to show him the waiting room by seating himself firmly on the typist's chair at one of the empty desks. "Like to talk to you," he said; and was immediately diverted by this unconscious echo of Vera Langhorne's style.

The mimicry must have been more accurate than he realized. Elsie gave him a quick smile before she asked, seriously: "About . . . about Fran?"

"That's the idea." The desk at which he was seated was at right angles to the fireplace, and facing the window. He put out a hand to twist the platen knob of the uncovered typewriter. "Is this where she worked?"

"Yes, it is." She had pushed her own machine away from her, and now sat with her elbows on the desk and her chin on her hands, regarding him. There was a certain wariness in her expression, and he wondered what caused it; but she could tell him—if anyone could—what Fran Gifford was really like.

"Are you on your own now? You must be busy."

"It can't be helped, can it? We have a girl in the mornings, but sometimes I think I'd get on better alone." She paused, watching him. "Fran will be coming back," she said.

The words startled him; he had been vividly aware of the accused girl as a person that morning, but now for the first time he began to see her in her own environment, the everyday scene for which the stark backdrop of the prison had been substituted so abruptly. "Do you think she'd want to?" he asked.

"If you mean the money, I don't think she'll take it."

"I didn't mean that." The chair was quite amazingly uncomfortable. He wondered how girls managed, perched on things like this all day.

"I knew, really." She dropped her hands, and began to fiddle with a pencil on her desk. "It's just something I don't want to face . . . that she might be acquitted, and people still think she did it." She raised her head, and this time her look was searching. "Mr. Davenant's in a fuss over the details of the brief. It does mean . . . you think you can help?"

So that was something else Vera Langhorne had been wrong about, for here was one friend at least who was still concerned for Fran Gifford. But what could he say to reassure her? That it was a poor hope at best? "What's the general opinion in the town?" he asked, on an impulse.

"It's horrible, the things they're saying. As if Fran had been scheming to get the money. And, of course, they think . . . the police don't make mistakes," she added wryly. "I don't blame them, really. But I know Fran, you see."

"Do the Randall family share that opinion?"

"I've only seen Hugo. He won't talk about it at all."

"What do you think happened, Miss Barber?"

"I don't know." She sounded angry now. "Sometimes I think it couldn't have happened . . . only it did. It's difficult to see how it could have been an accident."

"Very difficult. Were you surprised when Miss Gifford didn't turn up at the dance on New Year's Eve?"

"No, of course not. I wasn't in here when Mrs. Randall spoke to her, but she told me when I came back into the office."

"Was she disappointed?"

"N-no. I don't think so."

"It broke up your party, though, didn't it?"

"Hugo was angry," she admitted. "He didn't say so, but I could tell. I think he only came because he'd promised the twins . . . well, Mark despises dancing, but Marian was keen, of course."

"Had Hugo a—a partiality for your friend?"

Elsie took her time to think that out. "He was always very possessive," she said at last, "and when a crowd of us went somewhere it seemed to be taken for granted . . . it's difficult to explain."

"And the next question's difficult to ask, so I shall have to rely on your discretion." He waited a moment, and was reassured when she did not protest her reliability. "Were you all together at the dance—say, between ten and half past? I mean, could you be sure your whole party was at the Assembly Rooms?"

Again she did not pretend to misunderstand him. "We got there about nine-thirty," she said, "and after that I never noticed the time until just before midnight. I don't think Hugo left us for any length of time, but he did go outside for a smoke once or twice, and he might have been away longer than I thought. And because I'm telling you this," she added, without change of tone, "it doesn't mean I suspect him. He'd no motive, for one thing."

"What about the new codicil to Mrs. Randall's will?"

"He didn't know about it, and if he had he'd have wanted her to have time to change her mind."

"Do you think she would have?"

"She wasn't a will-maker, you know; some of our clients make a hobby of it. But if she was angry about something— she must have been, don't you think?—she'd have been bound to cool down sooner or later."

"Were you surprised, yourself, at the change?"

"Completely surprised."

"And as far as you know she didn't give Mr. Byron any reason—?"

"He might not have told me, but he said she didn't."

"I see. Did you tell Fran Gifford?"

"Of course not." She seemed amused at her own prim

tone. "Well, it would have been most improper, you know. And Mrs. Randall was in so often about one thing and another—investments mainly—that there wasn't any need to explain."

"She might have wondered, when you'd typed the draft, why you didn't ask her to call it to you."

"She wouldn't have spent much time wondering, anyway. We were both far too busy."

"Mr. Davenant tells me you aren't being called as a witness."

"No, I can't explain at all how she could have seen it. But it could be as she says, the draft might have been among some other things and she didn't know what it was."

"Where, for instance?"

"On Mr. Byron's desk, perhaps," she suggested.

"She wasn't his clerk."

"No, but lots of things might have taken her to his room. I never knew anything about all this, of course, until after she was arrested. In fact, I'd rather taken it for granted that Mrs. Randall had said something to her on the Monday afternoon, when she asked her to go to see her on New Year's Eve. I mean, Fran could have easily said she had a previous engagement, which was true. Why should she throw up the dance, just to go to Ravenscroft for an hour?"

It cannot be said that this echo of his own thoughts gave Antony any satisfaction. "Was Hugo Randall the only man she went out with?" he asked.

"Oh, no. She went out with other people sometimes, but—"

"But—what?" he prompted as she hesitated.

"I think she liked him best."

"Are you sure of that?"

She stiffened slightly at the sudden sharpness of his tone. "I'm not sure of anything. Fran is very reserved."

"There could have been, for instance, someone you knew nothing about?"

"Of course there could. That's one of the things they're saying in the town," she added reluctantly. "But before— before all this, you know—no one seemed to think there was anyone but Hugo."

"I see. Now, about Mrs. Randall's visits to the office, I suppose it was Mr. Byron she saw."

"Yes, of course. There wasn't anything unusual about the Friday visit, except that I was surprised to see her so soon after Christmas, and she did stay rather a long time. But then I thought she'd probably come in with Hugo— Friday is market day—so she'd have to wait until he could take her back."

"Did Mr. Byron send for you straightaway?"

"As soon as she'd gone," Elsie said. "I could tell he didn't like what she'd done, and he said he thought she might very well change her mind. So it would be very undesirable if Fran heard anything about it, he wouldn't like to raise false hopes. Well, I wouldn't have told her anyway; but I was specially careful with my notes, and the draft, and everything."

"You said," he prompted, "that there was nothing unusual about the Friday visit."

"Well, on Monday I was watching her more closely, I suppose. I couldn't think what had happened to make her cut out Hugo and the twins; I think I felt I must be able to tell something by looking at her."

"And could you?"

"She was always very polite, you know, but rather unbending. I thought perhaps she seemed even stiffer than usual, that day. She didn't say a word when Mr. Davenant and I went in to witness her signature, except 'Good afternoon' to him—she'd seen me before—and 'Thank you' to both of us when it was done. And when Mr. Byron started to ask her again if she was *sure*, she interrupted him quite sharply and said that nothing would alter her decision."

"Might not Fran have guessed from the fact that you were both called in—?"

"Oh, I don't think so. She might not even know Mr. Davenant had gone up to Mr. Byron's room."

"Did Mrs. Randall leave immediately after the codicil was signed?"

"No. I came away, and after a few minutes I heard Mr. Davenant come downstairs and go into his room. And almost immediately after that Mr. Byron rang for me, and when I got into the hall they were already halfway down the stairs. He said, 'I'll leave Mrs. Randall with you, Elsie,' and she never looked round or said good-by. I think he'd been trying again to make her change her mind, and that had offended her; and it might very well have decided her to tell Fran, just to be awkward.''

"Yes, I see. But you weren't in the office when she spoke to her?''

"No, I wasn't. Mr. Byron went back upstairs, and she stood at the bottom with her hand on the rail and looked ever so queer. So I asked her if she'd like me to bring her a cup of tea to the waiting room, but she said she was quite all right, she just wanted a word with Fran. So I went back and got some papers off my desk that Mr. Byron wanted and took them up to him; and when I came down again she had gone.''

"Did Miss Gifford tell you what had passed between them?''

Elsie shook her head. "Only that she might not be going to the dance after all, because Mrs. Randall wanted her to keep her company. And in the ordinary way, of course, I'd have said something, but everything was so queer I thought perhaps I'd better not try to persuade her, so I just asked if Hugo knew. She said, 'I shall tell him,' and began to type rather fast, as if she was angry. I went on with my work, too, and didn't ask her any more about it.''

"Was anything said next day?''

"Not a word. I was frightened of putting my foot in it; I mean, it *was* awkward. Fran was a bit quiet that day, but nothing out of the ordinary. And when we left she just said she hoped I'd have a lovely time, so I knew she hadn't changed her mind about coming.''

"When did you hear of Mrs. Randall's death?''

"About eleven o'clock on New Year's Day. I think it was Miss Randall who phoned Mr. Byron, and he went out to Ravenscroft straightaway; he just stopped in here for a moment to tell us.''

"How did Miss Gifford take the news?''

"She didn't say anything until he'd gone, and then she said, 'Oh, no! Oh, no!' over and over again, as if she was talking to herself. But you know, it must have been a shock to her, when she'd been with the old lady only the evening before. We didn't know then that Mrs. Randall had been poisoned; in fact, I didn't know that until the weekend, when the news got out that Fran had been arrested. And that seemed impossible, too.''

"I expect it did.'' He put the envelope on which he had been making a few indecipherable notes back into his pocket, and started to talk to her about life in Chedcombe. Five minutes later Tommy Davenant arrived back from his lunch.

IV

Ravenscroft lay southeast of the town, not more than three or four miles distant. It had started to snow again, though in a halfhearted way, just enough to make the road slippery. Davenant concentrated on his driving, and maintained an unbroken silence until he slowed to turn left from the main road into a narrow lane. "This is where the bus stops,'' he said. "Where Fran got off that night, and caught the ten-twenty into town after she left Mrs. Randall.''

"Do the conductors remember her?''

"There's just the driver, you pay him as you get on. They both knew Fran by sight, and remember seeing her on New Year's Eve. Not that that helps anybody, you know.''

"I just wondered.'' Maitland was at his vaguest. "We must be nearly there.''

"This is all Ravenscroft land.'' Davenant gestured with his right hand. Peering across him Antony could see a hedge, neatly laid, with a plowed field beyond. A moment later they were turning into an open driveway, well ditched at either side, with hedge and fence still in good order. The ground rose gently toward the house, more steeply beyond it where some sheep were grazing. There was nobody in sight, but in spite of this and the bleakness of that January day, there was no mistaking that the farm was alive, well cared for. Maitland left this fact for later consideration and looked forward through the windscreen toward the house.

A long building of gray stone, with leaded windows and a heavy oak front door. "Inconvenient,'' said Davenant, confirming Antony's thought, and braking a little too suddenly to bring the car to a halt in a convenient position. "But the individual rooms are comfortable enough."

"Where are the farm buildings?"

"At the back. The house is bigger than it looks . . . deeper. The rooms at the back are the kitchen quarters and the estate offices, with a door into the yard. In spite of its size, it's a farm first," he added.

"Yes, I can see that." They were both out of the car by this time, and Davenant went up to the door and banged the knocker. There was a pause after that, while the echoes died slowly, and Maitland had time to appreciate how quiet the countryside was around them; and to think—rather fancifully—that the house seemed to be holding its breath. Then the door was opened by a pretty woman with curly dark hair, and after a moment's hesitation she said, "Oh, it's you, Tommy," in a tone of relief, and pulled it wider.

"I'm sorry to bother you, Nell." Davenant stepped into the wide hall, and Antony followed and looked about him curiously. Paneled walls and a flagged floor with a good rug at the center; a degree of warmth and comfort beyond what he had expected. "Antony Maitland, one of Fran's counsel," the solicitor said, and paused as though he expected some protest; or at least, a question. When none came he added perfunctorily: "Miss Nell Randall," without turning his head. "Maitland wants to have a look round, Nell. And we'd like to see Hugo."

She was older than he had thought at first glance, but perhaps even more attractive; a slender woman with clear gray eyes, and thin expressive hands. She said now, breathlessly, "I'm sorry, I think he's about the farm somewhere," and sounded as though she was really distressed. "I'll go and find him, shall I?" she added, more hopefully, looking from one of them to the other.

Maitland contented himself with smiling at her; Davenant said again, "I'm sorry," which she interpreted, correctly, as an affirmative.

"Come in and wait," she told them. But when she started to move toward a door at the right of the hall, Tommy Davenant called her back.

"We'll look at the little sitting room while you're gone, and then wait for Hugo in the study, shall we?"

"Yes . . . of course. You know your way." She had an indecisive manner of speaking, and when she had finished she seemed to drift away from them as though she had no fixed intention of going.

"Damned awkward position," said Davenant, as a door at the back of the hall closed behind her. He sounded angry. Then he said, more purposefully, "We have to go through here," and turned left into a long room whose furniture was shrouded in dust sheets, crossed it briskly to the far end, and threw open a second door with a gesture. "This is where the old lady used to sit."

Antony followed more slowly, and stopped altogether when he noticed a framed photograph over the white-painted mantel. "Alice Randall?" he said.

Tommy came back to look. "That's the old girl," he assented. "Had it taken a year or so ago . . . Walter's idea, or so I understand." He watched Maitland's expression and his gloom seemed to lighten. "Proper old battle-ax, wouldn't you say?"

"I would indeed." A handsome, stern old lady, tight-lipped and cold of eye, her hair dressed neatly but with no concession to the style of a later day than her own. A fanatic, at a guess, the question was . . . "Was she really like that, or is it just how the photographer caught her?"

"It's an excellent likeness, the one she chose herself."

"I see. And that's the old lady you think would have changed her mind again?"

"She'd changed it once," Davenant pointed out.

"There must have been some very good reason." Something was bothering him, he seemed reluctant to leave the picture; but presently he sensed his companion's impatience and followed him through the door.

The little sitting room had a desolate air. It had obviously been cleaned after the police finished their activities; equally obviously it had not since been used. The big room they had passed through was waiting for an occasion that would inevitably arise to bring it back to life; the little room at the corner of the house had died, he thought, of despair. He found the idea disagreeable, and altogether too fantastic to be seriously entertained. And yet it stayed with him and would not be quite forgotten, even after they had left Ravenscroft and he was back in the solid, no-nonsense atmosphere of his room at the George.

He set himself to look around appraisingly, ignoring his uneasiness. An old lady's room, comfortably and not very tastefully furnished; probably refurnished, in fact, for Alice Randall when she came to the house as a bride. Maitland came halfway across, and stood staring down at the grate where a fire had been relaid; Davenant thought his expression sardonic, as though there was some wry amusement to be found in the situation, and hurried into speech as if the silence made him, in turn, uneasy.

"Mrs. Randall sat on the sofa there, the corner nearest the fire. That's what Fran says, and it was her usual place. Fran had the chair opposite, and the tray was on that small table, which had been pulled up close; and the kettle had been plugged in down there, also on her side of the hearth. But she doesn't deny all that, of course."

"No," said Antony, not very encouragingly. His eyes were busy. "I wonder where the workbox was put down while they were looking at the test tube."

"Fran couldn't remember. Beside the old lady on the sofa, I should think; that's where it was next morning."

"But nothing to show the test tube wasn't on the tray, for instance, while the toddy was being prepared." He pulled the inevitable envelope from his pocket, and went across to the old-fashioned bureau to use its surface to write on. "I'm told Appleton's good," he said, stooping.

"He won't miss any points," said Davenant gloomily, "if that's what you mean."

"It is, and I was afraid of it. There's material for a very graphic picture of what went on in this room that night; but I daresay you realize that."

"I didn't know if you did," said Davenant, with uncharacteristic bluntness.

"Because I believe our client when she says she's not guilty?" He straightened his back, and folded the envelope carefully. "It's damnably tricky, and I realize—I assure you—exactly what we're up against." He looked round the room again, and said more briskly: "Let's get the hell out of here!"

They got no farther than the hall when a girl came out of

the room opposite, and stood waiting for them to come up to her. A very young girl, as dark as the woman they had seen before, with a thin face, an eager expression, and restless movements. "Hallo, Tommy darling," she said. Antony wondered briefly whether there was anyone in Chedcombe and district who addressed the solicitor with any formality.

"Oh, hallo, Marian," said Davenant, without enthusiasm.

"I heard you were here. How's Uncle Freddy?" This was said with a sidelong glance, and it was so obvious she was trying to get a rise out of him that Maitland was surprised at the violence of his companion's reaction.

"That's a new one! Mr. Byron to you, my girl."

"He's going to marry Nell, isn't he? Won't that make him my uncle?"

"Nonsense!" said Davenant shortly.

"Is it? Is it, really?" The dark eyes were mocking, but after a moment, seeming abruptly to lose interest, she left the doorway and moved nearer to them, eyeing Antony with open curiosity. "Is this . . . Fran's *new* lawyer?" she asked, after a further hesitation apparently dedicated to the discovery of the *mot juste*.

Davenant ignored this. "Run along, there's a good girl," he told her.

"Don't be so stuffy, Tommy. I must say," she added, looking at Maitland and ignoring the lack of introduction, "I shall be very glad if you can help Fran. Things have been perfectly horrid, ever since Mark started to have a hate against her."

"Ever since Mark—?" said Davenant incautiously, his voice rising to an outraged squeak. "Don't be so silly!"

"If anyone's being silly," she flashed at him, "it's you!" She seemed to recollect herself and added, with a dignity that bordered upon the absurd: "If you'd read any psychology you'd know he has a guilt complex. I mean, he has to blame *someone* besides himself for Granny's death."

"Does he blame himself?" Davenant asked her.

"He wouldn't admit it, of course," said Marian, still in a very grown-up way. It struck Antony that she didn't seem particularly concerned, either about her grandmother's death or her brother's alleged emotion. "And now he says

it's all Fran's fault, and she must have wheedled Granny
. . . which she wouldn't. Though I must say it's very awkward,'' she went on, thoughtfully, ''not having any money,
or even a real home.''

The solicitor seemed to be struggling with embarrassment; Maitland thought it was time he took a hand. ''How
did you know who I am, Miss Randall?'' he asked her.

She turned to him eagerly; obviously it was not to talk to
Tommy Davenant that she had waylaid them. ''I don't know
your name,'' she admitted. ''But Walter told us . . . someone from London, he said, with a big reputation. And I must
say I thought you'd be older, but you look very like a lawyer.''

The sudden change from adult to child was bewildering,
but disarming too. ''It's very important to look the part,'' he
assured her.

''You can laugh if you like,'' she said, but without resentment. ''Walter said you'd be sure to come here, and he told
Hugo he'd better watch out because you might not be so easily satisfied as the police. But really, you know, the quarrel
he had with Granny was nothing out of the ordinary.''

''Old ladies,'' said Antony with apparent sympathy, ''are
often very difficult.'' Now, what was she trying to tell him:
about the quarrel, in case he hadn't heard of it, or did she
really want to assure him that it wasn't worth his consideration?

''Well, Granny was,'' said Marian. ''But, of course,
she'd have changed her mind again . . . about leaving Ravenscroft to Hugo, I mean. Which is really more important
than anything, because—'' She paused, and looked rather
apprehensively toward the back of the hall. ''There's Hugo
coming,'' she said, and immediately was poised for flight.
''He's *all right,* you know,'' she assured Maitland earnestly, ''even if he is positively archaic.'' And with these
words she disappeared without further ceremony up the
staircase. Antony had the impression that she paused at the
top, listening, but he couldn't be sure of this.

The door at the back of the hall had opened, but no one
had as yet come through. They heard Nell's voice, high-
pitched with agitation, ''But, Hugo, you must tell him . . .

you can't let him think—'' and a man's deeper tones answering her savagely.

"I'll tell him what I please. For God's sake, Nell, shut up!"

The door slammed open against the paneling and a dark young man came through into the hall with a black and white sheep dog at his heels.

V

It could not be said that the newcomer regarded either of the visitors with any great degree of amiability. In fact, he reminded Antony (who had seen a revival of the film version of *Wuthering Heights* not long before) of nothing so much as Olivier playing Heathcliff; there was the same lowering look, the same air of bewildered resentment. Davenant started an introduction, but this was waved aside as unnecessary, as indeed it was. "I've talked to the police," said Hugo Randall violently, "and I've talked to that woman you brought here, and I haven't anything to say that's to the point."

"The thing is," Maitland told him apologetically, "I've a weakness for seeing for myself. And hearing, of course."

Hugo seemed to find this mildness disconcerting. "I might have known you'd pull some trick like this," he said to Tommy Davenant; but he spoke now without rancor, and turned his head so that his eyes met Antony's with an oddly searching look. Perhaps he expected some further attempt at persuasion; when nothing was said he shrugged his shoulders and gestured curtly toward the door at the right of the hall. "We shall be more comfortable in the study," he remarked. "And more private too, if you think that's any consideration."

Davenant seemed to be momentarily at a loss; Maitland had his amused look again as he stepped back to allow Randall to precede him. The sheep dog looked up at him with wise brown eyes as she went past.

The study was a pleasant room, with books along one wall, chintz-covered chairs, and such varied signs of occupation as an untidy heap of magenta knitting, a woman's magazine lying open on the sofa, and a number of copies of the *Farmers' Weekly*, unmistakable in their yellow covers, strewn in disorder across the top of the wide desk. There was an outsize hypodermic on the coffee table, along with a machinery catalogue from a well-known firm; and the wall opposite the window had been wholly given over to display purposes, having a fine crop of rosettes of various colors and a number of silver trophies set out on brackets that had a decidedly homemade look. The desk was the only relic, perhaps, of the room's original purpose; there were plenty of books, but they had a jolly, almost rollicking air about them, in no way consonant with the word "study."

Hugo picked up the tangle of knitting from one of the chairs, eyed it moodily for a moment as though wondering whether the so far anonymous garment might, by some mischance, be intended for him, and then dumped it ruthlessly on the floor. He waved a hand in negligent invitation before seating himself. "I can't stay long," he told them. "Here, Floss!" He snapped his fingers, and the dog lay down at his feet.

"I'd hoped that at this time of year—" Maitland was at his vaguest.

"I've a sow pigging," said Randall shortly. "She won't stand Ken near her. And if you're thinking it's bad management to have her farrowing down at this time of year," he added belligerently, "I'm short of space and it can't be helped."

There had indeed been an inquiring gleam in Maitland's eye. If the way to this abrupt young man's heart was through a discussion of his stock, he was only too ready to oblige. "What breed?" he asked.

"Saddlebacks. They're hardly . . . well, they've need to be." He didn't sound as though he took much pleasure in the thought. "And if this goes on—" Antony followed his glance at the window, and saw the snow still falling gently.

"Too early in the year," he agreed, "to have to start foddering your sheep."

But Hugo was not so easily to be diverted. "You didn't come here to talk about the farm," he asserted, almost as surlily as before. Maitland grinned at him.

"Or to help with the milking. How did you guess?"

He thought for a moment he saw an answering smile in

Randall's eyes, but when Hugo snapped, "Well?" his tone was not encouraging.

"There are a number of things I have to ask you," said Antony, reverting to the diffident tone he had used before. "And I'm sorry if you find the repetition boring, but perhaps before we're through we'll break new ground." He paused, looking down at the fire. "When did your brother first introduce the digitalis into the family circle?" he asked, almost casually. And raised his eyes to Randall's face again.

"If you've read his statement you must know the answer to that. And it wasn't digitalis, it was digitoxin . . . or so he says."

"I'm asking you when first it came to your notice."

"On Boxing Day." He broke off there, but when he saw that Maitland was evidently prepared to let the silence lengthen he added reluctantly: "He pulled it out of his pocket at teatime . . . the little fool."

"Mrs. Randall was not amused?"

"Of course she wasn't! She read him a lecture and took it away from him." Again there was a pause. "We all saw her put it in her workbox," he said, as though in answer to a further question.

"It didn't occur to you it might be better destroyed."

"You didn't know my grandmother. I really had no say in the matter." He didn't like the subject; his voice had a ragged sound. "And I didn't know—how could I?—what was going to happen."

"Do you know now, Mr. Randall, exactly what occurred?"

"I know she's dead!"

"And you were in no doubt as to the deadly nature of the—er—preparation?"

"Mark said it was enough to kill the whole household. He doesn't joke about things like that; and he doesn't make mistakes."

"Wasn't it a joke, that he had it at all; or, at least, that he showed it to you?"

"Yes, of course. I meant, he wouldn't joke about—about its properties."

"I see. You quarreled with your grandmother, didn't you? When was that?"

"Often," said Hugo, with an air of gloomy triumph.

"Thank you. I wasn't aware of that." His tone was bland, and Randall's scowl deepened. "I meant, as I'm sure you know, during the Christmas holidays."

"Well, then, on Christmas Day. Any of the servants will tell you."

"What was the cause of the disagreement?"

"That's nobody's business but my own." He wasn't even trying to disguise his hostility. "The police asked me all this," he said, "but they know . . . everyone knows . . . it happened all the time."

"On this occasion, it seems, Mrs. Randall took the fact more seriously. Did she tell you she was going to change her will?"

"She did not."

"Did you, in fact, know it?"

"How could I? I told you she never said a word."

"Someone else might have informed you. Miss Gifford, for instance."

"She says she didn't know." He got up with an abrupt movement, stooped to throw a log on the fire, kicked it into place, and then stood gloomily regarding his handiwork. But Maitland's silence seemed to annoy him even more than the questions had done; he whirled round suddenly and said in an angry tone: "You're her counsel, aren't you? That means you've got to believe her!"

"You're making me curious, Mr. Randall. Do *you* think she's telling the truth?"

"How should I know?"

"You're a friend of hers, aren't you?" He was quickening the pace a little; the casual pose had served its turn.

"I suppose I was." By contrast, the reluctance in Hugo's voice was very marked.

"You were taking her to the dance on New Year's Eve."

"Yes."

"When did she tell you she didn't mean to attend?"

"She phoned me, the evening before." He hesitated. "I went into town to meet her. There's a shop that stays open, we had coffee there sometimes."

"What did she say?"

"Just . . . she was coming to Ravenscroft, not to the dance."

"You didn't question her decision?" Hugo sat staring at him, making no attempt to answer, and after a moment he twisted the question slightly. "Didn't you feel she was letting you down?"

"It was her affair, what she did. I wouldn't have gone at all if I hadn't promised Marian."

"Ah, yes, your sister. Did Mrs. Randall approve of her going to parties?"

"Good God, why should I have to answer all these questions?"

"Because if you don't I shall probably ask them in court," said Antony literally.

"But I understood . . . you told me, Tommy—"

"Changed my mind," said Davenant, with an echo of Vera Langhorne.

"So there you have it. As for the questions, it's only fair to say I may ask them in court in any case," Maitland added, with a show of honesty. And, surprisingly, Hugo laughed.

"Well, Grandmother didn't approve . . . of course she didn't. But it was my affair, not hers. I couldn't stop her saying what she thought, but I didn't let it affect what I did. Well, not often."

"In the circumstances that have been described to me—" said Maitland carefully.

"What does anyone know of the circumstances? It wasn't charity, if that's what you're thinking; she *needed* me. And as for what she did for the twins, I earned that, every penny of it."

"What did she do for them?"

"Fed them, clothed them, educated them." The words were thrown out defiantly. "Mark will get scholarships, I daresay, but he's erratic. I couldn't let him depend on that; besides the right place is important, he's clever, you know."

"So I've been told."

"Brilliant," said Tommy Davenant, suddenly re-entering the conversation. For a moment, Hugo seemed almost startled by the interruption, then he relaxed and went back to his chair again.

"That's what they tell me," he said. "I suppose it's a good thing, but it's a bit trying at times. He gets so fed up during his holidays." His glance flickered to Davenant's face, as though he expected—or perhaps even feared—some comment, but the solicitor was silent. Antony said, after a moment:

"And Marian . . . is she a student too?"

"Well, she's still at school. She says she finds it a dead bore."

"No need for further education in her case, then."

"A girl needs different things."

"Do you know what they are?"

"Of course I don't." He glanced uncertainly at Davenant. "And Nell knows about as much as I do about coping with a couple of teen-agers."

"More . . . surely?" said Tommy, shaken out of his silence again.

"It isn't that I'm not grateful to her. These last years, she's only stayed here because of the twins. One thing, Marian won't go over the line, I've told her . . . never mind!" He broke off, compressing his lips tightly and scowling at Maitland as if he had committed an indiscretion for which the other man was to blame. "You can't be interested in all this," he said.

"I don't know what I'm interested in . . . yet," Antony told him, with truth. "Is that why you stayed here when your parents died?"

"Not altogether."

"Well?"

"If you're determined on accuracy, you should have said, 'when my father died.' He divorced my mother when I was two years old, and as far as I know she's still alive."

"I see."

"As for why I stayed, it was my home, wasn't it? The farm needed me . . . I never owed her a thing." The bitterness was back in his voice again; full measure, pressed down and running over, thought Antony . . . and *that* quotation's got out of context somehow.

"And now?" he asked quietly.

"I'm not whining about what's happened. We'll manage."

"You knew about the previous will?"

"Oh, yes. She told me, when my father died."

"Did you drive your grandmother into town when she went to see her solicitor?"

"If you mean, during the last week, I took her on the Friday. I believe Nell drove her on the Monday."

"And still she told you nothing of her intentions?"

"I didn't even know she'd seen Byron. I dropped her at the Bank just after ten o'clock, and picked her up, two hours later, at the teashop."

"But later . . . you were contemplating some action, weren't you, to upset the will?" Hugo eyed him stonily, and he added in a sharper tone: "Isn't that right?"

"Have it your own way," said Hugo, shrugging. Then he suddenly burst out, as though a sense of grievance overcame him: "It was Walter's idea. When I knew he'd taken advice I told him I wouldn't have a thing to do with it. I meant it, too."

"So if Miss Gifford is acquitted you'll do nothing about the codicil?"

"I didn't say that. It's different now."

"In what way?"

"That won't help you, if you're working for Fran."

"If you've changed your mind there must have been a reason."

"Well, there is, but I'm not telling you that."

"You think, after all, Fran Gifford cheated you in some way?"

"I don't know! How can I know?" He was in earnest suddenly, desperately and unmistakably in earnest; and for the first time he spoke, Antony thought, without any consideration for the consequences of what he said. "I only know she turned on me like a tiger-cat and said she'd fight any action that was brought, every inch of the way."

Maitland glanced at Davenant, and met a look as startled as his own. "When was this?" he asked.

"The day after Grandmother died."

So much then for the girl's protests that Alice Randall's action hadn't been fair, that she had asked her to restore the position as it had been before. If Hugo was to be believed . . . but, "wait till you see him," Vera Langhorne had said. Revenge was an ugly word, he wasn't quite sure whether it was too ugly. "Why do you suppose she did that?" he asked.

Hugo shrugged. "Some man, of course." His tone was carefully casual.

"Can you suggest—?"

"How should I know? But what else can I think? There must be someone." His lack of interest didn't quite ring true. "Fran would never—"

"You think she isn't interested in money?"

"I didn't say that." The statement had an air of finality.

"That brings us back, then, to the quarrel you had with your grandmother," Antony said.

"That's queer," said Randall. "That's damned queer, when you come to think of it." He spoke slowly, as though he was thinking something out.

"What is?"

"Oh . . . the row we had?" He seemed to recall the question with difficulty. "If you want to know what I think, Walter'd been making mischief."

"Your uncle?"

"That's right. He wouldn't have been sorry to have stirred up trouble. But that doesn't explain—" He was still thoughtful. The sentence trailed off, uncompleted.

"Something you'd done, then, that your uncle knew about," Antony prompted after a while; and saw Hugo return to reality with what was obviously a sense of shock.

"I've said too much already." The sulky look was back again, his voice was bitter. "You've a damned insinuating way with you," he added, disagreeably. Davenant clicked his tongue in a reproving way, but Maitland met Hugo's belligerent stare serenely.

"It's really awfully easy to tell the truth," he said. "You must try it some time."

Randall ignored this, unless the angry gleam in his eye could be regarded as an answer. He said, much more quietly: "Why do you want my evidence?"

"I'm trying to prove Fran Gifford's innocence. Why

else?" He chose his words deliberately, and thought for a moment he was going to get a reaction. But Hugo only said:

"I don't see how I can help you."

"Perhaps you will, when you think it over." Maitland got to his feet as he spoke. "I mustn't keep you any longer from that sow of yours," he said, "but there's one thing I wish you'd tell me. What was Mrs. Randall really like?"

Hugo frowned. "She had her own ideas," he said shortly.

"Yes, I've gathered that. But I expect, like most of us, she was more tolerant on some points than on others. If there was one particular sin she abominated, for instance, what would you say it was?"

There followed a silence. Hugo's face was completely expressionless now. He sat looking up at Maitland and for a moment there wasn't even anger in his eyes, just a sort of flat despair; then he got up with one of his sudden movements.

"I have to go," he said. And without any further word of farewell marched out of the room with Floss at his heels, leaving the door wide open behind him.

Antony looked at Tommy Davenant, who was still seated and had rather a stupefied look on his face. "I can't help feeling that's a hint," he remarked. "We seem to have outstayed our welcome."

VI

Very little was said between them until they were back in Davenant's office, and Elsie Barber had brought them tea. Antony pulled his chair away from the desk and nearer the fire, and left his companion to look through the various papers that had accumulated in his absence. He was perfectly well aware that Tommy would have been glad to be rid of him, and he was willing to allow him a reasonable degree of latitude. But certain questions were going to be asked—and answered—before they parted company.

Perhaps Davenant realized this, perhaps he was merely unnerved by the other man's apparent calm. He pushed the papers aside at last, picked up his teacup, and asked fretfully: "Do you think all that was helpful?"

"Who lives may learn," said Maitland, and wasn't in a hurry with his next remark. "I didn't realize how well you knew the family at Ravenscroft."

"Well, you see, it's Nell," Davenant told him, as though that explained everything. "I told you the situation was awkward, but as things were, Byron felt we could hardly let Fran down."

"No, I see that. But perhaps you can tell me what Hugo meant when he said Miss Randall only stayed at Ravenscroft because of the twins."

"Just what he said. The old lady was difficult; I doubt if Nell would have stayed purely out of affection for her."

"A sense of duty, perhaps?"

"That didn't enter into it. It was convenient for Alice to have her at home, but Nell wasn't in any way necessary to her."

"I see." He was thinking that there might have been other factors, of which the solicitor knew nothing; that perhaps Hugo might have said, with greater truth, "she meant to stay at Ravenscroft until the old lady died." Perhaps something of this was reflected in the dryness of his tone. Davenant said quickly:

"It wasn't that she had no chance to get away. I happen to know—" He caught Maitland's eye and grinned sheepishly.

"An offer of a job . . . an offer of marriage?" Antony suggested, watching the other man's expression.

"Well, I do know what I'm talking about as a matter of fact," said Tommy, suddenly becoming voluble; though whether he felt a genuine urge to confide in his companion or merely despaired of the success of his evasive tactics, Antony couldn't decide. "She always said she couldn't consider getting married, not until the children left school. At least, I hope that's what she said. Because if she meant 'finish their education' it's all up. Young Mark looks to me like the sort of chap who'll spend so much time learning things he'll never have time to do anything at all."

For some reason, Maitland had put the solicitor down as a family man of long standing. "Is your partner a bachelor, too?" he asked, deliberately tactless; it seemed too good an opportunity to miss, to get a little information about Frederick Byron, whose character so far remained an enigma.

"He is," said Davenant. "My wife died five years ago
. . . cancer, poor girl." But his mind was still on the question. "He's a good-looking chap, mind you," he added,
with an obvious desire to be fair, "but fifty-five if he's a
day. A woman Nell's age doesn't need an older man." He
paused, brooding. "I think that wretched girl was just trying
to get a rise out of me, don't you?"

"I'm quite sure she was," Antony told him soothingly;
which was true, but the teasing remarks might still have had
some substance. He did not think, however, that his companion was in any real doubt as to Miss Randall's feelings,
and this was confirmed when Davenant said ingenuously:

"Lately I've rather thought Nell was weakening. About
waiting, you know. I haven't much time for all this self-sacrifice myself."

"A sad mistake. Do you agree with our client's estimate
of Marian's character, by the way?"

"She's flighty, but I don't know any real harm in her,"
said Tommy grudgingly. "And she seems a good friend to
Fran."

"Is Mark like his sister?"

"Same type, a little taller. And if you're going to say next
that everyone seems to have taken his part in all this without
turning a hair, I can only tell you it's nothing to be surprised
at. He's always messing about with chemicals, doesn't seem
to be interested in anything else."

In that case his likeness to Marian could be no more than
skin-deep. The girl was at a restless age, ready for any mischief; and from what he had heard of Nell Randall and the
little he had seen of her, Maitland wondered if she had any
idea at all of the explosive nature of the material she was
handling. Hugo knew all right; he wished suddenly he could
have come to grips with Hugo. If he had got an answer, for
instance, to the last question he had asked . . .

"Do you think Randall was telling us the truth?" he said
abruptly.

"I can't see what reason he had to lie."

"No, but . . . forget to be discreet for a moment and tell
me, do *you* think him capable of murdering his grandmother
for revenge?"

Davenant seemed to be regarding the query from all angles. "In the ordinary way I'd have said he wouldn't have *poisoned* her," he said at last. "But I have to say, yes, I do think he might have killed her for that reason; and the two seem to go together, don't they? Or am I being illogical?"

"I don't think so."

"But unless he knew about the will—"

"I think he did. I think Fran Gifford told him."

"Then why the hell do they *both* deny it? asked Davenant, with unaccustomed heat, and looked affronted when Maitland laughed.

"That's one of the things that make this job so interesting," he said. "You never know what's going to happen next."

"And a good time was had by all," Tommy agreed sourly.

"Let's change the subject, then. You say you witnessed Mrs. Randall's signature to the codicil."

"Yes. Elsie Barber and I." He paused, and then added as though reluctantly: "She was in a rare temper, I can tell you that. Alice, I mean."

"She didn't give any reason for the change she was making?"

"Not a word."

"I see. One more question, and I'll leave you in peace."

"Till tomorrow," said Davenant, uncomforted.

"Whose fault is that? But supposing I asked you to describe Mrs. Randall—?"

"I couldn't do any better than the things you've heard already . . . self-righteous . . . overbearing—"

"I see." Suddenly he was anxious to be gone. "I'll get back to Miss Langhorne's notes, then, and see what I can make of the medical evidence." He put his cup down carefully on the tray that Elsie had left on a table near the door. "Do *you* know the difference between digitalis and digitoxin?" he asked.

VII

After a couple of hours spent in earnest consideration of a hastily assembled brief, with the accompanying proofs and appendices and Vera Langhorne's commendably legible comments on the whole, it was a relief to go down to the small dining room allocated to the Bar Mess during the period of the Assize, and find his friend Wellesley waiting for him, and his drink already ordered.

"How did you know I'd still be here?" Maitland inquired as the waiter retired again.

"The penalty of fame, my lad. Haven't you seen the evening paper?" Wellesley was plump and jovial, with very bright blue eyes that could, on occasion, be uncomfortably piercing.

"Oh, lord . . . no!"

"Well, I admit I was looking for the paragraph. I wanted to know if our Vera got her way. And you can't blame the local newshound; we haven't had a murder trial here since 1872."

"What do you know about my dealings with Miss Langhorne? Cheers," he added, and raised his glass. "That's much better," he went on a moment later. "I can probably bear the truth now."

Wellesley was happy to enlighten him. "We all knew she was after Davenant to get hold of you, once she knew you were down here on that smash-and-grab." Antony grimaced; the case had been one he resented, and he hadn't quite forgiven his clerk yet for accepting the brief. "As a matter of fact, there were a few bets laid . . . whether she'd get her way, you know."

"Were there, indeed? I gather you won," said Maitland, gesturing with his glass.

"I thought," said his friend smugly, "you'd probably be in need of some refreshment."

"To tell you the truth, I'm frightened to death of her," Antony complained. "And what with being continually told both by my instructing solicitor *and* my learned junior that life is real and earnest, just in case I might forget the fact—" He broke off, and stood looking down at his glass, and said in an altered tone: "I don't quite understand why she wanted me; I'm damned sure she thinks I'm irresponsible."

Wellesley's thoughts apparently gave him some pleasure. "I can tell you that, all right. She likes the results you get, but she's scared of your methods."

"I don't quite see—"

"Don't you? She feels as if she's conjured up the devil, and she isn't quite sure what the harvest will be."

Maitland took a moment to consider this; then he smiled. "How salutary it is to have a candid friend," he remarked.

"If you want to show your appreciation, there are two things *I* want to know. Why did you agree? And what do you think you can do at this short notice?"

"To answer the second question first, I don't know. As for why—" He hesitated. "They take it so seriously, Davenant and Miss Langhorne, but I don't think either of them has the least idea . . . well, I like the girl, you see," he concluded lamely.

"I don't see," said Wellesley, in a dissatisfied tone. "They're a good firm, mind you, Byron and Davenant, but no experience in this kind of thing."

"How could they have?"

"How, indeed? And the local gossip may amuse you; they're both said to be courting Nell Randall." Maitland stared at him. "Everybody knows everything in Chedcombe," Wellesley added blandly.

"So it seems. It's queer she never married," said Maitland in a thoughtful tone.

"Is it? I don't know the lady." He glanced inquiringly at his friend, and smiled at his serious look. "Opinion is divided as to which of the two she'll accept."

"I thought you said the old cats knew everything."

"It's a tricky point, apparently. Byron has all the advantages of an assured position in the community—"

"How nice for him!"

"—and is, besides, a handsome chap. Something of a ladies' man, from what I hear. Davenant, however, has a more romantic background, being a widower; and Miss Randall is reputed to be a kindhearted creature."

"She'd hardly marry him just because he lost his wife," Maitland objected.

"After a long and painful illness. Of course she'd sympathize," said Wellesley firmly. He saw the waiter in the doorway, and waved to him in a peremptory way. "Same again?" he asked.

"Since you're in such a generous mood . . . it must have been a profitable bet." He turned and surveyed the room, which was far emptier than it had been the previous evening. "Is Appleton here?" he asked.

"Don't you know him? No, he isn't here." He was grinning to himself as he spoke.

"What's so funny?" Wellesley shook his head. "Well, then, what's he like?"

"Excitable," said Wellesley, thoughtfully; and saw a considering gleam in his companion's eye. "Make the most of the information," he invited generously.

"I shall. Indeed, I shall," said Antony irrepressibly. He turned as the waiter came up to his elbow. "Halford, of course, I know," he added a moment later. "The most sedate of Her Majesty's judges, Uncle Nick once called him. But I don't think I've seen him since he was at the Bar himself."

"That must be a good time ago."

"It is. There are advantages in being bred to the law, but the disadvantage is that you meet too many eminent men too soon."

"Is that a disadvantage?"

"Oh, yes. So many chaps who are on the bench now, so many senior members of my own and other Inns, have known me since I was at school. It takes a good deal of living down," he went on sadly.

Soon after that, dinner was served, and around the table the talk became general. Maitland was aware of the interest his presence aroused, an increased interest since he had undertaken this new commitment; there was amusement, too, that he had fallen for Vera's blandishments. She was something of a celebrity, he gathered, and her fellow members of the West Midland Circuit took a perverse pride in her eccentricities. But they were curious—some of them nearly as openly curious as Wellesley had been—about his own motives. He began to wish, rather wryly, that he understood them himself.

He went up to his room soon after eleven, and thought perhaps he would ring Jenny before he settled down to Fran Gifford's affairs again. Wellesley had followed him up the stairs. "I'll see you at breakfast, I expect," he was saying as they reached the door of Antony's room. "After that . . . I say, it's like a hothouse in here."

An overzealous chambermaid had turned on the heat to its fullest extent. Antony crossed to the window, pulled back the curtains, and began to struggle rather angrily with the cock of the radiator. Seeing him using his left hand, Wellesley remembered for the first time that evening that his friend had only a limited use of his right arm. He also remembered that, for one reason or another, Maitland resented any reference to this, and would be extremely unlikely to ask for help. "What you really need," he said, crossing the room in his turn, "is a breath of fresh air."

This was only too obviously true. Antony controlled his annoyance and stepped aside; he knew already that the window was far from smooth-running. He watched Wellesley put up a hand to the catch, and thought idly that the George obviously hadn't had sashes all its life. Then there was the sharp sound of breaking glass, Wellesley gave a grunt of pain and staggered back with a hand to his shoulder, and something heavy fell to the floor, its impact deadened by the thick pile of the old-fashioned Turkey carpet.

He saw in a moment that his friend was more startled than hurt, and went to the window to peer out into the darkness. The snow had stopped, and the cobbles were clear and shiny where the light from the hotel spilled into the square; but beyond that the shadows were heavy. He thought he saw a movement, but it might easily have been imagination. On the pavement below a man had stepped back to look up at the window, thinking the noise he had heard came from there, not from outside; Antony recognized a junior member of the Circuit, and made a beckoning gesture as well as he could through the hole in the glass. Otherwise, as far as he could see, the square was deserted.

Wellesley had been swearing steadily, but he stopped now and said, "Here, look at this!" And then, as Maitland drew the curtains again and turned from the window: "Who do you suppose is chucking rocks at you?"

It lay on the floor, a piece of jagged stone about five inches by three, with a folded paper encircling it and fastened with fine string. "That could have done some damage," said Wellesley, a little grimly. And then, glancing again at the window, "Did you see anyone?"

"Only Sutton. No, I don't think he threw it, you idiot, but he might have seen who did. Let's go and ask him."

"We ought to phone the police."

"Do you think . . . without taking a look at the doings? It may not have been meant as an offensive weapon at all," said Antony, at his most persuasive.

"That's all you know about it. It hurt like hell."

"I know. I'm sorry, really I am." He was down on his knees now, his handkerchief in his hand. "If I pull this thread—" he remarked. Wellesley watched him in a disapproving silence.

Opened out, it proved to be a piece of lined paper torn from a cheap notebook. The message had been cut from a newspaper, which perhaps accounted for its brevity.

neither Shall A wicked Woman have
LIBERTY to go abroad

"Now, isn't that nice," said Maitland in an admiring tone.

But Wellesley was already at the telephone. Antony shook his head at him, and went out to find Sutton. He met him on the stairs.

THURSDAY, 30TH JANUARY

MR. SUTTON had seen nothing suspicious, and neither had his colleague, Mr. Dennis, in whose company he had been leaving the hotel for a breath of air before retiring. The manager was inclined to be apologetic, and said so many times that such a thing had *never* happened before that Maitland lost all interest and went and sat on the bed, leaving it to Wellesley to act as spokesman.

Wellesley was indignant over what had happened, and only too ready to answer all the questions the police sergeant had to ask. The sergeant found him pleasant and helpful; but then, he was a Northdean man, not a foreigner from London like the other chap. He thought Maitland supercilious, and considered—with more justification—that he wasn't as open as his friend. If it hadn't come under the heading of disorderly conduct, he'd have been almost inclined to sympathize with the culprit; not that he approved of throwing stones, of course, but it all went to show what could happen when outsiders mixed themselves up in a purely local affair.

He returned to the hotel the following morning just as Antony was finishing his breakfast, with some purely negative information. There was no clue to be found in the message: the notebook from which the paper had been torn was of a type on sale at Woolworth's, the string was in use in half the stores in town, and the words forming the message had been cut from the local paper, which came out on Fridays . . . and no use thinking they could search every wastepaper basket in the place for a mutilated copy, said the sergeant, forestalling criticism. There were no fingerprints at all, either on the paper or on the stone. He then refused a cup of coffee, rather as though he were being invited to assist at an orgy, and went away; leaving Wellesley, who had strolled into the dining room while they were talking, to say to his friend that he gathered there was nothing to be learned about the incident.

"Oh, I wouldn't say that. How's the shoulder?"

"A bruise the size of my fist," said Wellesley, seating himself; he sounded rather pleased than otherwise.

"I'm sorry about that."

"Never mind. What would you say then?"

"About the stone thrower? A chap with a good eye, probably a cricketer at some time in his life. Local, of course; prejudiced . . . I think I should say violently prejudiced, for some reason, against my client; knows I've accepted the brief—"

"The whole town knows that."

"Well . . . perhaps. Is either a biblical scholar, or—more likely—has access to a Dictionary of Quotations. And though he couldn't have expected to do any serious damage, he obviously didn't care whether he did or not."

"Do you think it was meant as a warning?" It was obvious that Wellesley considered the idea melodramatic, and resented being in a position where he had to take it seriously.

"I shouldn't be surprised."

"I don't like the sound of that. He may try something else."

"Don't lose any sleep over it," Maitland advised. He drank the last of his coffee, and got up reluctantly.

"Well, all these deductions sound very fine, but they don't really help," Wellesley grumbled.

"I never said they did." He thought for a moment before he added: "The real problem is, how did he know my room?"

"It would be easy enough to find out," said Wellesley dryly. "Any of the hotel staff would have pointed out the window—first floor, to the left of the entrance—and never thought twice about it."

"You may be right. I wish . . . oh, well! I'd better be off."

"Must you go this minute?"

"You wouldn't like me to keep Miss Langhorne waiting? Are you leaving this morning?"

"As soon as I've eaten." He eyed his companion uneasily. "You'd better look out, you know."

Antony grinned, and left him.

II

The case was called sufficiently early to get the preliminaries over before the luncheon recess; and Herbert Appleton, Q.C., appearing for the Crown, was halfway through his opening speech when the court adjourned.

Mr. Justice Halford was sorry for the necessity of interrupting him, but there was really no knowing how long he meant to go on. The Judge was an elderly man; old enough, in fact, to regard many of his distinguished colleagues as mere youngsters. He was tall and thin, and stooped slightly, so that he looked as if his robes were too heavy for him; under his wig, his face was lined and a little peevish. He was not, by nature, a disciplinarian, but had become one—paradoxically enough—because of his strong sense of propriety. It was little wonder that he was not altogether pleased to find Maitland leading Vera Langhorne for the defense. He really didn't know what the outcome would be, but one thing was certain . . . here was the reason for Appleton's unusual eloquence. Counsel for the Prosecution was saying everything three times, going back and explaining his points over and over again; as though the jury were in any danger of misunderstanding what the Crown intended to prove.

Over the years Halford had earnestly practiced, and had now nearly perfected, the art of never knowing anything that was going on outside his own immediate sphere, so he had been surprised to see Maitland that morning. Even in his determined isolation, echoes of one or two of his cases had reached the Judge, and Halford had felt almost in sympathy with Sir Nicholas Harding until he remembered that Maitland had always been unpredictable, even as a boy, and his uncle should surely have known better than to encourage him to follow the staid pathways of the law. He took a little hope from the fact that Counsel had behaved very properly when he appeared before him earlier in the week; but he wasn't completely comforted by the reflection.

Maitland was sitting quietly in his place, and drawing idly on the back of his brief. This was contrary to his usual practice while his opponent was stating his case, but when he had composed himself as though for slumber his learned junior had dug him violently in the ribs, so that there had been nothing for it but to abandon the pose.

Appleton had been cordial enough when they met that morning, but decidedly wary. He was a rather pompous little man, with a sad eye and a sallow complexion, and so far showed no signs of the tendency to excitability which Wellesley had attributed to him. As to that, time would tell. What was immediately obvious was that he knew his stuff; he might be repeating himself, but he was doing so without self-contradiction . . . which, when you came to think of it, argued an extraordinarily clear brain. He was speaking to his brief, of course, but unless Antony was very much mistaken he believed his case implicitly, and that in itself made him dangerous. His junior was a sharp-faced young man with an alert look about him, and an air of self-satisfaction so pronounced as to make one genuinely curious to know its cause. Maitland raised his eyes for a moment from his sketch, and turned his head to glance at his own junior; he found, to his discomfort, that she was staring at him somberly, as though his presence gave her no pleasure at all.

Vera Langhorne met his look resentfully. She had pulled her wig on at an even more rakish angle today, and her gown still looked as though it had been rolled up in the bottom of a dusty cupboard for several weeks. In spite of this she was feeling some annoyance over the fact that Maitland seemed to have so little regard for the impression he made on the jury . . . if only he would abandon that studiedly casual attitude (as though the outcome of the case was no concern of his!) and stop drawing—what was he drawing, anyway? Pigs!—all over his brief. She had seen to it that her own clearly written notes came into court with the other papers, and he had accepted them with his most disarming smile; but now she saw that he had produced a sheaf of tattered envelopes from his pocket, and placed them on top of the foolscap sheets she had given him. And if he could himself read what was scrawled across them she'd be very much surprised. Like the Judge, she took what comfort she could from recalling his performance in this same court the previous Tuesday, and she was beginning to feel that the stories she had heard about her leader's unorthodox ways were more than a little exaggerated. On the whole, this was a relief; she only hoped his ability hadn't been overrated, too.

Sitting behind them, Tommy Davenant watched his team with trepidation. He had been sitting by all the morning, while they thrashed out the question of tactics; and Maitland had been very willing to listen, but he wouldn't mind betting that Maitland had his own ideas and would quietly carry them out when the time came. He had said, quite clearly, the day before, that he believed in Fran's innocence; Davenant, who thought the evidence overwhelming, couldn't quite credit that. An actor, he thought, getting into the skin of his part.

Fran Gifford was seated in the dock, staring down at her hands and the small square of embroidered linen twisted between them. Just for a moment when she came into the court she had looked around her, had seen the judge's scarlet and raised her eyes for a moment to meet his courteous, impersonal gaze; then she had looked down into the body of the hall and seen Mr. Davenant smiling at her, and remembered "he doesn't believe me," and told herself—clutching angrily at her courage—that at least he'd never said so. On the bench in front of him counsel's robes were confusing for a moment; Miss Langhorne was looking up at her and nodding encouragingly; Mr. Maitland gave her the very briefest of smiles before he turned away. She thought he was looking enigmatic, and kept her eyes fixed on his face for a long moment while she remembered what he had said to her the day before. And then she looked down at her hands again, and twisted her handkerchief into a tight cord. All that morning she had seemed to be moving in a dream world, where nothing was real, nothing mattered; but now, suddenly, the shadows had substance and her fears came crowding back.

By keeping her head bent she could ignore the eyes that watched her, even if she couldn't forget them, but she was aware now of the hostility of the spectators as an almost tangible thing. And she couldn't ignore Herbert Appleton's voice, or fail to hear the things he was saying, the dreadful things about what she had done. She thought if she had never been in the little sitting room at Ravenscroft she could still have visualized it clearly, from his description; and as for what he said had happened there on New Year's Eve, so much of it was true. But none of his hearers—not the Judge, nor the jury, nor anyone in court—could see Aunt Alice as she had, unsmiling and implacable. Yet that was how it had been, with herself in the role of a suppliant. "You're an unholy little liar," her counsel had said to her. She wondered what his comment would have been if, instead, she'd told him the truth.

Now, as she listened to Counsel for the Prosecution, she recognized, as Maitland had done, the sincerity that was implicit in his tone, so that every word seemed not only accusation but condemnation too, and by the time the adjournment came she felt almost suffocated with terror.

Still in his place after the Judge had retired, Maitland turned to say to Davenant: "You'd better go and tell that child we shall have our say later, Miss Langhorne and I."

"Fran Gifford?" The solicitor sounded surprised. He hadn't thought Maitland had looked at his client after that first quick glance when she came into the dock. "The case for the prosecution can't help but sound bad," he added.

"Well, tell her that." He moved out into the aisle and stood waiting for Vera Langhorne to follow him; and couldn't help noticing that she paused to move his papers so that the inexpert sketch he had made was no longer in open view.

III

On the whole, the police evidence sounded very much like Appleton's speech, translated into official language. Detective Inspector Camden had been informed by Dr. Firmont, early on New Year's Day, that old Mrs. Randall was dead, and that a quantity of poison was missing. In the circumstances he had considered it proper to institute inquiries immediately, and had been given every facility by the bereaved family. As a consequence of these inquiries he had, when the doctors' report was at length received, taken a statement from the accused. . . .

There was no doubt about it, the case had been well prepared and—besides bidding fair to be damning—offered very little room for maneuver by the defense. There were certain facts that couldn't be denied, and certain matters of opinion where denial was essential but would obviously sound unconvincing.

The Inspector, a dark man, rather short for a policeman, whose face looked as if it had been inexpertly carved out of a piece of wood, showed no signs of being discomposed by Miss Langhorne's cross-examination. Competent, Maitland thought as he listened to his colleague; if there was a fault it must lie in the lack of imagination to which she had admitted. She was an intelligent woman, but blinded by the prejudices of her class and upbringing; even her apparent perception where Fran Gifford was concerned was based, he believed, on a false concept of the girl's character. For all that, he liked both her stubbornness and her honesty, and the amusement he so often felt in her company was already almost affectionate.

There followed Sergeant Webb, who looked young to be an expert in fingerprints, but who was uncomfortably sure of himself and his facts. To try to cast doubt on his evidence would only serve to emphasize it, and the points he made weren't really under dispute. Antony printed "LEAVE IT" on a fresh note pad that appeared at his elbow, and pushed it in front of Vera. She nodded, without looking at him; he couldn't tell if she agreed with the advice, or not.

In the small hours of that morning, Maitland had brushed up his chemistry sufficiently—he hoped—to be able to cross-examine the medical witnesses without provoking their open scorn. He had done this mainly at the prompting of his conscience, because it was a subject he found difficult and distasteful; and it was lucky he hadn't expected any dramatic opportunities, at least he wasn't disappointed. The police doctor who had assisted at the post-mortem examination spoke of the Scrophulariaceae, of purified glycosidal fractions, of Keller's Test and Baljet's Reaction, in the obvious confidence that the court was as familiar with the subject as he was. Maitland could not forbear from remarking dryly, when the matter had been elucidated somewhat, that the medical examiners had been fortunate in having a fair idea what they were looking for, as eleven persons had been murdered by this means in Liège in 1938 before any suspicion of poisoning arose. To which the witness replied with unshakable complacency that things were very different now. He did not add, "and of course that was abroad," but it seemed fairly obvious that he was thinking it.

Dr. Maurice Firmont was a big, shaggy man with a square, good-humored face. Unlike his colleague, he wasn't at all happy in the position in which he found himself, and his evidence was only dragged from him reluctantly in response to Appleton's questions; so that it was all Antony could do to withstand the mischievous temptation to indicate to his learned friend that a request to be allowed to treat the witness as hostile would meet no objection from the defense. When his own turn came, Firmont turned to face him with a look of almost comical alarm; the doctor had heard, of course, of the stranger in their midst, and didn't find the quiet, almost diffident tone of Maitland's first questions particularly reassuring.

"Were you surprised when you were called to attend Mrs. Randall at Ravenscroft on New Year's morning?"

"Very surprised."

"Even though she was your patient, and seventy-five years old?"

"She was rarely ill. I knew she was starting a cold, but she wouldn't have called me for that." Maitland said nothing, but the doctor, who was himself of a humorous turn of mind, had the momentary impression of a character in a strip cartoon with a question mark over his head. He added, forgetting his unwillingness: "Miss Randall had dined with my wife and myself that evening. That was how I heard."

"Thank you, doctor. Now, you have described Mrs. Randall's symptoms in some detail to my friend. Leaving aside their distressing nature, would you have suspected poison in the normal way?"

"It certainly didn't occur to me at first. Then I thought . . . in a farmhouse, you know . . . there might well have been an accident."

"Yes, I see. Sheep dip, for instance, or one of the chemical sprays that are now in such common use?"

"Something like that."

"But the symptoms you observed . . . these things would not contain digitalis in any form." He sensed, rather than saw, that Appleton was beginning to fidget. "Could they have produced a similar reaction?"

"I am not really familiar—"

The witness was allowed to get no further. Appleton had jerked upright, almost as though he moved against his will. "My lord!"

The Judge said nothing, but turned his eyes on Counsel for the Defense with a look of courteous inquiry. Maitland said deferentially: "Dr. Firmont has been called by the prosecution as an expert, as well as a witness to matters of fact." From his tone you might have thought him almost completely uninterested in the outcome of the protest. "I will confine myself to the latter, if your lordship would prefer that I do so."

Halford frowned at him. "You may proceed, Mr. Maitland," he said. Appleton bundled his gown around him and sat down again with a disconsolate air, and Antony annoyed them both by ignoring the permission and abandoning his question unanswered.

"We have established, doctor, that you had some questions in your mind about the cause of Mrs. Randall's illness."

"That was why I asked Miss Randall if there was anything she could have taken by accident."

"And when she had replied, what did you do?"

"Went down to the old lady's sitting room."

"Both of you?"

"Yes."

"What then?"

"Miss Randall opened her mother's workbox, which was lying on the sofa. Just inside there was a test tube, nearly empty. I told her to close the box again, to leave everything as she found it."

"And then?"

"She began to cry," said the witness precisely. "But it seemed to me . . . I couldn't see how the old lady could have taken that by accident; so I locked the sitting-room door when we left, and took the first opportunity of informing the police.''

"When all this happened the old lady was already dead?''

"I should not have left her otherwise.''

"At what time did she die?''

"Just before five-thirty A.M.''

"A short illness, compared with some that are recorded.''

"You must remember she had taken a heavy dose. And an old lady of seventy-five, even a healthy old lady, would have less resistance than a younger person.''

"What time did Miss Randall phone you?''

The doctor looked a little taken aback by this abrupt change of subject. "About two-thirty in the morning.''

"And you reached Ravenscroft—''

"I didn't notice exactly. About half an hour later, I imagine.''

"Miss Randall herself let you in?''

"Yes.''

"And took you to her mother's room? And assisted you—as you have told us—until the old lady died?''

"That is quite correct.''

"During that time, what other members of the household did you see?''

"Why . . . nobody else.''

"Did that not seem rather strange to you?''

"Not at the time.''

"But upon further consideration—''

"My lord—'' said Appleton, bouncing to his feet this time without any hesitation at all. Antony gave him a benign smile, and sat down again.

"Have you any further questions for the witness, Mr. Appleton?'' asked Halford.

"I had not, my lord. But as the point has been raised,'' said Counsel for the Prosecution, beginning to see where his incautious intervention had led him, "did you require any other assistance, doctor, than that which Miss Randall could give you?''

"There was nothing anyone could have done, and quite frankly a crowd of people can only be an embarrassment on these occasions. Miss Randall was able to provide me with everything I needed, and as we were both fully occupied, I doubt if either of us thought—''

''That is *exactly* what I meant to ask the witness, your lordship,'' said Maitland, more in sorrow than in anger. ''If my learned friend is permitted this license, perhaps I may be allowed one further question.''

''If it is in order . . . certainly, Mr. Maitland.'' Mr. Justice Halford was perfectly well aware that Counsel had, in fact, intervened because he didn't altogether relish what the doctor was saying, but his protest was reasonable enough, even if he had deliberately maneuvered to put his opponent in the wrong.

''If my friend has nothing more to interpolate into my cross-examination—'' The look that accompanied those words could hardly have been more courteous, but there was no mistaking their provocative intent. ''Afterward, doctor, after Mrs. Randall died—''

''Why, then, of course, the household was aroused.''

''Mr. Hugo Randall among them?''

''I did not see him until later in the day.''

''Do you know if Miss Randall had attempted to rouse any member of the household before she telephoned you?''

''My lord, this is intolerable!'' Appleton broke in, before the witness could elaborate his reply. Maitland waited for the Judge's strictures with a look of patient resignation which Halford mistrusted profoundly, and then said only, ''Thank you, doctor,'' before he seated himself again. It seemed to him that Firmont's look, before he stepped down from the witness box, was surprisingly full of comprehension. He took what comfort he could from this: his junior was scowling at him, and Tommy Davenant leaned forward to say in his ear: ''What the hell do you think you're doing?''

''Looking for the truth,'' Maitland said gently. ''Can *you* answer the question for me: where was Hugo Randall while his grandmother was dying?''

''I never asked him,'' said Davenant sulkily.

''So I noticed. Nor did the police. But I want to know, you see,'' Antony told him; and again his tone had a deceptive mildness.

Vera Langhorne said gruffly: "Woman's a scatterbrain,
but better not let her see what you're at."

"If I knew myself—"

"Don't you?" she asked him bluntly. "Don't you?" But
by this time Nell Randall was in the witness box, and Maitland turned his attention to Appleton's examination.

He had noticed before the strong resemblance between
Marian and Hugo Randall. Nell was as dark as her niece and
nephew, but that was as far as the likeness went; and she had
a charm of manner, a gentleness, which he had certainly not
observed in either of the others. She was relating in a low
and rather breathless voice how she had arrived home at
about one o'clock on New Year's morning, and gone
straight to bed. It had been some time after two when she
was aroused by a sound . . . a sort of choking, moaning
sound . . . from her mother's room, across the corridor
from hers. She had run across, and found her mother half out
of bed and moaning and throwing herself about as if she was
in great pain. No, she wasn't sick at that time, the vomiting
had occurred previously, but she seemed to have some difficulty in getting her breath. As soon as she was a little quieter
Nell had telephoned Dr. Firmont and asked him to come at
once.

There was an odd little pause here, as though Appleton
couldn't quite make up his mind whether to take up the
question the defense had raised with the previous witness.
Maitland turned his head in time to meet a far from friendly
look, and then Appleton shrugged and seated himself.
Counsel for the Defense came to his feet in a leisurely way,
and suddenly, unexpectedly, the crowded hall was silent.

The queer thing was, she wasn't nervous, she returned his
regard with a look as steady as his own. The breathless way
of speaking was a mannerism only, not a symptom of some
inner disquiet. She wasn't nervous, but he realized as he
looked at her that she was deeply unhappy. Just for a moment he felt a strong revulsion from his own part in the affair, and his thoughts seemed to spin away from the
courtroom: the logical place to start is with the family . . .
she needed me, I didn't owe her a thing . . . revenge is an
ugly word . . . neither shall a wicked woman have liberty . . .

. . . and Fran Gifford herself was afraid of the truth.

He was aware that the Judge's eye was on him, and that the silence had lengthened unduly. "Did you go into Chedcombe on the 30th December last?" he asked.

"The 30th? Oh . . . yes."

"Please tell us about that visit, Miss Randall."

"Mother wanted to go into town, so I took her."

"When was that arranged?"

"At lunchtime."

"When all the members of the family were present?"

"I think . . . I'm sure . . . they were all there."

"Mr. Hugo Randall, and his brother and sister."

"Yes." She was eying him doubtfully. Appleton said, rather too loudly:

"My lord, these questions are irrelevant."

"Irrelevant?" Maitland swung round to face his opponent, and then turned to look up at the Judge. "Irrelevant?" he said again.

"Are they not, Mr. Maitland?"

"I submit, my lord, that is for my friend to prove. I am not yet ready to address the jury on the point I have in mind."

"If the defense are going to ask us to believe that the deceased was poisoned at lunchtime, thirty-six hours before she died—" said Appleton scornfully, and just for a moment Antony forgot that he had been doing his best to annoy the other man and felt an answering stab of anger at his tone.

"When I ask my l-learned and skeptical friend to b-believe a thing," he said, "be sure I s-shall be ready to p-prove it."

The Judge smiled at him, and made a note on his pad. (Probably, thought Antony, a reminder to hold me to my promise.) "That sounds very satisfactory, Mr. Maitland. You may proceed."

"Thank you, my lord. I was about to ask you, Miss Randall, whether Mrs. Randall gave any reason—"

"Yes, she said she wanted to see Mr. Byron. She had an appointment with him for half past three."

"So you drove her into Chedcombe."

"Yes. We went a little early, because she wanted to call in at the Bank."

"Did you know the purpose of her visit to Mr. Byron?"

"She often went to see him. He was her solicitor."

"But on this particular occasion—?"

"She didn't say why she wanted to go."

"You know the reason now . . . don't you? To sign the codicil to her will." He paused, and gave Appleton an amused look, his irritation forgotten. "Well, perhaps I should have said: you have been told that was the purpose of her visit?"

"Yes, I have been told that."

"Did you have any inkling before of her intention?"

"Oh, no."

"Tell me, Miss Randall, when you heard what she had done, were you surprised?"

"I—" Her eyes met his questioningly; and, oddly, he thought he read in them a sort of appeal.

"There's no hurry," he told her. "Take your time. I don't suppose you've thought about it before, and now—"

"You don't have to remind me," she said. "I've sworn to tell the truth. Well, then . . . I wasn't surprised."

"May I ask you to be a little more precise?"

Mr. Justice Halford cleared his throat. "I am willing to give the defense a good deal of latitude," he remarked, apparently to someone sitting among the rafters. Maitland chose to take him literally.

"I am grateful for your lordship's forbearance."

"We seem to be getting into the realms of conjecture, Mr. Maitland," Halford pointed out gently.

"Yes, my lord." He turned again to the witness. "You were out, weren't you, on New Year's Eve?"

"Yes, I went out at seven o'clock." She hesitated and then, surprisingly, volunteered the answer to what would have been his next question. "I offered to stay with my mother, but she said she was expecting Fran."

"Did she tell you why she had invited Miss Gifford?"

"No . . . she didn't."

There was something in her tone that he didn't understand. He said slowly, "But you thought perhaps you knew—" and was so absorbed for the moment that Appleton's furious protest took him completely unawares. He made his apologies in a vague way that further irritated his opponent. "How was Mrs. Randall that night? Did she seem to have anything on her mind?"

"She was . . . very much as usual."

"Not upset in any way?"

"My mother would have said she didn't permit circumstances to upset her."

"Well, then, would you say she had anything on her mind?"

"If anything the—the unreliability of the legal profession. I think Mr. Byron had upset her by trying to persuade her not to change her will."

"Nothing else?" He found the picture intriguing, but Appleton was quivering on the verge of another objection; no use rousing him again so soon.

"Nothing else," said Nell sadly.

"Then—I am sorry to return to the subject, Miss Randall—perhaps you will tell us why you did not call on any other member of the household for help, when you found your mother so ill."

"The servants sleep at the other end of the house. I hadn't time—"

"There were three members of your family at home," he reminded her. "Or hadn't they come back from the dance?"

"They were in bed by then. Hugo would never have let Marian stay out so late."

"But still you didn't—"

"They're much too young; and there was nothing they could do." She found his eyes still on her, and added more emphatically: "There really wasn't anything to be done."

"Moral support?" he suggested; and smiled at her.

"Well, I'd have been glad if Hugo . . . but one of the cows was sick, you see; I knocked on his door when I went to telephone, but he wasn't in his room."

"Thank you, Miss Randall; that makes everything quite clear." Maitland turned his head to look up at the Judge, but finding no encouragement in Halford's eye, bowed slightly and sat down again.

Counsel for the Prosecution disclaimed any desire to re-examine. He sounded a little put out, but perhaps that was because he couldn't make up his mind what the defense were trying to prove.

IV

It was already late when Nell Randall left the witness box, and the court rose with some alacrity when the Judge announced the adjournment. Now that his attention was released, Antony was aware again of Miss Langhorne's heavy breathing beside him; he spent rather longer than was necessary piling his papers together, because if she was going to tick him off about the line he was taking he felt suddenly too tired to argue the point . . . to tell her again that he was groping in the dark with no clear idea of where he was going. He'd done his best to make her understand, but it seemed she wouldn't believe him.

But if Vera had anything to say, she wasn't in a hurry. He became aware that Davenant was muttering something about "having a word with Nell," and turned quickly to veto the suggestion.

"I'm sorry, I want to see our client. It won't take long."

"Oh, very well!" But it seemed he regretted his ungracious tone, because as he turned away he grinned suddenly and said over his shoulder: "Did you see Appleton's face?" He did not mention the cross-examination that had just ended, so presumably all was forgiven; the thought crossed Antony's mind that the solicitor's reaction was one of relief, as though he had been afraid that—somehow or other—Nell Randall would give herself away.

The room which was used for interviews at the Shire Hall was no more cheerful than any of its kind, and a good deal colder than most. Vera established herself in a chair at the head of the long table; she was still silent, and Antony decided uneasily that something was brewing. Tommy Davenant came in and joined her, and said something in a low voice . . . about the Judge . . . about Appleton . . . he wasn't really listening. His whole attention was already focused on Fran Gifford when the door opened and a wardress stood aside to let her come into the room.

She had a blind look, he thought; he wouldn't have been surprised to see her feeling her way with hands outstretched in front of her. He pulled a chair out from the table and set it as near as possible to the tepid radiator under the window.

Fran crossed the room toward him and put an ice-cold hand into his for an instant, and smiled up at him with mechanical courtesy. Perhaps it was only the movement he had made that attracted her notice; she didn't seem to realize that there was anyone else in the room. He said the first thing that came into his mind, and perhaps the most unexpected.

"That's a nice dress. The color suits you." It was a dark, warm red, with a softly flowing line much more attractive than the one she had worn when he saw her at the prison; in the court some of the warmth seemed to have been reflected in her cheeks, but here, under the harsher light of a single, unshaded bulb, her pallor was almost ghastly.

Fran was looking at him blankly, as though the words, if she heard them at all, were meaningless. "Nell sent it to me," she said at last (it was queer, he thought, how the rules of conventional politeness would assert themselves). And then she added, frowning: "She's always so kind. Why did you ask her those questions?" She seemed like a sleep-walker who had been wakened too abruptly.

"I can only give you the obvious answer. I wanted to find out—"

"Yes, of course." She sounded docile and uncomprehending. "Do you want to talk to me again?"

"Just two questions. Sit down, Miss Gifford. I'm sorry it's so cold in here."

"It is, isn't it?" This was said still with her air of vague courtesy. She came forward and took the chair he indicated and spread her hands against the radiator. He cast about in his mind for a question sharp enough to bring her back to reality.

"Tell me, Fran, there's a man, isn't there? Someone you hope to marry."

The brown eyes were raised quickly to meet his intent look. "Who told you that?"

"The question is," said Antony, "is it true?"

"No, it isn't. You asked me that before."

"So I did, but I hadn't talked to Hugo Randall then."

She was very still now, her eyes watchful. "What did Hugo say to you?"

"It was only an opinion, after all," he said casually.

"But there isn't anybody . . . really there isn't. He's just making it up."

"There was something else he told me." He paused, and after a while she said, as though she couldn't help herself:

"About me?"

"Yes."

"What was it?"

"He says you told him you'd fight any action the family might take to upset the will. Was he lying about that, too?"

"I didn't say—" She broke off and looked down at her hands; they were streaked with dust from the radiator, and she began to rub them together, trying to get it off. The task seemed to absorb her, or perhaps she didn't want to meet his eyes.

"Was he lying?" Maitland asked again.

"No, I . . . I told him that."

"When?"

"The day after Aunt Alice died."

"When did you see him?"

"In the evening. He picked me up, and we drove to—to Daneshill, and sat in the car and talked."

"I'm interested to know how the conversation reached that point."

"I don't remember exactly." She was staring at the window now, though there was nothing to be seen beyond it but the stone wall of the house at the other side of the alley. "I was furious because Mr. Byron had told me they were going to bring an action."

"You told me you'd tried to persuade Mrs. Randall to change her will back again," Antony reminded her.

"Well, so I did." There was nothing in the least vague about her reactions now. "I changed my mind, that's all," she added positively, and raised her eyes at last to his.

He seemed to have no desire to press the question. "We'll leave it there," he said lightly. And then: "You're not making it any easier, are you? You want my help, but you want it on your own terms."

She sat staring up at him, and her defiance melted. Her mind was in confusion. She wanted his help—the thought came like an echo—but she was afraid of him, too. . . .

His expression changed. "What is it?" he asked her urgently. "You mustn't worry about Appleton, you know, it's his job to talk like that."

"He believes I killed her." She seemed to have difficulty forming the words. "But that isn't it. I didn't know *they* felt like that."

So her unhappiness was no armor against the hostility he had sensed in the courtroom. He said angrily: "You can't change human nature. It's always like that." But he knew as he spoke that the statement was misleading.

"It's a little because I seemed to be getting something for nothing," she explained carefully, as though she hadn't heard him. "And then . . . poison; I don't blame them really."

"It isn't anything personal," he insisted, almost with desperation.

"You know that isn't true," said Fran, silencing him for a moment. "I always rather liked living in a small town, but now . . . I'm afraid."

"If you'd only trust me," he said; and saw again the flicker of fear in her eyes.

"I'm grateful to you," she told him, with a return of formality. "I know you'll do what you can." She stood up as she spoke, and said, like a child: "Is there anything else? May I go now?"

Her composure had a brittle quality that disturbed him, even while he was irritated by her stubbornness. When he did not reply she moved away from him, and paused for a moment to speak to Miss Langhorne and Davenant. "You're both very kind," she said. "I'm sorry—" Her politeness was still that of a self-possessed child, who had been taught what was right and obeyed without understanding.

A moment later she was making for the door. She didn't look at Antony again.

When she had gone, Vera Langhorne got up from her place near the table. "Going home," she said. And then: "Like to see you later, Maitland."

"Very well." She sounded belligerent, he thought, but it was easier to agree than to argue. "I'm going to see Walter Randall after dinner, as I told you. But after that—"

"Yes," she said. "Walter." She seemed to be thinking

deeply, but when she finally spoke she said only, "Any time. Give you coffee," and tramped out of the room.

Antony sighed, and looked at Davenant with an eyebrow raised inquiringly. "Do you suppose there'll be strychnine in it?" he asked in a resigned tone.

V

John Willett, the clerk who had brought down the "malicious wounding" papers for Maitland's attention, was waiting in the hall of the George when his principal went in. He was a cheerfully efficient young man who had taken, of recent years, a good deal of the weight off Mr. Mallory's shoulders, without in any way allowing the old man to feel that the tyranny with which he ruled Sir Nicholas's chambers was any less absolute than before. There was a theory about Willett that he never walked where he could run, and rarely stopped talking for any reason whatever; but on this particular evening he remained perfectly still at the side of the hall for perhaps fifteen seconds before he moved forward to bring himself to Maitland's attention, and had time to notice the slight stiffness with which the other man moved, the frown of concentration between his eyes. He knew the signs only too well.

The frown disappeared, the laughter lines deepened on Antony's face as he caught sight of the clerk. "Good to see you, Willett. Come up to my room, we'll have a drink." He was already pulling off his tie as he went up the staircase, quite forgetful of the fact that he was still in the public part of the hotel.

The window had been mended and his room had warmed up again since morning. An extra suitcase stood in the corner. "Mrs. Maitland thought you'd need some things," said Willett, following his glance.

"I do, of course. I hadn't thought of it." He waved a hand toward the telephone. "Order whatever you like. I need a Scotch—Black Label." He disappeared into the bathroom and turned on both taps full.

The George was not noted for the speed of its service, and he arrived back in his dressing-gown just as the waiter was leaving. He accepted the sherry that seemed to have been ordered for him with no other comment than a humorous look. "You oughtn't to drink spirits if you've got a headache," said Willett defensively.

"As a matter of fact, I haven't. Never mind. The way to hell is paved with good intentions," said Antony. Willett picked up his tankard and refrained from further apology.

"I'll have to leave in half an hour to catch my train," he said. "Unless, of course—" He trailed the sentence invitingly, but added, when no answer was forthcoming: "I hear you had some trouble here last night."

"Nothing much. I don't really need a bodyguard."

"Of course not, Mr. Maitland."

"Well, don't let my uncle hear of it through you, that's all," said Antony repressively.

Willett's eyes were reproachful. "I'm not one to talk, sir, as you very well know," he said, severely. As it stood, this statement was palpably untrue. "If you're thinking Mrs. Maitland would be worried, that's all right; Sir Nicholas will hear of it sooner or later, but probably not until you're back in town."

Which was true enough. Wellesley was unlikely to keep the story to himself, and the legal grapevine would do the rest. And Uncle Nick would have some caustic comments to make, quite regardless of the fact that Maitland's behavior since he came to Chedcombe had been—he considered—almost painfully correct. "But he wouldn't tell Jenny," he said aloud; and then, catching Willett's eye and remembering his presence again: "It's the sort of thing that might have happened to anyone."

If Willett thought that in the light of past events this was stretching the facts a little he didn't say so. "I've only been here an hour or two, but I've heard talk," he said. "Seems they've made up their minds here, and don't want any interference." Then, as Maitland seemed unresponsive to this gambit, he gave it up and added: "I nearly forgot. I brought you some money."

"That's good. I was expecting to have to do battle with the local Bank tomorrow." He accepted an envelope and weighed it in his hand. "How much?" he asked.

"Fifty quid."

Antony closed his eyes and indulged in a little mental

arithmetic. "You didn't get that from Jenny," he said, opening them again. "Or from the petty cash."

"Well, I won't say Mr. Mallory is feeling very happy," Willett admitted. "And he says he never heard of Byron and Davenant—"

"And if no good comes of it, *he* won't be responsible," Antony concluded crossly. "You don't have to tell me that."

"That's just about it, Mr. Maitland," said Willett. And drank the rest of his beer.

VI

Maitland sent his apologies to the Mess, and ate early in the public dining room. Before he had finished he saw Tommy Davenant standing in the doorway; the solicitor had an impatient look, he thought, and he abandoned his coffee, which was still too hot to drink. He noticed as he crossed the room that several conversations were interrupted as he passed, only to break out again in whispers behind his back; his expression was so forbidding as they passed through the hall that the reception clerk's salutation died on his lips.

The Humber was parked out in the center of the square. "We may as well walk," said Davenant, and Antony fell into step beside him. It was much milder tonight, not at all unpleasant, though the air had still a feeling of dampness. They crossed the stream and made for North Street, a narrow and inconvenient thoroughfare which was still one of the main roads out of the town. Past the turning into Westgate, and on the opposite corner a building that had been only slightly modernized bore a discreet sign: FROST'S BANK LIMITED. "Old-fashioned arrangement," said Davenant, pulling the bell. "Lives over the shop."

A little, colorless woman came down to let them in, and Antony felt a stab of surprise when she was introduced as "Mrs. Walter." He couldn't help wondering how she managed to keep her end up with her in-laws. Upstairs the flat was warm and bright and unimaginative; he could see now that she was expensively dressed, though with a complete lack of taste. Or perhaps it was just that she was uninterested in fashion. She led the way to a fair-sized sitting room, so full of furniture that movement of any kind was almost impossible, and having turned off the television set in the corner was about to go out again when her husband called her back.

"There's no need for you to leave us, my dear."

"Very well, Walter." She did not question his decision, or even glance inquiringly at the two men who had followed her into the room, but crossed without hesitation to the corner of the chesterfield nearest the fire, where she sat down and folded her hands in her lap. Her face was still completely without expression. From the wall above the fireplace, Alice Randall's photograph looked down at them unsmilingly.

Walter Randall was as dark-haired as the rest of his family, a big man with a pasty complexion and a spreading waistline. He greeted Davenant as a familiar, and his other guest with the sort of professional affability Antony could imagine him employing towards a respectable customer of long standing who nevertheless might—just possibly—be about to ask for an overdraft. "A bad business," he said when they were all seated. "But I don't see what I can do about it."

As Davenant had obviously no intention of answering this, Antony was left to make his own explanations. "I need some background information."

"There's no chance of your wanting to call me as a witness, I take it . . . anything like that?"

"That's up to Davenant. As far as I can tell at present, no chance at all."

Walter seemed to relax a little. "I'll tell you frankly, I've no wish to be involved in any way. In my position—"

"But you'll not object to a little informal gossip? Just between"—he glanced at the silent Mrs. Randall—"just between the four of us."

"As long as it stays that way."

"The feeling in the town is strong, I take it . . . against Fran Gifford." He was anxious to establish the fact in Walter's mind that he wasn't solely interested in the Randall family, but there was no knowing what was going on behind that pudding face of his.

Randall glanced at Tommy Davenant before he replied, a deprecating, almost an apologetic look. "Very strong, very bitter," he said.

"Do you understand why?"

"A young girl, not bad-looking, living alone—"

"She's lodging with one of the most respectable families in town," Davenant protested.

"That makes no difference. You've got to understand the Chedcombe people," said Walter earnestly. "I do . . . which is why the Bank sent me back here, against their usual policy, you know. But, as I was saying, there's the lack of conformity straightaway: one, alone, in a crowd. You ought to understand that, Tommy; I've heard the old tabbies dissecting Fred Byron often enough. *And* you."

"We were talking about Fran Gifford," said Davenant shortly.

"Yes, well, that's one thing. And then she wormed her way into the old lady's graces, which is a grievance that I share with them. And instead of showing gratitude—" A gesture completed the sentence; he looked, for a moment, preternaturally solemn, and Antony was suddenly curious. Did the man feel anything at all?

"You're not in sympathy with the defense, Mr. Randall?" he asked bluntly.

"Why should I be? After all, my mother—"

"I know. I'm sorry. But Miss Gifford hasn't been convicted yet."

"Not yet. That little bitch," said Walter venomously, "is guilty all right. You'll see."

It wasn't very clear what arguments Tommy Davenant had used to bring about this interview. "It doesn't make it very easy for me," said Antony with a dejected look. Walter's eyes were on him, speculatively.

"You'll do your best," he said in a condescending way. "I told Tommy I'd give you the background details, so as long as you don't get any wrong ideas in your head—"

"I won't," said Maitland earnestly. His tone was no clue to what he was thinking. He hoped he had got over tolerably well the impression of a man working not only against odds, but against his own conviction.

"Well, they may have a point," said Randall, apparently satisfied. "The people who say she's guilty, you know. They say there's a man, and that's why she did it. She's no money of her own, not at all a good catch, matrimonially speaking."

The days were not so far in the past, it seemed, when a marriage announcement would carry, in parentheses, the amount of the bride's fortune. Antony stored this away for future consideration, and went straight to the point that interested him most. "Do they also say who the man is?"

"Now that," said Walter regretfully, "I haven't heard. Mrs. Harlow will have it Fran was in the habit of slipping out of an evening; said she was going for a walk, but sometimes she wouldn't get back till quite late. And you don't know Chedcombe if you think there was more than one interpretation to be put on that."

"I'd have thought there'd have been some surmise, at least, as to whom she was meeting."

"Well, up to the time of the old lady's death," said Walter, "they'd have guessed—as I did—that it was my nephew Hugo." There was something almost vindictive in his tone. "But the change of will made nonsense of that, of course."

"I don't quite see—"

"It couldn't have mattered less to Fran if the old lady was threatening to cut her out again . . . if she'd really got Hugo in her pocket."

"I suppose not. Have you any idea why the change was made in the first place?"

"That's obvious, I should have thought. Hugo quarreled with her once too often."

"Do you know why?"

"He says it was about the operation of the farm," said Walter doubtfully.

"The land looks in good heart."

"That's not the point. Hugo says he can't operate at a profit without more stock, more equipment. Well, he could build up the stock gradually, without any capital outlay; but the thing is, he says he'd have nowhere to house the beasts if he did."

"I see. Was Mrs. Randall also dissatisfied with the position?"

"In a way. She used to say, 'in your grandfather's time' . . . wouldn't admit things had been different then. And I've heard her accuse him of lining his own pockets, but I don't think she really believed it. Why, I told her myself—" He broke off, and laughed self-consciously. "Trade secrets," he said.

"When did you first know of the new codicil?"

"The day after Mother died. Byron told me. I took him out to Ravenscroft right away."

"And then?"

"Well, I asked him about the position, of course, but he was cagey about it. Can't blame him, really, what could the poor chap say?"

"It was certainly difficult."

"To tell you the truth," said Walter, suddenly confidential, "I wasn't all that sorry to see Hugo put in his place. But it's a good property, you know, Ravenscroft, it ought to stay in the family; and there's the money as well. Besides the fact that it would be damned inconvenient to have those brats of Allan's without a penny of their own. So I talked to Neale when I got back to town, told him to do whatever was necessary to start proceedings."

"Did Hugo agree?"

"I took his agreement for granted, of course. But when he heard—"

"He came here that evening and swore at you," said Mrs. Randall, in a dead voice. She had been silent for so long that the simple statement seemed to have a quite disproportionate effect. Antony turned and smiled at her, but she met his look without any expression at all.

"Yes, well, we aren't exactly in sympathy," said Walter; his tone was probably intended to be jovial.

"Is Hugo still against any action being taken?"

"I wouldn't say that, quite. He won't talk about it at all. But there's nothing to be done until the verdict's in, you know."

"And even then, the situation will probably be complicated." But that, thank goodness, wasn't his affair. "If you think the original change followed a quarrel with Hugo," he said thoughtfully, "why did she cut out Mark and Marian too?"

"A whim, I suppose. She wasn't very pleased with Mark over that digitalis business."

"Everyone tells me that was quite characteristic."

"Oh, yes. Too brainy by half, and now see what's happened. I don't know where he got his ideas from."

"Not from his father?"

"From Allan . . . oh, no! He had a knack with women, and with animals as it turned out; nothing more."

"Someone told me his first wife is still alive."

"Cathie? I think so. She was living in Dover, the last I heard. I can't think why," he added, as though the thought had only just struck him. "She's still there, as far as I know."

"Doesn't your nephew hear from her?"

"Hugo? Not that I know of." He paused, and seemed for the first time to be considering the precise form of what he was about to say. "It wasn't an amicable divorce. Allan brought the action, and there was never any question of her getting custody of the child."

"How long ago was this?"

"Before the war."

"In 1938," said Mrs. Randall, making another of her unexpected darts into the conversation. "Hugo was two years old." Again when he looked at her, Antony could find no trace of emotion in her face; it was as though a statue had spoken. "Cathie wasn't a *nice* woman," she added primly.

"Was Allan living at Ravenscroft at that time?"

"I'd better start at the beginning," said Walter. There was a kind of relish in his tone, as though the story was one he would enjoy telling. "I hadn't much time for my brother, as you may have guessed, he was a bit of a clod if you see what I mean. But the eldest son, of course.

"Well, Father always farmed in a dilettante sort of way . . . left things to the bailiff, didn't need to concern himself. But he knew the land, and he expected Allan to know it too. But nothing would do for him but to go to London and take some half-baked job on a newspaper—it was different for me, I had to go. And he met Cathie, and married her when he was twenty. Our parents didn't like that much, but it was nothing to the row there was after the divorce."

"They disapproved?"

"Mother did. I don't think I ever knew what my father really thought. And it didn't make a bit of difference to her when she knew what Cathie was like . . . Allan was a man, and therefore in the wrong."

"How delightfully simple."

"Wasn't it? Well, I'm not too clear how he got on in the years immediately after the divorce. I believe he had a housekeeper, or something of the sort. But then he joined up when the war started, and as soon as the blitz got going Nell took herself up to town and more or less kidnaped Hugo. It wasn't as easy as that, of course, because she still had Mother to reckon with; the old lady didn't give in until Nell announced her intention of leaving home and taking a job in a factory so that she could keep Hugo with her. Mind you, I think she was misguided, but it took some doing, standing up to Mother.''

"How old was your sister then?"

"In 1940? Nineteen, or thereabouts. She stayed home right through the war, looking after Hugo and working as a sort of land girl. And in the later years Allan came home once or twice on leave . . . that was after Father died and I suppose the old lady could see she was going to need him, so there was a reconciliation of sorts. Anyway, Allan met Mary Trevor on one of his visits and married her as soon as he was demobbed . . . no, it must have been before that, he was back in England in 1945, I remember.''

"And the whole family stayed at Ravenscroft?"

"What else? Journalism was a broken reed, so far as Allan was concerned, he never really made the grade. And now he had a family to support. So he concluded a truce with the old lady, and settled down to learn farming like a good boy.''

"And died—let's see—twelve years later?"

"That's right. Leaving the twins to Hugo's tender mercies . . . and Nell's, of course.''

"At least, Nell had some experience.''

"Not of brats that age. Once Allan was home for good she didn't interfere. She was afraid of getting on the wrong side of Mary, you know.''

"I see. How did it work out?"

"As you'd imagine.'' Well then, a difficult household, and it was with Nell that his sympathies lay. But strangely, considering his previous enthusiasm, Walter did not seem inclined to enlarge on the topic. It was Mrs. Randall who said, in her sudden way:

"She ought to have left home then. Afterward, your mother would never have let her go.''

"Oh, come now, my dear, she wasn't as difficult as all that.'' He waited a moment, but went on when it was quite obvious she wasn't going to speak again. "Hugo went to the grammar school here, and spent all his spare time hanging around the farmyard. Made it natural that he should take over when Allan died . . . and just as well he took to the life, if you aak me," added Walter, spitefully. "I doubt if he'd have mcasured up to a more civilized profession; certainly not to one where he had to mix with people."

"What about the twins?"

"Marian lives at home and comes into town to school; Mark is at Brantford, but he's home now, of course, because of having to give evidence. The school has a very fine scholarship record, I understand, particularly in the sciences. I wouldn't lift a finger to help send him to university myself . . . do him all the good in the world to get down to a job of work."

"Were you at Ravenscroft on . . . Boxing Day, wasn't it? When he produced the digitalis, I mean."

"Digitoxin," corrected Walter automatically. Mark Randall had obviously drilled his family well. "We were having tea there. He was just showing off, you know . . . and I'll say this for him, it would have been a good deal safer in his hands than hers. But there you are, the old lady lost her temper."

"Did she put it in her workbox then and there?"

"That sounds like a leading question," said Walter, inaccurately, but still with good humor. "She did, because it happened to be handy. But no one could have known she'd leave it there, could they?"

"Of course not. Did you hear about the quarrel Hugo had with his grandmother on Christmas Day?"

"Nobody told me. I could tell there'd been one, the atmosphere was unmistakable."

"But no hint of the reason? Or of Mrs. Randall's intention of changing her will?" He kept finding the phrase "the old lady" on the tip of his tongue, but Walter seemed to regard that as synonymous with "mother."

"No hint at all. And she'd have got over it, you know, put things right again," said Walter, confidently. For a moment Antony wondered just what his version of "right" would have been. "If she'd lived," added Randall; and sighed.

"I'm sorry to harp on this, but do you yourself know of anything that might have led to the quarrel?" He met the other man's suddenly suspicious stare and added carefully: "You see, it has been suggested to me—"

"That *I* told the old lady something? Well, I don't know

anything about Hugo's affairs, and don't want to," stated Walter flatly.

"No, of course," said Antony meaninglessly. "Did you see your mother at all on the Friday after Christmas?"

"The Friday . . . the day she went to see Fred Byron? She came into the Bank that morning, as she often did on market day, to make a withdrawal. And she stayed in my office about half an hour, talking."

"Did she tell you where she was going?"

"She said she hadn't made an appointment, and hoped Fred wouldn't try to pretend he was busy. But she didn't tell me why she wanted to see him, and you may be sure I wasn't asking questions out of turn. She was still in a devil of a temper, you know."

"I see. And after that?"

"We were up to the house for tea on Sunday as usual. You were there yourself, Tommy. Nothing happened that was out of the way."

"Well, I'm very grateful for your patience, Mr. Randall—" Maitland seemed more downcast than ever, and Walter—apparently taking heart from the fact—smiled with renewed condescension.

"I'm afraid I wasn't very much help," he said, "but I don't really know what you expected. And at least you and Tommy will have the satisfaction of knowing you've done everything possible—"

The words "when your client is convicted" weren't actually spoken, but the implication was very clear indeed. Antony took his leave with a depressed conviction that Walter was probably right, at that.

VII

As they left the Bank Tommy seemed disinclined for conversation, but remarked grumpily that he was like Walter, he didn't know what Maitland had expected.

"What I don't see," said Antony, ignoring this, "is why he consented to talk to me at all."

"Wendy," said Tommy briefly; and added irritably as his companion stared at him: "Mrs. Walter. She runs the show, really."

"It isn't very obvious."

"I suppose not." It seemed he was talking himself out of his ill-humor, for he added, more expansively: "She's pro-Fran, you see. And she wouldn't set up her opinion against Walter's in public, but when they're alone—"

"You're guessing."

"Common knowledge," said Davenant. "True as I stand here."

"Old Mrs. Randall's influence, perhaps? I gather she was a feminist."

"In theory, yes. She didn't let it inhibit her in any way in her dealings with her own sex."

"I don't suppose she did. Look here, could Walter be hard up?"

"He's nothing besides his salary, so far as I know. But I've never heard of any extravagances." He was looking curiously at Maitland as he spoke. "What are you thinking?"

"That there's nothing quite so convincing as a money motive. And Fran Gifford wasn't the only person to benefit under Mrs. Randall's will."

"But, look here—"

"Don't take me too seriously at this stage. How do I get to Miss Langhorne's?"

"Next on the left . . . the Causeway . . . third door on the right. Number six, you can't miss it." Tommy had a doubtful look, but it seemed he had no desire to carry the conversation any further. He turned back toward the square with a muttered "Good night."

The Causeway was narrow and cobbled, with a high wall on one side and on the other a row of tiny cottages which seemed to have come at some fairly recent date under the renovator's hand. Number six had a green front door with a Lincoln Imp on the knocker . . . a leering, self-satisfied imp, thought Antony resentfully, even though it was so far from home. He raised his hand and tapped respectfully, and was glad he hadn't taken a more vigorous line when Vera Langhorne opened the door and he saw that it led straight into the living room.

It wasn't, after all, so small a room as the exterior of the cottage suggested. A door on the right led, presumably, to a closed-in staircase; another, opposite, to the kitchen . . . or so he supposed from the enticing aroma of coffee. The furniture had clearly come from a much bigger house . . . good, solid stuff. There was a bright fire on the hearth and an easy chair pulled close to it; its fellow, opposite, was pushed back almost against the wall. The sort of chairs a woman would choose, he thought . . . soft enough, but made for perching, not for sprawling at ease. Incongruous in the corner a record player of excellent tone was discoursing Tchaikovsky's *Piano Concerto* . . . *No. 1,* he thought, and remembered the composer's statement that a concerto should be a battle between piano and orchestra. Perhaps the music had been chosen in sympathy with his hostess's mood.

He turned to find her eying him, watching his reactions. ''I like your house,'' he said.

She seemed to consider the compliment, and then treated it with her usual gruffness. ''So do I,'' she told him. ''You'd better sit down, I'll just fetch the tray.''

She waved him to the chair near the fire, and surprisingly it was comfortable. He could relax here, it seemed days since he had been able to do so. He leaned back and thought that if he had the energy he would walk across and look at the rows of books ranged along the opposite wall; but if they were inherited, as the furniture seemed to have been, they would provide no further clue to Vera's character. And perhaps, after all, the music told him enough.

He was nearly asleep when she came stumping back. The tray went down with a clatter on a coffee table which he had suspected on sight of being an old plant stand cut down. Vera went over to the record player and lowered the volume a little, and then came back and stood looking down at him with an odd expression; a mixture, he thought hazily, of disapproval and respect. After a moment, apparently satisfied with her scrutiny, she slumped down in the chair opposite and began to pour the coffee. ''Got to hand it to you . . . doing your best,'' she said.

He sat up to take the cup she was offering him, and somewhere at the back of his mind the phrase she had used struggled for recognition. Walter had said something very much like it, but whatever you thought of Vera you couldn't accuse her of condescension. She might not like him, he was pretty sure now she didn't, but for some reason she had produced the words as a tribute.

"I'm sorry—" he said.

Afterward he was never sure just how the apology would have ended. She cut him short, saying bluntly: "Thing is, not at all sure I was right about Fran Gifford. Didn't like what I heard in court today."

"In court?" Antony struggled with this for a moment. "There was nothing you didn't know already," he said at last.

"Your talk with her. Not . . . not a simple girl," she told him. "Wouldn't surprise me if you were right about the man."

"Well, it wouldn't surprise me, exactly. But does it really make any difference?"

"Could mean I misled you. Based my conclusions on a faulty premise, you know."

"That doesn't matter, either, if your conclusions were right."

"You really believe that, don't you? Thought at first . . . disingenuous," she said.

"I shouldn't have stayed if I hadn't believed it," he pointed out.

There was a pause, and then she smiled at him; and he realized, with surprise, that it was the first time she had done so. "And now you're caught," she said.

This was so exactly true that it startled him. He said carefully: "I want to do my best for her."

"So do I, of course. But what I wanted to say to you, if you're laying grounds for a counterattack . . . won't be a popular move."

"It never is." He picked up his cup, found the coffee too hot still for drinking, and set it down again.

"In this case, more than ever. Don't think you realize the depth of feeling in the town." She paused, and then added reluctantly: "Got to admit, Nell Randall knows something about Hugo that she doesn't want to tell."

"Do you think she'd stand by, if she knew Fran was innocent?"

"She couldn't know that."

He was silent for a while, and then said with a directness

that matched her own: "Miss Langhorne . . . why did you ask me to stay?"

"Thought I explained."

"It was obvious from the beginning that if we weren't just going to try to get Fran off for lack of evidence—which you could have handled perfectly well yourself—we had to go all out to prove someone else killed Alice Randall. Which is, in any case, the only defense worth a damn. To do that, I've got to ask questions, and as far as the prosecution witnesses are concerned I have to do the best I can in court." He paused, as if inviting comment, and then added ruefully: "When all's said, I may be no wiser in the end. But what else is there to do?"

She seemed to be thinking this out. "What I thought, you could show someone else could have done it as well as Fran . . . not any particular person."

"I may be reduced to that. But while there's any hope at all—"

"Even if you antagonize the jury?" she asked him; and watched with an interest that was not altogether without sympathy while he gave the idea his undivided attention.

"I think it's a risk we've got to take," he said at last. "Which brings me to something I've been wondering, Miss Langhorne. Why didn't you try to get the trial shifted on grounds of local prejudice?"

"Thought about it, of course; talked it over with Tommy. Think he was right though, no real grounds."

"No, really—!"

"How often have you known an application for change of venue succeed?"

"Not often," he admitted.

"Didn't much fancy the idea of arguing about something as intangible as public opinion; all talk, the press behaved very properly . . . nothing there."

"I know the kind of thing," said Maitland dryly.

"If we made the application and failed . . . unfavorable reaction," Vera told him.

"Yes, well, it'll be a point for the Court of Appeal. We may do better there." He leaned forward and picked up his cup again. "You're stuck with me now, you know. *And* my methods."

"Can see that, all right," said Vera grimly. And let the silence lengthen.

Antony did not speak again until he had drunk his coffee and passed his cup for a refill. The concerto was nearing its end; he was happy enough to listen, but the peaceful mood had been for a moment only, it was broken now. When the last notes had died away and the machine had shut itself off with an incongruous click, he said casually: "There's one thing I've been wondering, about Nell Randall."

"Tommy knows her. I don't."

"Yes, but I couldn't ask him this, and I daresay it's common knowledge. Why did she never marry?"

"She was engaged once, man was killed in the war. Tragic thing . . . 1945 . . . nearly over."

"That might make a bond—wouldn't you say?—between her and Davenant." He thought of Wellesley as he spoke.

Vera gave him another of her rare smiles. "Been listening to gossip," she said.

"Yes, of course."

"Women don't marry for that sort of reason." She paused, considering the statement. "Shouldn't say that, no personal experience. But don't see it myself."

"I expect you're right."

"Mind you, wouldn't wonder at her taking him. Like to see it myself; bad luck, losing his wife like that. Very devoted couple, can't think it's good for him to be alone." After a moment she added, with a penetrating look: "But you're more concerned with Nell Randall."

"She's unhappy," said Antony. He sounded apologetic. "But I was wondering how the old lady'd have taken it if she'd got married, you know. And whether Davenant, or any other of her suitors, could have made a shot at keeping her in the style to which—"

"That gentle creature," said Vera, appalled.

"Why not?"

"For one thing she was dining with the Firmonts."

"As far as the family are concerned, their alibis, or lack of them, doesn't matter a damn. Supposing what Fran saw in the test tube was only half the quantity of poison that confounded boy manufactured? If the remainder was already in the rum, for instance; or mixed with the sugar—"

"The rest could have been emptied later. But—"

"The doctors were vague as to the exact quantity she'd taken," he reminded her.

"That could apply just as well to Hugo."

"Even better," he agreed. "That must have been one hell of a household, at Ravenscroft."

But he couldn't get her agreement to this; she shook her head stubbornly and said it was "a very natural arrangement." He could only be thankful that no further argument arose that evening about the conduct of the defense.

VIII

Back at the George he collected his key, and two envelopes which the desk clerk said had been delivered by hand. The first contained a note from the Judge's Marshal, commanding his presence at dinner the following evening. At least, that's what it amounts to, he thought ungratefully, and threw the note down on the bed while he went to investigate what Jenny had sent him in the way of shirts.

Reassured on this point, he tried the telephone next and asked for his own number; and it wasn't until he had finally resigned himself to the fact that his wife was still out that he remembered the second envelope and went to look for it.

Not an official communication of any kind. The address was printed in rough capitals, and the purplish ink had blurred on the cheap paper. Inside, the message, too, was printed.

WE DON'T WANT ANY INTERFERENCE
WE CAN SETTLE OUR OWN AFFAIRS

ALL WICKEDNESS IS BUT LITTLE TO
THE WICKEDNESS OF A WOMAN

And then, a little below the rest, as though somehow he might have missed the point:

SHE ISN'T ANY GOOD, YOU KNOW

This is getting monotonous, said Antony to himself. He folded the note carefully and put it away in his wallet. He'd have to do something about it, he supposed, but it was a damned nuisance just now.

FRIDAY, 31ST JANUARY

LOOKING back, he was even more irritated by the necessity he had been under of explaining himself to Vera Langhorne. By comparison Davenant, who in theory was instructing him, was willing to give him a much freer hand; though he had to admit that this was probably because the solicitor was of a more easygoing temperament . . . not to say more lazy. The feeling of dissatisfaction was in his mind when he awoke, and stayed with him while he dressed. It wasn't until he was downstairs in the dining room, waiting for his breakfast kipper, that he remembered the anonymous message and took it out to have another look. But when he spread it open on the table the message had disappeared.

He tried the fire first, holding the sheet of paper open to the blaze, and thought as he did so that it was a good thing Wellesley had left; no one else seemed at all interested in what he was doing. It was different when the waiter returned; he seemed to regard it as the height of eccentricity that his customer should have poured milk into his saucer in order to soak a blank piece of paper. The experiment seemed to be an absorbing one. Maitland gave him a vague look and asked for a clean saucer. When it came he had hung the paper over the toast rack to dry and was already eating the kipper, though in a thoughtful way. There was still no sign of the printing that had been so clear the night before.

There were a couple of writing tables in the smaller lounge, and he went in there after breakfast to reply to the Judge's invitation. The thought of his anonymous correspondent was an ugly background in his mind. When the note was written he went into the hall again to arrange for its delivery to the Judge's Lodgings. It would have been easier to take it himself to the Shire Hall, and find a messenger there, but as the invitation had been delivered to his hotel perhaps the more formal approach would be in order. And while he was talking to the clerk at the desk there were two women whispering together at the bottom of the staircase, and he caught the words ". . . from London." And then, with unmistakable tartness: "I think it's a disgrace. They say his clients are *never* convicted."

"Wicked, I call it," said the second voice, not mincing matters. He knew who they were, now, two elderly ladies who resided in the hotel; this one spoke in a naturally penetrating tone which was clearly audible in spite of being lowered. "It's all a matter of money. If you can pay enough you can get away with murder."

"She ought to be made an example of . . . a girl like that. They say some man was keeping her, right here in town. Some of these young people—"

"Quite shameless." The whispering stopped as Maitland handed over his letter and turned away from the desk.

So that was what "they" were saying. He ought to have found it merely amusing, but for some reason the hushed voices filled him with anger and disgust. If Fran Gifford had had a hundred lovers . . .

The extravagance of the thought brought him down to earth again. Human nature, he'd said, trying to reassure the girl; so why take it so to heart? The accusations against her were just as absurd as the idea that he always won his cases. But somehow, at that moment, the situation didn't seem to have in it any of the elements of humor.

II

The prosecution, that morning, were dealing with routine matters, and the reporters who had arrived overnight— impelled by who knew what vulturine instinct—were having a dull time of it. Nobody was trying to deny that Sophie had admitted Fran Gifford to Ravenscroft at three minutes past nine on New Year's Eve, or that she was sure of the time because Bob was late and she had her eye on the kitchen clock. Nobody was even interested in the cook's vague confirmation of this, or in the fact that she was a little hard of hearing and hadn't noticed anything out of the way all night. And the evidence of the two bus drivers was completely superfluous. Maitland, abandoning the farmyard, produced an ill-executed sketch of a stiff-backed old lady with a censorious expression, which turned out so unlike the photograph he had seen of Alice`Randall that when he sat back and regarded it dispassionately he wondered for an uneasy moment if his junior might take it for a libel on herself. But Miss Langhorne kept her eyes averted, her attention on the witnesses and on the few questions that could usefully be asked in cross-examination.

Appleton himself was quiescent this morning, the faint pomposity of his manner very marked. The Judge looked somnolent; the jury . . . what were the jury making of all this, anyway? A dull-looking bunch, he'd been wrong about people's occupations so often that he wasn't making any guesses, but they were locals, of course; that woman in the tweed coat might have been the sister of the tart-voiced woman at the hotel. The men looked respectable, rather stodgy; it was a measure of his own lack of the commonplace virtues, he thought, that the description should sound to him like a reproach. Shameless . . . wicked . . . an absolute disgrace . . . they were right, at that, to poison an old woman was all these things, and more. But suddenly his mind was groping for an allusion, something only half remembered; it would give him, he thought, the clue to the whole affair, and for a moment he was almost panic-stricken because he couldn't recall . . . but that, of course, was nonsense.

There was a stir of interest when Mrs. Harlow went into the witness box, but there was to be no gossip this morning, just a plain story of how she had heard Fran Gifford come in soon after half past ten on New Year's Eve, and had called out to her without receiving a reply. So she'd taken up a hot drink anyway, when she thought the girl had had time to get to bed; but Fran hadn't even started to get undressed, and though she kept her face averted it was very obvious she had been crying. Maitland scribbled a note on his pad and pushed it across in front of Vera Langhorne: "Ask if she might not have been peeling onions." But the suggestion was rightly ignored.

And so it went on. There was no complication about the case the prosecution were building up: following, emphasizing, interpreting Appleton's opening remarks, it had a clarity that was hideously simple. Fran had seen the new draft, glimpsed briefly the allure of riches, but already when she came to sign the codicil old Mrs. Randall was having a change of heart; perhaps if her solicitor hadn't been pressing her she would already have admitted her mistake. Elsie Barber's story would have helped them here, presumably she had never told the police that the old lady looked upset when she left Mr. Byron's office that afternoon. But—sure enough—here was a friend of Fran's . . . no, a fellow boarder . . . with a silly little tale of a conversation about what they'd both do if they were rich. Fran, it seemed, would have liked—just once!—to buy some new clothes without having to ask the price. And she wanted to travel . . . seemed to have quite a thing about it really. It was all too silly . . . he shook his head slightly at Vera Langhorne's inquiring look and got up himself when Appleton's learned junior sat down again.

"What was your own contribution to this—er—this fantasy?" A hard-faced wench, he thought, and smiled at her in a friendly way. "Diamonds? Furs? Dinner at the Ritz?"

"Oh, yes. I'd like to have a good time."

"Ten thousand a year and a handsome husband?"

"That's right." She was smiling back at him now, completely at her ease.

"But that's just a dream, isn't it? We all have our dreams. And I don't suppose Miss Gifford is any older than you are."

But it was after the luncheon recess that the interest quickened, when Mark Randall was called. He was dark and a little taller than his sister, perhaps no thinner, but with the bony structure of his face more clearly defined. In fact, he was a bony creature altogether. Like Marian, he had an air of restless energy, but there was a sulkiness, a guarded expression, that Maitland had not noticed in the girl.

Mark was ready enough to expatiate on his experiment with *digitalis purpurea,* and even more didactic than the expert witness had been about the properties of the substance he had produced. He was inclined to shy away from a discussion of teatime on Boxing Day, but there was a little resentment, too. "If she'd left it with me nothing like this would have happened," he insisted; but his grievance seemed to be that people would blame him, rather than that he blamed himself.

Maitland, who had already taken in every detail of his appearance without seeming to do so, stood eying him in silence for a while when he rose to cross-examine. Just for the moment it was very quiet in the court; he could hear Vera's breathing; at the other end of the counsel's bench Appleton began to drum his fingers nervously on the table; the Judge coughed . . . an obvious rebuke to an unwarranted delay. "When did you conduct this experiment, Mr. Randall?"

"Last summer. August, I suppose."

"During your school holidays?"

"While I was home. Yes."

"Why?"

"I often work at home. One has to do something."

"Surely something of a less deadly nature—?"

"What difference does that make?" asked the witness reasonably.

"None, I suppose, if a proper control is kept."

"I couldn't help that. And even when she took it, if she hadn't been fool enough to show it to Fran—"

"By 'she,' do you mean your grandmother?" asked Maitland coldly. The sulky look deepened about Mark Randall's mouth.

"Yes, I do."

If he wanted to display his spite, by all means let him have the opportunity to do so. "And that very improper remark about Miss Gifford . . . I take it when you manufactured this substance you had no idea of its ever being used?"

"Of course I hadn't!"

"Not even when you handed it over to your grandmother on Boxing Day?"

"How could I? I didn't know then that Fran had been getting round Grannie to cut us all out."

"Now, I'm very glad to have that explained, Mr. Randall." Counsel's tone was cordiality itself. "I was wondering what lay behind your sense of grievance against my client, but of course, in the circumstances—"

"It isn't that at all."

"I don't quite understand you. Er—what isn't what?"

"I only meant, I didn't know she was that kind of girl."

"Can you really imagine anyone exerting undue influence over your grandmother, Mr. Randall?"

"Well, I . . . well, no," said Mark. And suddenly he grinned. It came as such a surprise to Maitland that he hardly heard Appleton's objection; but this didn't really matter, because it was a foregone conclusion that he would object. And that the Judge would uphold him . . .

But he had got his effect. The fact that the sullen look settled quickly on the witness's face again wasn't going to spoil it, and his muttered "I don't know what Fran told her—" was lost in what Counsel for the Prosecution was saying. But Maitland wasn't listening to that, his mind was fixed still on Mark Randall . . . not on what he could tell the court, it wasn't very likely that would be important, but on what he himself could learn of the boy.

"If your experiment was completed last August, had you been carrying the poison in your pocket ever since?" His tone was more friendly now, but Mark treated the question scornfully.

"Of course I hadn't!"

"Did you take it back to school with you?"

"I left it in my desk at home . . . locked up."

"And when did you take it out again?"

"At the beginning of the . . . when I came home for Christmas."

"Why did you do that?"

"Well . . . I wanted to."

"That is hardly an explanation, Mr. Randall." There was one thing he had learned about Mark, at least . . . he didn't like being reminded of his status as a schoolboy. And—perhaps because it had some particular association for him—he seemed to find this blend of politeness and sarcasm especially galling. "If you wish me to spell it out for you . . . why did you want it?"

"If you must know, I got interested in vegetable poisons." His tone was an ungracious as ever, but the subject was one on which he was willing to enlarge. "There's a lot of work to be done with quite common herbs, particularly among the less lethal alkaloids. It seems to me that with proper care . . . anyway, I thought next summer I'd get down to some really original work. The digitoxin was child's play, you know.''

It had sometimes seemed to Maitland, in the course of his researches, that there was nothing original left to be done when it came to extracting poisonous substances from the hedgerow; there they all were, foxglove and monkshood and deadly nightshade, and man's ingenuity more than sufficient to exploit their murderous qualities, even if he had been a little slow to split the atom or find a cure for the common cold. ''Doesn't it strike you as rather a morbid occupation?'' he asked.

''Not at all.'' Mark was on his dignity again. ''A good many of these things have a medicinal application; that's what I had in mind.''

''A benefit to humanity, in fact.'' He found the Judge's eye resting meditatively on him, and spared a moment to wonder why Appleton was holding his peace. ''So you carried the test tube about in your pocket for several days before you brought it to your family's notice.''

''Yes, I did.''

''And on Boxing Day, at teatime . . . why did you produce it then?''

''I don't really know.'' He was scowling again. ''For a lark, I suppose.''

''And because all the family were there at that time, to be impressed . . . or frightened.''

''I didn't think of it like that. It was nothing to be scared of, anyway.''

''You'd been handling the test tube, I suppose. It would have your fingerprints on it?''

''Of course.''

''Did you explain to your family exactly what was in it?''

''I just said there was enough poison there to kill everyone in the house.'' His attempt to sound offhand was not altogether successful.

''And you told them how it had been obtained.''

''It wouldn't have been any good explaining. I told them it came from the common foxglove.''

''What did Mrs. Randall say to that?''

''Just . . . she was angry.''

"Yes, you have told us that before, and I don't find it very surprising. Exactly what did she say to you?"

"That it wasn't safe for me to have it." And suddenly his resentment seemed to come to boiling point. "As if I'm not dealing with poisonous things every day of my life! But she never could see—"

"What did she say to you, Mr. Randall?"

"I don't see . . . oh, very well! She said she never believed in children being allowed to play with dangerous toys."

Maitland grinned at that, not sympathetically. "That was cutting you down to size, wasn't it?" he observed. "Have you any other childish hobbies, Mr. Randall?"

"It was a serious experiment," said the witness hotly.

"Child's play . . . you said."

"That was just a manner of speaking."

"You've outgrown such childish pastimes as . . . throwing stones, for instance?" Mark was suddenly very still.

"I don't know what you mean."

"You were making invisible ink in your kindergarten, I must suppose. Visible ink which later disappears is an interesting variant, I admit."

Mark eyed him sullenly for a moment, and then gave a crack of quite genuine laughter. "Try to prove it!" he said.

Mr. Justice Halford was looking plaintive. Appleton bounced to his feet and said loudly, forgetting formality: "What nonsense is this?" Maitland looked at the witness and said, smiling: "It really isn't worth while." He looked up at the Judge, as though Halford had given voice to his discontent, and added: "I have no more questions, my lord."

"Really, Mr. Maitland, I don't understand this line of questioning at all."

"Your lordship must forgive my somewhat fumbling approach. I have had—er—very little time to study my brief."

"It seemed to me you had something definite in mind," said the Judge querulously. Antony made no attempt to reply. "Oh, very well, very well! Have you any more questions, Mr. Appleton?"

"Don't know what you're at," said Vera Langhorne

quietly as Maitland sat down again, "but it won't make a good impression, treating the boy like that."

Behind them Davenant, puzzled himself and increasingly uneasy, saw counsel turn to his junior, and heard the quick, angry stammer in his voice as he replied: "I d-don't want to m-make a good impression. I just w-want to p-prove our client's innocence. R-remember?"

The last witness that afternoon was Frederick Byron, and his evidence was obviously intended to be the climax of the prosecution's case. Antony had to admit to himself that it was effective: opportunity had already been proved, and now the jury's attention was to be turned to motive and perhaps this was, after all, the strongest link in the chain. But even as he thought this, it occurred to him that the most telling point in the case for the Crown had been made by implication only. Here was a girl with good reason to commit the crime, who visited the old lady in exceptional circumstances and mixed the drink in which the poison was administered; would it not be an incredible coincidence if someone else had chosen that very evening . . . ?

Byron was, as Tommy Davenant had admitted, a handsome man, and if he was fifty-five he didn't look it. His fair hair was thick, and waved in an orderly way that immediately aroused Antony's envy; he had regular features, a rather ruddy complexion, and vividly blue eyes. He was tallish, a little portly, but no more than lent him dignity. And he was immaculately turned out, down to the last detail. It would be an odd thing if Chedcombe didn't count his appearance as being in his favor in the matrimonial stakes . . . that is, if they were right about his intentions toward Nell Randall.

There was nothing unexpected in the evidence, though much of it would be new to the jury. Mrs. Alice Randall was an old and valued client; she had come to his office on the morning of Friday, December 27th, without an appointment, arriving at about a quarter to eleven.

"Were you at all surprised to see her?" In spite of his occasional explosiveness, Appleton was a versatile chap; this was a smooth, man-to-man approach, and Byron responded with equal affability.

"No, not at all. I don't think it ever occurred to her, you

know, that I might have other commitments." He spoke indulgently, with a half-smile for the vagaries of an old lady.

"Were you, in fact, engaged?"

"As it happened, no."

"And what was her purpose in visiting you, Mr. Byron?"

"She wished to add a codicil to her will."

"Please tell us exactly—"

The witness complied, going into some detail over the original dispositions and the change which was proposed; his natural verbosity encouraged, Maitland thought resentfully, by the questions with which Appleton was plying him. At last,

"What was your own reaction to this, Mr. Byron?"

"I was very worried about it. I think I may say I was appalled. I ventured to remonstrate with her, I felt it to be my duty. But her mind was quite made up."

"Did she give you any reason why Miss Gifford should be favored in this way?"

"My lord," suggested Maitland, waking up, "my friend might care to rephrase his question."

"Perhaps, Mr. Appleton, it would be more satisfactory if you ask merely the reason for the change. Will that content you, Mr. Maitland?"

"If it contents your lordship."

"She refused to give me any explanation at all," said the witness, obviously indignant at the recollection. "I could only hope that she would think better of it in the interval between giving me her instructions and signing the codicil. But I could not persuade her to delay the matter beyond the following Monday—and then only, I am sure, because the weekend supervened."

"Did you inform the accused of her good fortune?"

"Most certainly not!"

"Even though she worked in your office?"

"That made no difference to the position. I dictated the revision to my own clerk; I believe she came in on Saturday to type the fair copy."

"The office is not open on Saturdays?"

"Not as a general rule."

"And where was this codicil in the interval between typing and signature?"

"On my desk, the engrossment and draft together. I took the precaution of piling some other papers on top of them, in case Miss Gifford had occasion to come in."

"Did she, in fact, do so?"

"Not to my knowledge."

"And when Mrs. Randall came in on Monday, she had not yet changed her mind."

"There is no evidence, my lord," said Counsel for the Defense, in a bored tone, "that the deceased lady ever had second thoughts in the matter."

"Are you not being overcritical, Mr. Maitland?"

"The question, my lord, is capable of more than one interpretation. If my learned friend would care to be more explicit—"

"Had Mrs. Randall changed her mind when she came to your office on Monday the 30th December?" said Appleton, in a goaded tone. Maitland smiled at him disarmingly, and sat down again.

"No, she had not."

"What had transpired on that occasion?"

"I read the codicil to her, and she signed it. My partner, Mr. Davenant, and my clerk, Miss Barber, witnessed her signature."

"Did you again bring up this question of restoring the position?"

But the afternoon was drawing on; the Judge had already glanced several times at the electric clock that had been affixed, incongruously, to the wall of the court. "I think, perhaps, we should pursue these matters after a recess, Mr. Appleton," he remarked apologetically. "The court will adjourn until Monday . . ."

III

Antony waited for the crowds to disperse a little before he made any attempt to leave the hall. He was frowning to himself as he piled his papers together; if the case for the prosecution could have been completed that afternoon, he'd have been ready to waive cross-examining Frederick Byron, rather than recall his testimony to the jury on Monday morning. After all, there was nothing in his proof that could possibly help the defense; nothing that would answer his own urgent questions. Now, of course, Appleton would go over the whole thing again . . .

"Going to sit here all night?" inquired Vera Langhorne, beside him.

"Sorry. I was thinking." Even Davenant had gone, he realized, and got up in a hurry and followed her out into the aisle. He hoped she wasn't going to catechize him about his plans for the weekend, but she plodded along a little ahead of him in silence, making no attempt to speak.

The street lamps had been lit long since; they didn't afford any very dazzling illumination. Several groups of people still stood about on the pavement, and Frederick Byron and his partner were going down the steps ahead of them, slowly, and in earnest consultation. Antony didn't notice the girl until he heard his name spoken, and turned to see her move out from the shadow of one of the pillars. "You'll be Fran Gifford's London lawyer?" she said; and answered her own question before he could speak. "Well, I know you are. I saw you inside."

He could see now that she was very young, not much older than Marian Randall, but of a very different type. A little thing, with a fair, rather fluffy prettiness; but then he saw her eyes, china blue, and fixed on him with a hard, almost calculating look. He said, "Can I do something for you?" and thought with impatience that the words meant nothing at all. But they couldn't stand here staring at each other, and she seemed to be waiting for him to speak.

Beside him, Vera Langhorne said brusquely: "Now then, Nancy. You can't be up to your tricks here."

"That's all you know about it," said the girl. "I've got business with him . . . see?"

"What *can* I do for you?" asked Maitland again.

"You can get Fran Gifford out of this. You can do that, can't you? That's what you're here for."

"I think perhaps . . . do you know this lady?" he asked, turning his head to look at Vera Langhorne.

"She's well known in Chedcombe," said Vera grimly. "And if her business is what I think it is—"

"Well, it's not, then. I told him—"

"You're a friend of Miss Gifford's, perhaps?"

She laughed at that, an uncomfortably mirthless sound. "I just want to know you'll get her off," she said again.

"Well . . . why?"

"Hasn't she told you?"

"I still don't know your name," said Antony irritably.

"Selkirk." She was very close to him now, looking up at him intently. "None the wiser, are you? Well, ask Fran Gifford . . . ask her!"

"What am I to ask her?"

"About the money. And then you can come and tell me, can't you? Anyone'll tell you where I live."

"If you would explain exactly—"

"I might be able to help you, at that." The thought seemed to be new to her. "But you find out first," she said, "and then I'll think about it." She ran down the steps without waiting for his reply; paused to look up at him, so that he saw her face for an instant, a white blur in the darkness, then she was out of sight and her light footsteps were dying away in the distance.

"What on earth was all that about?" he asked.

"Up to no good," said Vera Langhorne gruffly.

"But she said—"

"Wanted to get your interest. Out for anything new."

"Oh," said Antony, rather blankly. And then: "She's very young."

"Bad reputation," said Vera, warming to her theme. "Take my advice, don't get mixed up with her."

"I've no intention—" But the absurdity of the situation struck him suddenly, and he began to laugh. "Why is her reputation bad?" he asked.

She began to move down the steps again. "Never was good," she said at last. "Had a baby last year, should have been still in school. Defiant attitude, made it worse."

"She isn't married, then? The father—?"

"Could have been one of several. *She* wouldn't say."

"What did Chedcombe make of the problem?" His tone was sarcastic; he didn't care, just then, if he offended her.

"They didn't like it," said Vera, missing the point. "Mother's a fool; girl's been running wild ever since."

"Well, what did she have to do with Fran Gifford?"

"Nothing. That's why I told you—" She obviously had no patience with his obtuseness.

"If you think she was making a pass at me," said Antony bluntly, "she wasn't!"

She stopped in her tracks, and stood eying him, obviously trying to assess his capability to speak as an expert witness. "I suppose you'd know," she said doubtfully.

"I think I should," he told her gravely.

"Now you're laughing at me," she said, without resentment, and was silent for a moment. When she spoke it was to change the subject. "Why did you bully young Mark?"

"Did I bully him?"

"You know very well—"

"It would give me a good deal of pleasure to wring his neck," said Antony, "but I didn't think Halford would altogether approve. Contempt of court, or something," he added vaguely.

Vera gave one of her rare laughs. "Do you really suppose it was Mark who broke your window?"

"Yes, of course. And sent me a damn silly anonymous letter besides."

"Did you take it to the police?"

"There wasn't much point. The writing had disappeared this morning."

"Oh, I see," she said doubtfully. "But I don't see why—"

"Neither do I. I wish I did."

"Was it wise to let him see that you knew?"

"The idea," he told her patiently, "was to discourage him from any further action."

Again she thought for a moment before replying. "Should have done that, all right," she agreed.

IV

But, setting out on foot for the Judge's Lodgings that evening, Maitland became aware of uneasiness. When he turned from Market Square into Abbot's Walk there seemed to be an echo to his footsteps. He was so convinced of this that he drew back once into the shadow of a doorway, and waited; but the steps behind came on firmly and passed him, and a moment later, when he saw the man under a lamp, he was sure it was a stranger.

What was worrying him, anyway? He had done his best to anger Mark Randall, and partly that had been because he felt he had a score to pay. There had been a note of genuine amusement in the boy's laughter, but he had laughed because he was nervous. So it was of all things the most unlikely that Mark would be in Chedcombe that evening; besides which he'd decided—hadn't he?—that no one was following him at all.

Abbot's Walk was hardly more than a passage, really, leading into the Close, where the Judge's Lodgings held an honorable place. Everyone had told him he must see the Cathedral, but he hadn't really meant to do so by moonlight; the sky was cloudless and it was much colder, and the moon—in its second quarter—gave a fair illumination here, as it had done in the square. He walked on, past the welcoming lantern outside the Judge's door, and after a while was able to gaze up at the dark mass of the Cathedral, silhouetted against the sky.

So now he could say he had seen it, and Halford, he imagined, would frown on a tardy arrival. He turned and walked back past the old, elegant houses, and thought that as the Close looked tonight it had looked three hundred years ago, with the moon shining down through bare branches; and suddenly he was aware again, more strongly than before, of the feeling that something was wrong. He had no idea why he felt this, if there had been a movement in the shadows ahead he had not observed it consciously, but this time he wasn't in any doubt at all.

He did not slacken his pace or give any other sign of what was in his mind. The pavement was dry tonight, and in the cold air his steps rang clearly. And then he became aware of the other footsteps, no echo now, a slower, more ponderous tread; a moment later his learned friend, Mr. Appleton, marched out into the moonlight, bound—of course!—for the same destination as himself.

There was a square of grass in front of the lodgings, with a neat, narrow path leading across it to the door. If he wasn't wrong, if he wasn't letting his own imagination scare him, the only place for an ambush was in the shrubbery beyond.

He met Appleton at the foot of the path, and took his arm in a friendly way that must have surprised him; and swept him toward the door, protesting slightly, at a quite undignified speed. There was an old-fashioned bell pull; somewhere in the depths of the house he could hear an answering chime, and then—quite distinctly—the stealthy movement of frozen branches. He flung himself down, and somehow dragged Appleton with him, a stiff, reluctant figure. And the whole world seemed to explode in the sound of a shot. The bullet slammed into the stonework, a little to the left of the door, and rebounded harmlessly into the darkness. For a moment Maitland's only thought was relief that he hadn't made a fool of himself.

The noise had been so shattering in the stillness of the Close that he wasn't surprised to find Halford and his Marshal hovering in the background when the butler opened the door. They both went back a pace as the two men erupted into the hall; Antony released Appleton's arm, slammed the door, and leaned back against it, panting a little.

"What the . . . Mr. Maitland!" said the Judge; rather unfairly seeming to absolve the Crown counsel from responsibility for the disturbance. "What has happened?"

"Someone shot at us. I suppose we ought to tell the police, but he'll be gone now, of course."

The Marshal, who was a conscientious young man, began to move away down the hall. He didn't want to miss any excitement, but he knew where his duty lay. "Call the Chief Constable," Halford called after him. And then, looking from one of the newcomers to the other: "This is an outrage!"

"I'm sorry, Judge," Maitland apologized. His eyes were bright with excitement, but he managed to sound properly concerned. "I hope I didn't hurt you, Appleton. I think the shot was meant for me, but I couldn't be sure how good his aim was."

"I suppose," said Appleton coldly, "I must thank you for saving my life." He looked like a dumpy pigeon with all its feathers ruffled, and without thinking Antony half turned toward the Judge, ready to share the joke.

Looking at him, Halford had the strangest feeling, one which surprised him even more than the younger man's tempestuous entry had done. He wasn't going to admit to himself that it was envy. "You're telling us someone tried to kill you?"

"It's just that I think I was followed from the George."

"I see. You don't think . . . a personal matter?" he added, almost hopefully.

"I don't think so, Judge."

"No doubt the police will be interested in your reasons. As for me"— Halford's mouth was set in a thin, unforgiving line—"if an attempt has been made to interfere with the course of justice you may be sure I shall take cognizance of the fact."

The Chief Constable and his minions arrived with commendable speed, doubtless galvanized by this dreadful example of *lèse-majesté.* The Judge's demands were peremptory, he insisted on a guarantee of safety for all concerned and a complete absence of publicity. Antony listened, and made as little as he could of his story when his turn came. The Chief Constable, with one eye on Her Majesty's representative, treated him warily, and was obviously relieved when he was able, at last, to bow himself out of the presence; but it was noticeable that the Inspector who accompanied him had a reproachful look.

Mr. Justice Halford was silent while they ate their dinner, and Appleton showed signs of still feeling affronted by what had happened. Antony was thankful enough for the opportunity of concentrating on a plate of rather overdone beef and the confusion of his own thoughts. It wasn't until the port was circulating and the servants had withdrawn that the Judge looked up and said, as though he had reached a decision:

"I think, gentlemen, that an official consultation is called for; and I hope I need not apologize for dealing with the matter on what I had intended to be a purely social occasion."

Appleton said, "It is certainly quite serious enough to warrant—" and seemed to forget how he had meant the sentence to end; Maitland bowed; the Marshal, who knew his place, contrived to convey that he was both alert and uninterested.

"Very well then. From what you told the Chief Constable, Mr. Maitland, it would seem that there have been certain other episodes since you came to Chedcombe.''

"I think I must say, Judge, since I accepted the brief in the Gifford case.''

"Yes, precisely. Do you think, then, that tonight's incident was also connected with that case?''

"I'm afraid I do.''

"And even if you were wrong, if you, Appleton, were the intended victim . . . the situation is quite intolerable,'' he added, almost pettishly.

"In either event,'' said Appleton, "it seems there must be some connection with the case in which we are both concerned. An attempt to prejudice the court in favor of the accused, who admittedly cannot be held personally responsible—''

"Or an attempt to put an end to any further inquiries,'' Maitland interrupted, with something of a snap.

"Do you really believe that?'' asked Halford, looking at him curiously.

"It's possible, Judge. I'm not sure.''

"Not a very efficient assassin, surely,'' said Appleton with some sarcasm in his tone.

"You may be right.'' Maitland sounded vague again, but he added after a moment's consideration, "If he meant to kill he'd have aimed for the head . . . not exactly an easy shot. And you must remember that we took evasive action.''

"I hadn't forgotten it.'' This was obviously still a source of grievance. The Judge looked from one of his guests to the other and said a trifle testily:

"Well, frankly, gentlemen, I realize these possibilities exist; but it seems far more likely that the local prejudice that prompted the first two incidents was responsible also for the third. In any event, it makes very little real difference to the situation.''

"No,'' said Maitland. He picked up his glass, and remembered as he did so that Uncle Nick had always said Halford had no palate.

"In fairness, then''— the Judge sounded exasperated—"it seems I must be prepared to consider an application to transfer the trial. Do you agree, Mr. Appleton?''

"With respect, Judge, I should like time to consider. The proceedings having gone so far—"

"I've spilled my wine," said Maitland, in an odd voice. For a moment his whole attention seemed to be taken by the stain which was spreading across the damask; then he reached for the salt cellar, and began to cover the spot carefully. "I too should like time to consider," he said, not looking up.

"Well, really!" said Halford, completely taken aback. Maitland looked up and smiled at him.

"I appreciate your consideration, Judge. In fact, I have wondered why no such application was previously made by the defense, but my colleagues assure me no sufficient grounds existed."

"Then why, in heaven's name—?"

"I must consult my instructing solicitor, of course."

"He'll hardly object, if you feel it advisable."

"No, I . . . may I have time to think it over?"

"Certainly, if that is what you wish." A coldness had crept into Halford's manner. "Let us say, I shall be prepared to consider an application on Monday morning, when the court assembles."

"Thank you." Now, why was it so difficult to explain? "I may be only too glad to avail myself of your kindness," he added. The prospect seemed to depress him.

"Then I have only to ask you—both—to cooperate with the Chief Constable in whatever measures he deems necessary for your protection."

Appleton said: "Certainly, Judge. Certainly." Maitland, his spirits apparently restored, met Halford's suspicious look with an innocent one. After a moment the Judge turned away, and asked his Marshal, a little peevishly, to circulate the decanter.

Saturday, 1st February

Maitland had strained his shoulder in the fall, but not too badly. After a while he went to sleep, and awoke rather late the next morning with only a confused memory of a dream in which the pigs he had drawn on the back of his brief had mysteriously become a bunch of old-fashioned anarchists. He lay for a moment pondering this, but it didn't seem to make any sense at all, and it passed from his mind when he went downstairs and found the hotel manager hovering near the reception desk: a little, precise man, no longer apologetic but rather stiff in his manner.

"I understand, Mr. Maitland, you would like a change of room."

"No, why? I'm very comfortable."

"Inspector Arkwright thought perhaps . . . a nice room at the back of the house." Maitland suggested, briefly, a course of action for Inspector Arkwright that made the manager look disapprovingly down his nose. "I don't like the responsibility, and that's a fact. If you felt you'd be more comfortable somewhere else—"

There must be something worrying him beyond a mere visitation from the police. "What's the matter?" asked Antony. "People are talking, I know, but that won't hurt *your* reputation. And you can't be really concerned what happens to me."

"Oh, I assure you—" But the protest was perfunctory. "It was bad enough having the windows broken, but when it comes to paint all over the front of the hotel—"

"What?"

"Well, actually, on the pavement, but right outside the door. *Green* paint," said the manager, as though somehow this was the final indignity. "I've got two men out there scrubbing, because it wouldn't be nice if the ladies were to see it."

"A picture? A message?"

"A message . . . if you could call it that. Which I would not sully my tongue to repeat," said the manager austerely.

"Then I'd better have a look."

"I think . . . I hope . . . that by now it is illegible."

"Well, why blame me?"

"It is not exactly a matter of blame, Mr. Maitland. The meaning was clear enough." He paused a moment, obviously for purposes of translation. "The message reflected on—er—the moral code pertaining in the metropolis. And added a suggestion that outside interference was unwelcome here."

"Tell the police about it. It's their worry, not ours."

"I have done so." He added huffily: "I can't offer you a *bath*, I'm afraid, but I'll give instructions for your things to be moved."

"I don't think so, thank you." Antony had a fair idea what "a nice room at the back" would be like. "Don't worry . . . I'll tell Inspector Arkwright you did your best to oblige him."

Both Miss Langhorne and Tommy Davenant telephoned before he had finished breakfast, so obviously the story of the shooting was already all over town, the Judge's commands notwithstanding. Maitland took the hint and phoned Sir Nicholas as soon as he had concluded a rather acrimonious conversation with the police Inspector and was back in his room again.

When he had finished telling his uncle what had happened, the silence at the other end of the line was not encouraging. "I thought perhaps you'd tell Jenny," he said.

"Yes. Yes, of course," said Sir Nicholas testily. And then: "The Judge's Lodgings? You couldn't possibly have contrived better."

"An error in judgment," Antony admitted.

"And one which will ensure the maximum publicity," agreed Sir Nicholas cordially. "Er—what did Halford say?"

"An outrage!" Antony told him primly. "And he told the

Chief Constable no statement was to be made to the press, but I'm afraid it's got out somehow.''

"As was to be expected. The national papers had already taken up the Gifford case.''

"Yes, so I noticed. Uncle Nick, he offered—Halford did—to agree to a change of venue.''

"Very properly.''

"Yes, well—''

"Didn't you jump at the chance?''

"Not exactly.''

"The more fool you.''

"I've got till Monday to decide whether to make application.''

"If this girl is really innocent,'' said Sir Nicholas skeptically, "wouldn't it help to have more time?''

"The thing is, I don't see my way.''

"What chance have you of getting an acquittal?''

"None at all, so far as I can see. And it wouldn't satisfy me anyway. I want to prove—''

"I might have known it!'' Sir Nicholas's voice was bitter. "Another injured innocent.''

"Well, sir, I think—''

"You don't have to tell me, Antony, I've heard it all before.''

"You haven't heard the local tabbies; they've got the whole thing sewn up.''

"That doesn't prove they're wrong.''

"I suppose it doesn't,'' Antony agreed in a tone of discontent.

"And to return to what happened last night, what did the police have to say?''

"They were treading warily, Halford was so obviously ready to erupt at any moment. But the local Inspector seems to think it natural enough that one of his parishioners should be taking potshots at me,'' said Antony, and moved the receiver rapidly away from his ear to avoid being deafened by his uncle's laughter. "Which is a chastening thought,'' he added, "but he says things were quiet enough before—''

"Is that all that's happened?'' asked Sir Nicholas, suddenly suspicious.

"Isn't it enough?''

"*What* else?"

"Well . . . someone heaved a brick through my bedroom window." He went on to describe the anonymous messages, and the activity of the pavement artist the night before.

"The same person?"

"I don't know."

"You're slipping," said Sir Nicholas satirically.

"You don't like my guesses, sir," Antony reminded him. "Anyway, you won't let Jenny worry, will you?"

"How do you propose I should stop her?"

The question was unanswerable; a change of subject seemed indicated. "What's she doing with herself, Uncle Nick?"

"Do you really want to know?"

"Yes, of course. When I spoke to her yesterday she was too busy telling me about a letter from Nan—"

"I thought Gibbs was going to give notice at last," said Sir Nicholas. They had all been trying to achieve this effect for years; Gibbs was something in the nature of a family heirloom, a saintly looking old man whose disposition— never saintly—had been further soured when the house in Kempenfeldt Square was divided to make an upstairs flat for the Maitlands. It now seemed unlikely that he would ever reconcile himself to the arrangement, but he preferred to continue working for Sir Nicholas, and most unfairly to assume the airs of a martyr in consequence.

"Well, that's a good thing, anyway."

"It didn't come to that. But he disserted for twenty minutes by the clock on the inconvenience of having a quantity of teak planks, ten feet in length, delivered to the house; which was not—if he might say so—the sort of thing to which he was accustomed."

"Teak planks?" repeated Antony, bewildered.

"Not to mention the noise," said Sir Nicholas inexorably. "But you can't deny you needed some new bookshelves in the living room," he added in a reasonable tone that didn't even start to ring true.

"Bookshelves? Oh, no! Uncle Nick, why didn't you stop her?"

"I never interfere," said his uncle virtuously.

"No, but . . . you know what happens when Jenny starts measuring things."

"She told me they weren't turning out *quite* as she had expected," admitted Sir Nicholas thoughtfully. "When do you think you'll be home?"

"In time to clear up the mess, I should imagine." But that brought him up against his problem again. "Even if we apply for a transfer, there'd be arrangements to make for the new trial."

"What about your junior—Langhorne, is that the name? Is he competent?"

"Not 'he,' Uncle Nick. It's a woman."

"Heaven preserve us!" said Sir Nicholas weakly. And then, more forcefully: "Is that why you stayed?"

"In a way," Antony admitted, truthfully enough. "And she's extremely competent, I should say; this just doesn't happen to be her line."

"The whole affair appears to have been grossly mismanaged," said Sir Nicholas severely. And then, in a resigned way: "You'd better tell me—"

By the time he had finished explaining himself, Antony was glad enough to put down the receiver and turn to the papers in the malicious wounding case, which was showing every sign of becoming, in its own way, a pretty fair headache. But when he bundled them back into his briefcase again later, he couldn't flatter himself that he had made any progress at all.

II

He went down to lunch early, and had finished in time to catch the one-thirty bus for Southleach. Inspector Arkwright had proved adamant on the subject of "protection," and when Maitland had reconnoitered after breakfast he had found an uncommonly burly man assisting the two hotel employees in their task of removing the pavement artist's message. He had concluded, with some annoyance, that this was his bodyguard, so now he caused a flutter in the kitchens by going out the back way, and took a circuitous route to the bus stop. He hadn't really any objection to reasonable caution, but rather drew the line at being followed about cross-country.

He was set down in due course at the corner of the lane which led to Ravenscroft; he had noticed a stile when he drove that way with Davenant, and took to the fields as soon as he reached it.

Following last night's promise, it was a cold, bright day. He was walking for the pleasure of it, but also he told himself it would be a good idea to see a little more of the terrain. Eventually he'd go to the house, but if he happened in the meantime casually to encounter some member of the family it would lend a touch of authenticity to the apologies he would owe Tommy for this informal approach. So he was rather relieved than otherwise when he came out on a cart truck that bounded a wide expanse of plowland and saw Hugo Randall coming down the hill towards him. Floss was walking close at heel, and two younger dogs followed at a respectful distance. He paused, waiting for Randall to come up with him. "Am I trespassing?" he asked.

"It's a right of way," said Hugo shortly. The encounter did not seem to afford him any pleasure. He stood scowling at Antony for a moment before he added: "I suppose it isn't just chance, our meeting like this."

"I was on my way to Ravenscroft," Maitland admitted. He was quite clear in his own mind that he had to talk to Hugo, and equally clear that it would have been worse than useless to attempt it with Davenant in tow.

"Does that mean . . . more questions?"

"I'm afraid it does."

"Oh, God!" said Hugo unemotionally. He turned and began to walk down the track, and Antony fell into step beside him. After a moment he added reluctantly: "I've been thinking since I saw you. But I don't know what to do."

"If you'd only tell me—"

"About my quarrel with Granny?"

"That's the main thing, certainly." Hugo didn't reply, and Maitland was content to let the silence lengthen. They skirted the plowland and crossed another stile into a field where ewes were grazing; Floss gave them a knowledgeable look and pressed closer to her master's heels. "Fran knew," said Hugo abruptly. "Why didn't she tell you?"

"She told me a number of lies," said Antony casually.

"It made me wonder—" That was another sentence that was never destined to be completed. He stopped, and swung round to his companion, and asked urgently: "Did she do it? That's what matters really. Do you think she's guilty?"

Maitland looked at him. He had an uncomfortable feeling that the question was sincere. "No, I don't," he said, emphasizing the words.

Hugo was frowning still, but he didn't seem angry now, only bewildered. "You said, 'a number of lies.' But why . . . if she's innocent?"

"I can only guess, Mr. Randall. Perhaps to protect someone else."

"Who—?" He had talked glibly enough about "some man" the other day; now his lips tightened at the suggestion. Maitland said deliberately:

"You tell me she knew why Mrs. Randall cut you out of her will. Who else but you could have been harmed by *that* knowledge?"

"I see. I've been afraid of that, since you were here on Wednesday." His voice was very low now, but he spoke carefully, as though each word was important.

"Not before that?"

"No." He stared at Maitland a moment longer, and then turned abruptly and began to move across the field again. "I thought I understood . . . when she said she'd fight if I disputed the will . . . I thought there was someone else."

"But you backed her story that she didn't know about the new codicil until New Year's Eve."

"What else could I do? I couldn't call her a liar. Whatever she'd done—" He paused, and then added dispassionately: "That was a trick, wasn't it? You didn't know."

"It wasn't a very difficult deduction."

"She told me on Monday night," said Hugo. "She said that was why she wasn't going to the dance . . . it would give her a chance to ask Grandmother to put things right. I told her I didn't want that, I begged her not to say anything. But I wasn't angry with her then . . . not really."

"Did you say anything to Mrs. Randall?"

"No . . . no, how could I?" They had reached the side of the field, and he paused with his hand on the gate. "As for Fran," he said, with a sudden violence that more nearly matched his previous mood, "it was a fool's trick, wasn't it, not to tell the truth?"

"Not very sensible, certainly." Hugo swung the gate open and the three dogs went through ahead of them. "I wish you'd trust me," said Maitland, following; and remembered as he spoke that he had made the same demand of Fran Gifford, which was all very well if their interests happened to lie together . . .

"I don't seem to have much choice. I've got to know . . . I've got to understand." He closed the gate carefully and signaled to the dogs with a jerk of his hand. Floss trotted away with the proud, purposeful gait of the well-trained sheep dog, the others frisked off together, momentarily intoxicated by their freedom. They were on a broad expanse of turf now, that stretched away in both directions between hedges of hawthorn. "One of the old 'green lanes,' " said Hugo. He wasn't looking at his companion now. "It isn't the quickest way home."

"That suits me." The grass was springy underfoot, but Maitland hardly noticed his surroundings any longer. His mind was as deeply concentrated on the other man as ever upon a witness in court.

"All right then. About Fran . . . can you get her acquitted?" Hugo asked, and moved away in the direction the dogs had taken.

"I don't think I can, unless I know the truth."

"And you want me to help you?" The words were softly spoken, but his mouth had a bitter twist.

"I think you must."

"One way out would be to provide the court with a scapegoat." He gave a sidelong glance at his companion. "Me, for instance," he suggested. "Is that the idea?"

"Not unless it's true that you killed her."

"It isn't," said Hugo, still watching him.

"I'm relieved to hear it," Antony told him tartly. And suddenly Randall laughed. "I don't expect you to believe me," he asserted. "But I'll tell you . . . about that, anyway. About the quarrel." He walked on in silence for some time before he added: "If you could call it that."

"It takes two—" said Maitland, at his vaguest.

"That's right. I didn't really have very much to say." He was frowning heavily now, choosing his words. "There was a girl in Chedcombe who'd had a baby. Someone told Granny I was the father. I was paying her maintenance, I expect that's how they knew."

Antony's first reaction was one of pure astonishment. He said: "Good God, Randall, is that what you've been jibbing at?"

"It isn't quite so simple." Hugo took the interruption calmly enough. "For one thing she was only a schoolgirl; when the child was born, I mean. For another, there was my grandmother's outlook on these things. You asked me the other day what particular sin she hated; I thought then that you knew."

"I just had an idea she looked . . . a fanatic," said Maitland. For some reason he sounded apologetic. "So I wondered—"

"Well, now you know."

"When did all this happen?"

"If you mean the child, it was born last May."

"And you've been paying the mother ever since, without your grandmother's knowledge?"

"Yes. That's why I thought perhaps Walter had found out and told her . . . I mean, through being curious about the cash withdrawals from my account."

"You don't think the girl herself—?"

"It hadn't occurred to me. But she might have, at that. You see, I'd had to tell her . . . I was doing what I could but I'd pretty well used up my reserves."

"Did Miss Randall know?"

"She's never said so. And if you're thinking Nell might have told Granny, she wouldn't."

"It seemed to me she knew something that made her unhappy," Maitland told him.

"Then I expect Granny told *her*. That's much more likely."

"I see. Well, what matters for the moment is that Mrs. Randall did find out. On Christmas Day?"

"That might just have been the first chance she had of—of taxing me with it," said Hugo.

"What did she say?"

"She asked me if it was true. Well, I couldn't deny it. So then she said I'd have to marry the girl."

"You didn't want that?"

"That little tramp!" Hugo laughed shortly. "Anyway, Granny changed her mind after that. Said she supposed I'd no more moral sense than my father had, and was the relationship continuing? I told her it wasn't, but I ought to have known then that she took the whole thing even more seriously than I supposed."

"How could you have known?"

"For one thing because she started talking about my responsibility in the matter, for setting the girl on the downward path, you know. And because she mentioned my father; she never forgave him for his divorce." They had been climbing steadily for some time now; the two young dogs were running ahead, in the happy certainty that they were clearing the path of any possible danger, but Floss had come back to her master's side, and as he spoke more freely, her brown eyes seemed to become more watchful. "Grandmother could never see past events to the people concerned in them." He was speaking earnestly now, trying to explain. "Happiness was only a word, and didn't matter; it didn't matter, either, if you got to the stage where you just couldn't take any more. That way out was sinful . . . scandalous . . . I don't know which was worse. I always knew she felt like that, of course, but I never realized quite how deep it went."

"Did she tell you she was going to change her will?"

"Not a word. I didn't know until Fran told me."

"I don't see why she should disinherit your brother and sister too."

"To punish me . . . can't you see that? I could always manage, but I wouldn't get very far keeping those two on a farm laborer's pay."

"But you love Ravenscroft, don't you?" His gesture was expansive enough to embrace the whole property, not just the fields between which they were walking.

"Is it so obvious?" Hugo asked after a moment.

"I think it is."

"She didn't understand that, you see." There was a gate on their left; he moved toward it as though he couldn't help himself, and stood looking out across the valley. Antony came up beside him and saw the orderly progression of fields, sloping steeply at first and then more gently down to the road and the river beyond. "Ravensburn," said Hugo, as though he were answering a question. And then: "You can see the house quite well from here."

The green lane had passed behind Ravenscroft as it climbed the hill. The farmstead lay below them now, a little to the left; they could see the square of buildings that formed the yard, and the depth of the house itself, much bigger than it appeared from the front. And its fields lay all about it, quiet in the afternoon sun. Antony wanted to ask, "What will you do now?" but the question would be too cruel. So he said the first thing that came into his mind: "What acreage have you?"

"Just over three hundred; and common rights, of course. That's where I'd been when we met, to see the shepherd. We've some blackfaces up there, tougher stock than the gently bred ladies you saw just now." His tone was gently mocking, but he grinned as he spoke; as though for the moment he saw in Maitland no more than a companion upon whose understanding he could rely. "There isn't much top soil up here, you know, but it's good grazing for them. And the lower fields are fertile enough."

"What other stock—?"

"Half a dozen Jerseys in milk, three heifers, nine breeding sows. We could feed more, off the land, but we've nowhere to house them; and building costs money." He broke off there, and then said slowly: "I keep forgetting."

It was easy to see that to Hugo at least the shock of dispossession must have been very great. Maitland turned from the view and looked again at him directly. "Why did she choose Fran Gifford?" he asked, and saw Randall's expression close and guarded. When there was no answer he added, in a resigned voice: "Then tell me the rest of the story."

"That's all." Hugo's voice was bitter again. "If you think I'm going to try to excuse myself—"

"I shouldn't be interested. But I should like to know why you lied about it."

"Isn't it obvious?"

"Not to me."

"I was afraid I'd be suspected of killing her," said Hugo savagely. "It seems that Fran thought I might have been angry enough to do so, even if it didn't occur to anyone else. Or else I was embarrassed. Take your pick!"

"I'm sorry, neither appeals to me." He watched Hugo's expression darken. "You forgot one perfectly good reason," he added helpfully. "You didn't want your sister to know."

"I'll remember that," said Hugo, tight-lipped, "next time someone asks me."

"Well, if you won't tell me the reason . . . who was the girl?"

"Does it matter?"

"Not really. I suppose it was Nancy Selkirk."

"How the hell did you know that?"

"She spoke to me last night as I was leaving court. At the time I couldn't think why."

"She didn't tell you—?" He broke off, and to Antony it seemed that he had drawn back a little, as though afraid of the results of a too-impetuous question.

"She seemed very anxious about Fran Gifford."

"Did she, though? A lot of use that is."

"I can't be sure—" began Maitland, watching him.

"Look here!" Hugo sounded desperate now. "I'll tell any tale you like in court . . . anything! Just leave Nancy out of this."

"Can't you get it into your head," said Antony irritably, "that if we call you at all I want you to tell the truth."

"Well, I will . . . but how will that help Fran?"

"There's the question of motive. If we can persuade the jury Alice Randall wasn't likely to change her mind—"

"She wasn't," said Hugo positively.

Maitland looked at him curiously. "Are you still trying to protect Fran in some way?"

"I never did that exactly. Only to back her up about not knowing what Granny had done about her will."

"I see. Well, if you'll take a little advice, Mr. Randall, you'll tell me the rest of it."

"There's nothing else." He didn't even try to sound convincing.

"You seem very anxious I shouldn't talk to Nancy Selkirk. Is that where you were on New Year's Eve . . . New Year's morning, I should say . . . while your grandmother was dying?"

"No!"

"Oh, well, it isn't where you were that matters so much as where Miss Randall thought you were."

"You don't wrap things up, do you? I really was with Lesser."

"One of the cows?" said Antony doubtfully.

"A joke of Marian's. I suppose"—he seemed to be considering the matter—"not a very good one. But I particularly wanted a heifer calf out of Celandine, so when she dropped one—"

"Yes, I see. And *she* was with you, no doubt"— he nodded toward Floss, who was lying down now with her chin on her paws—"and I wouldn't accept her evidence where you were concerned, even if she could give it."

"I daresay you're right, at that." Hugo was looking down at the dog, and his expression was hard to read. "She's mine, anyway . . . not part of the estate."

"Which brings us back to the question, why did your grandmother decide to make Fran Gifford one of her legatees?"

Hugo moistened his lips. "I don't know," he said. His eyes met Maitland's for a moment, and then he was looking away again, out across the valley.

"If you can't make a very good guess, you must be a bigger fool than I take you for," said Antony tartly.

"What do you mean?"

"If you don't know, I'll tell you . . . and here's something else I won't wrap up. I think your grandmother acted as she did because she knew very well you're in love with Fran Gifford, and this way she was quite sure you'd never marry her."

There was a silence. After a while Hugo twisted round, still with one elbow leaning on top of the gate, so that he could look at his companion. "Damn you, it isn't true," he said. In spite of the words, his voice was oddly devoid of feeling.

"I can't think of any other reason," said Maitland

thoughtfully, "for her to act exactly in that way. But you'd known Fran a long time; why had you never told her?" And suddenly Hugo's defenses were down; he didn't make any attempt to hide the fact, except that when he found his hands were shaking he thrust them into his pockets. He kept his eyes fixed on Antony's face and said in a quick, shaken voice:

"I couldn't ask her to live at Ravenscroft, could I? It wasn't—it wasn't a happy place. I had to wait—"

"And so you were caught."

"That's just how it was. When I knew what Granny had done . . . Fran was so worried about it, I couldn't tell her why it was so dreadful. And afterward, even if I'd pocketed my pride . . . she knew about Nancy by then. And I couldn't tell her—"

"What couldn't you tell her?" Maitland prompted after a moment.

"I must have been mad, I think. I never realized that might be why she said she'd fight to keep the legacy . . . just because she was so angry. And she had a right to be. When we knew how Granny died I never thought Fran could have done it; but then it seemed there was no one else, and I knew she wasn't telling the truth . . . I knew she wouldn't have done it on her own, but I thought if she was in love she might have been persuaded."

"And now?"

"I'll do anything . . . anything at all!"

"You've already offered to lie for her, but you won't tell me all the truth."

"There's nothing more," said Hugo. He sounded exhausted now.

"Very well."

"And you'll call me as a witness?"

"I've got to think about it."

"But you said . . . Granny wouldn't have changed her mind, you know. Once she knew about Nancy she'd never have forgiven me." His voice was bitter again as he added: "She never gave anyone a second chance."

"There could be complications." Maitland was irritable again. The last thing he wanted was to find himself in sympathy with this difficult young man. He'd have to see

Nancy, he thought; and what then? Fall back on Vera Lang-horne's suggestion, and try to get the girl acquitted for lack of evidence . . . thereby handing her over alive to every malicious tongue in Chedcombe? Or accept the Judge's of-fer . . . ? "I'll be damned if I do that," he said aloud; and shivered, as though he were only now aware that the after-noon was cold. "Who else could have killed Mrs. Ran-dall?" he asked, finding Hugo's eyes fixed on him speculatively.

"I've been thinking about that, but I don't seem to get anywhere."

"Could it possibly have been an accident?"

"I wish I thought so. There was a cork in the test tube, you know, and it was a pretty tight fit."

"Or suicide?"

"She had no reason. Besides, she thought it was a sin."

"Temporary insanity?"

"She wasn't mad," said Hugo positively.

"Then . . . someone who knew the house, knew where she would be sitting, and arrived almost immediately after Fran left."

"You mean, otherwise she'd have drunk her toddy and gone to bed."

"Exactly. And I think we have to add, someone who came to Ravenscroft with intent to murder; because Fran didn't see anyone in the lane, which means he was taking care to avoid an encounter."

"Someone who knew the digitalis was in the workbox," said Hugo, and again his voice was cold and expressionless.

"Five days after she put it there a lot of people must have known," Maitland told him, and watched him relax again. "If we go down to the house," Antony added casually, "do you think I could see Mark?"

"I thought Tommy said you couldn't talk to the prosecu-tion witnesses."

"It would be highly improper. But this isn't about the case, you see."

"I'm bound to say, he isn't in a very amiable mood," said Hugo. He sounded puzzled, and a little suspicious; but also, in a queer way, resigned.

"I'll have to risk that."

"This is the quickest way, then." He opened the gate; Floss was through in an instant, and turned a reproving eye on her two supporters as they scampered after her.

"I gather you've had some success at the shows," said Maitland as they started across the field. "The trophies in the study," he explained.

"Oh, I see. Yes, we haven't done badly at all." He accepted the change of subject without comment, but Antony realized suddenly that he'd been wrong in thinking Hugo in any way resigned. There was a tautness about him, as though he expected the worst and was braced to meet it; and he hadn't referred at all to Mark's appearance in court, though Nell must have told him, even if his brother had avoided the subject, that the defense had not been quite so kindly disposed as the prosecution.

"Celandine and her sisters?" Maitland asked, still negligently.

"Partly, yes; the cups are mostly for show jumping." He was answering at random, but still in that tense way. "Grandmother said it was a waste of time," he added. It was obvious that old Mrs. Randall was never far from his mind.

"Does Mark ride?"

"For convenience only. But Marian's interested, she's done quite well."

A nice, safe outlet for her energies, Antony thought; but he didn't say it aloud. "Do you get any shooting?" he said.

"Just for the pot." Each question, it seemed, was being passed as harmless, but with the mental reservation that perhaps the next one . . .

"Is Mark a good shot?"

"Yes, he is. In a casual, absent-minded way that I find intensely annoying," Hugo admitted. "The trouble is, you see, he doesn't really care about anything except these experiments of his."

"Don't you think so?" Something in Maitland's tone made Hugo look at him quickly.

"What do you mean?"

"I think he's trying, rather desperately, to protect *you*. The question is, you see, why should he think you need defending?"

"You'll have to explain that," said Hugo in a tight voice.

"I'll give him credit for having genuinely convinced himself that Fran Gifford killed your grandmother. But he's still afraid of what may come to light . . . if I ask too many questions, for instance."

"How do you know that?"

"Because he's been trying to discourage me . . . not very cleverly. In fact, I found his activities almost amusing, until last night."

Another gate. They were approaching the outbuildings now. "I don't understand," said Hugo mechanically.

"We'll let him explain, shall we?"

"Very well." He had been walking slowly, and more slowly, but now he quickened his pace again; through the door in the high wall, across the cobbled yard. A square-built, dark man was trundling a milk churn, obviously empty; the door of the cowshed stood open to the sunlight, there was a faint, companionable sound of movement beyond; nearer the house, on the same side of the yard, a handsome roan looked out over the half-door of the stable; in one of the buildings on the left the new litter of piglets squealed demandingly; a number of Rhode Island Reds had discovered a trail of spilled corn, but scattered indignantly at their passing. Hugo went straight across to a door at the back of the house, gestured toward a room on the right—"Wait there, will you?"—and then strode off down the flagged passage with Floss at his heels.

Antony went into the room, and the two young dogs tumbled in after him. A workmanlike place, with no concessions to comfort: three wooden chairs, a long deal table with some ledgerlike books spread open, a metal filing cabinet, a large-scale map on the wall. He went over to the window and looked out over the yard again. The dark man had gone back for another churn, and the brown hens were pecking placidly at the corn again, as though nothing could ever disturb them. He turned when he heard footsteps, and Mark came in. Hugo followed, paused for a moment while Floss slipped past him, and closed the door carefully. "Now!" he said, and leaned back against it. He had what seemed an uncharacteristic air of patience now, and looked prepared to wait all day.

Mark had come in with an unconvincing air of bravado. He scowled when he saw Antony and said ungraciously: "What do you want?" And then, more forcefully: "Didn't you say enough to me in court?"

"I thought so, certainly. It seems I was wrong."

"What do you mean?"

"Until last night I thought your actions ill-considered, no more. But what good do you think it would have done, even if Fran Gifford were guilty—?"

"If she was guilty . . . that's a good one!" Hugo said, "Mark," quietly and without emphasis, and he hunched an impatient shoulder and added petulantly: "Oh, all right! I know you don't like me to say it."

"What have you been doing?"

Mark looked quickly at Maitland, and hesitated as though waiting for him to speak. Then he said airily: "I just wrote him a couple of letters . . . that's all." Hugo was staring at him as though the words made no sense at all. "Oh, well . . . I chucked one through his bedroom window at the George. I thought it would have more—more impact that way."

The word was so apt that Antony might have found it amusing if the look on Hugo's face hadn't sobered him. "What else?" asked Hugo; and when his brother did not reply, repeated urgently: "What else?"

"Somebody shot at him in the Close last night. I suppose he thinks I did that too."

"And did you?"

"Nothing to do with me," said Mark. "I was in my room all the evening, reading."

"Then how do you know—?"

"I went into town this morning. Everyone knows," he added expansively. Hugo looked at him in silence for a moment, and then turned to Maitland again.

"Is this true?"

"It's certainly true that someone tried to shoot me." He spoke almost casually, but his eyes were intent on Mark's face. "Were you alone in your room yesterday evening?"

"Well . . . yes, of course."

"And there is on the premises, I've no doubt, at least one point twenty-two caliber rifle?"

"I don't see what that proves."

"Nothing, in itself. But there was another message, you know, written in green paint on the pavement in front of the George."

"That wasn't me. I didn't even . . . what did it say?"

"It was cleaned up before I saw it."

"We use black paint here, mostly; some white at the front of the house."

"So I noticed. Well, I don't want you to admit anything, but if there's any more violence—"

"I tell you, I didn't—"

"Forget it! I'm sorry," he added, and looked for a moment at Hugo. "That's all, I think. I'd better be getting along."

Hugo straightened himself. He did not look at his brother, or speak to him, but pulled the door open and waited for Antony to go through, and then followed him out into the yard. Halfway across he said abruptly, "It won't happen again," and as they reached the door in the wall he halted and asked: "Would you like Ken to drive you?"

"I'd rather walk. Can I get back to town across country, or must I stick to the road?"

"There's a short cut. I'll show you." He gave Maitland a rather odd look as he fell into step beside him.

"It was kind of you to offer me a lift, in the circumstances," said Antony lightly. "I'm sorry about that, you know." He wanted suddenly, almost with desperation, to break through the wall of reserve with which Hugo had again surrounded himself. "Boys get some queer ideas, I shouldn't—"

"Was the shot meant to kill you?"

"I'm afraid it was." He found himself adding: "I don't know it was Mark; in fact, to be honest, I've got a sort of 'what is wrong with this picture' feeling about it."

Hugo didn't seem to hear any of this beyond the answer to his own question. "It isn't that. It isn't only that," he corrected himself. "You said . . . he was trying to protect me."

"I think he may have had some idea—" He broke off then, and added: "You needn't worry about the police, you know."

"Why not?"

"The bullet was flattened, they just think it was a point twenty-two caliber from the weight. There'll be a check on all rifles licensed in the district . . . and a lot of good it will do them."

"Then why—?"

"Mark didn't tell you the incident took place on the Judge's doorstep. That puts the Chief Constable on the spot, you see. He has to try everything, useful or not." But the words reminded him of his own dilemma, and the uncomfortable fact that he was no nearer a decision than he had been the night before.

They had circled the buildings and were halfway down the drive before Hugo spoke again. He said painfully: "You see, I'm wondering if it really was that."

"What then?" But in answer to his inquiring look Hugo only shook his head. They reached the lane and crossed it, and Antony clambered over the fence.

"If you keep along the side of the hedge here, there's a bridge at the bottom; and a cart track at the other side."

"Thank you." He hesitated. "What's troubling you?" he said. "Are you going to tell me?

Hugo was looking past him, somewhere over his right shoulder. The sun was lower now and the shadows were lengthening. "When I thought it was Fran," he said slowly, "I still wouldn't have done anything to harm her."

"No," Antony agreed. He wasn't quite sure of the point of this remark, and his doubt sounded in his voice.

"I'm trying to explain," said Hugo, "but it isn't really so easy." His voice was quite expressionless. "You see, it seems to be a matter of choosing . . . who to betray."

"I can't make that choice for you, I'm afraid."

"No, I . . . I said nothing mattered but Fran, didn't I? So I've got to tell you I was wondering—" He paused, and then added in a rush: "If Mark has been raising a smoke screen . . . suppose it was just to protect himself."

Antony stood very still for a moment. There was an appeal here, a desperate need of reassurance; and how could he answer it when he knew so little? He said at last, slowly, "You've felt responsible for your brother and sister for a long time, haven't you?" and didn't realize, until he saw

Hugo's startled look, how irrelevant the comment must have seemed.

"I suppose I have. But—"

"Then don't you think it's time you started thinking about your own affairs for a change?"

Hugo gave a hard laugh, and said in a tone that was almost flippant: "It's rather late for that." Floss whined uneasily and pressed herself closer against his side.

They were still standing there by the fence when Antony turned and left them. He found the short cut easily enough, but he didn't really enjoy the walk back to town.

III

He knew he should phone Tommy Davenant, but managed to persuade himself that tomorrow would do; or perhaps he would talk to him later that evening. By the time he had finished his tea he had quite made up his mind: he was going to see Nancy Selkirk alone, though what Vera Langhorne's comments would be when he told her didn't bear thinking about.

He had an address from the phone book; Mrs. Mary Selkirk, of 17 Carlton Crescent, was the only one of her name listed, and he hoped to goodness she was the "fool of a woman" Miss Langhorne had referred to. He had no wish to provoke an argument by asking either of his colleagues where the girl was to be found. Finally he decided to check up with his watchdog, who seemed a little put out at being accosted, but was helpful enough once he realized his quarry bore him no malice. It ended by their walking round to the Selkirks' together, while Antony thought with pleasure that, with any luck, the expedition would provide a puzzle for Inspector Arkwright's leisure hours.

Carlton Crescent was part of a housing development on the western side of the town, a carefully planned estate of mock-Olde English houses; that was the only description Antony could find for them, they didn't seem to conform to any known architectural period. He found the district depressing, and was thankful he wasn't seeing it by daylight.

The front windows of No. 17 were all in darkness, but when he walked down the path at the side of the house, through a pergola-type erection which could only have been designed genteelly to screen the dustbins, he found himself facing another door with a lighted lattice window beside it. There was a black-painted knocker inappropriately shaped like a fish; he ignored it and pressed the bell, and was rewarded by a jarring, buzzing noise immediately inside. There followed a moment's dead silence, then the sound of footsteps; a moment later the door opened and Nancy Selkirk said reproachfully: "I didn't think you'd come so soon." Then, as the light streamed out and she saw him clearly for the first time, she broke off with a gasp and added, startled: "Oh, it's you!"

"I'd like to talk to you, Miss Selkirk, if I may."

"You'd better come in." She backed away from the door, leaving it open for him to follow her. It led straight into the kitchen, and here the olde worlde atmosphere the planning authorities had tried so hard to achieve had been ruthlessly abandoned. The room looked as if "our home expert" from one of the glossier women's magazines had been let run riot in it. The electric stove was shining and corpulent, the sink stainless steel and obviously nearly new; there were far too many cupboards, and what are known—to advertisers, if to no one else—as "working surfaces" gleamed in a particularly distressing shade of mustard yellow. It was a pity that Nancy herself should spoil the picture; her hair was in rollers, her nose unpowdered, and she had obviously been interrupted in the middle of manicuring her nails. A good deal of paraphernalia was spread about on the center table, which also had a yellow top.

She had recovered from her surprise now, and her natural instincts were reasserting themselves. "You ought to have let me know," she said; it wasn't really sensible to pat her hair as she spoke, but perhaps the gesture gave her some satisfaction. "You see, I was getting ready—"

"I'm sorry to interrupt you," said Antony amiably.

"Well, that's all right." She glanced at the clock as she spoke. "If you'll give me a moment—" She picked up a pink plastic tray which held some spare rollers, and swept out of the room without allowing him any chance to speak. Antony pulled out a chair and sat down near the table; as he waited he was wondering partly what on earth he was going to say to her when she returned, but mostly whether they ever ate at all in this house, the kitchen was so unnaturally tidy; except for Nancy's clutter, which was hardly appetizing.

She was gone for ten minutes, and when she came back she made an entrance that was obviously intended to impress. Her hair, freed from the confining rollers, was soft and fluffy, her face was delicately made up, and the blue dress she had chosen to wear suited her to perfection; she looked, in fact, enchantingly pretty . . . and obviously she knew it.

"I can't think why I left you sitting here," she said in a very grand way. "Won't you come into the sitting room?"

He was finding the kitchen oppressive, but the other room would probably be as bad in its own way, and most likely cold as well. "I'm quite comfortable," he told her, making no move to accept the invitation. "Why not sit down and finish your nails?"

"Oh, very well." She wasn't quite pleased to find him unimpressed by the vision she presented, but the suggestion was obviously a good one as she had already painted the nails on her right hand a startling vermilion, but the left remained unadorned. She seated herself, therefore, and picked up the bottle of varnish. Her eyes were on her visitor appraisingly as he went back to his chair again. "Have you talked to Fran Gifford?" she asked.

"Not since I saw you."

"Then, why—?"

"You didn't explain very well what you wanted. I hope you'll tell me a little more."

"When you've seen her . . . p'raps I will."

"Now," he insisted. Oddly, his quiet tone seemed to anger her.

"I have my rights," she told him. "Even if it wasn't all done legal."

"Your right . . . to what?"

"Money." The china-blue eyes were calculating, the charming expression for the moment almost ugly. Or was that just an illusion? He ought to remember . . . and as though she read his thought she added primly: "I'm not thinking of myself, you know."

"Why should Miss Gifford give you money?"

"Because that's why the old woman left it to her. Isn't it obvious?"

"I'm afraid I'm very dull," he apologized.

"Are you?" The anger had given way to a hint of dryness; so that he had yet another view of her, and wondered, with as much sympathy as curiosity, what she had been like before. . . .

"I expect if you explained to me—" he said, and smiled at her. "For instance, how did you know about Mrs. Randall's will?"

The painting of her thumbnail seemed to be a tricky business, requiring concentration. "I'm not telling you anything, not until you've talked to Fran."

"You said you wanted to see her acquitted," he pointed out.

"So I do. But I can't help you about that."

"How do you know?"

"I . . . well, I do know, that's all." She held out her hand to consider the effect of the varnish, and then looked up at him briefly with a mocking little smile. "A smart lawyer can get anyone off . . . that's what they're saying."

"A smarter man than I am, then," said Antony ruefully, disliking the word as he repeated it. "Besides, it isn't true."

"Isn't it?" She sounded indifferent. "Well, I don't know anything about the murder, though I wouldn't have thought it of Fran Gifford. But maybe she did us both a good turn."

"You understand there's no question of her inheriting, if she's found guilty?"

"Of course I do." She was glad to air her knowledge. "And it wouldn't do Hugo any good either . . . not necessarily. The court would have to decide." She found his eyes fixed on her, and gave a self-conscious laugh. "But you won't let it happen, will you?"

It was an effort to stay where he was, in the chair by the kitchen table; to answer her casually. As always when anything disturbed him, he wanted to get up and walk restlessly about the room. "I may have no choice," he said. Perhaps it was something in his tone that moved her to say, inconsequently:

"I was surprised you decided to stay."

"Well . . . as I did . . . wouldn't it be as well to answer my questions?" he said. "You can let me worry about whether you're helping or not."

She painted the nail of her little finger before she replied. "Would it be right," she asked primly, "to help you to—to defeat the ends of justice?"

It wasn't any use protesting at her assumption of Fran's guilt. "There's always the money," he reminded her cynically.

The little brush went back into the bottle. "It would depend, wouldn't it, on what you wanted to ask me?"

"For one thing, how did you know about the will?"

"She told me, of course."

"She . . . Fran?" Nancy shook her head sharply. "Mrs. Randall, then?" The incredulity in his tone made her smile a little. "When?"

"The second time she came here." There was a pause while she worked it out. "The Friday, that was . . . the day after Boxing Day."

"Did Nell . . . did Miss Randall bring her?" He was frowning over the information.

"She came in a taxi, both times. It waited for her. She didn't stay long."

"The first time—?"

"On Christmas Eve."

"Why did she come?"

"That's something else, isn't it?"

"I've been told about your . . . about the baby."

Her lips twisted into a bitter smile. "Then let's say, she wanted to see her great-grandson."

"Was that why she came?"

"In a way. She asked me if it was true."

"Did she tell you who had given her the information?"

"I've wondered that myself."

"And when you told her—?"

"She was a proper old cat, you know, but I'll say this for her, she didn't see it all one-sided. She said Hugo'd have to marry me. Well, I had to laugh."

"Would you have agreed?"

"Why should I? A father for Jimmy . . . what do I care? Not that he isn't a good kid," she added, with sudden earnestness. "He's always like this, not a sound out of him once he's had his feed. No trouble."

"For your own sake—" said Antony, a little helplessly.

"I'm damned anyway, as far as Chedcombe is concerned."

"But at the time . . . when first you knew the baby was coming?"

"I don't say that wasn't different. Hugo wasn't best pleased, but he's been good to me."

"If he'd asked you then, would you have accepted him?"

"Well, I might . . . if he'd asked me!" She grinned as she spoke.

"Marriage would give you a home, a certain position—"

"That's what you think. Besides—" She glanced up at the clock again.

"You've other fish to fry," said Antony crudely.

"What if I have?" Her eyes met his and she laughed. "I like older men," she told him. Her look was friendly and appraising; he hoped he was right in believing it also impersonal.

"Did you tell Mrs. Randall you weren't interested in her proposal?" he asked.

"What do you take me for? I told her to see what Hugo had to say."

"And she came back a second time to tell you?"

"That's right." Again there was the considering look; he had the feeling that every word was deliberately chosen. "So she said she was ashamed of Hugo, but she'd see we were looked after, Jimmy and me."

"By Fran Gifford?"

"She didn't want any scandal." There was a hardness in her tone now. "That's a laugh, isn't it?"

"I suppose it was natural that she didn't want to start any gossip about her own family."

"You can't stop it," said Nancy. "Not in a place like this. And, of course, she didn't think she was going to die. But I agree she didn't want this story to get about. She kept talking about 'iniquity' . . . which isn't a nice word," she added, suddenly prim again. "And she said it ought to be 'published abroad,' " she went on, with an obvious effort of recollection. "Well, I was glad enough she decided not to."

"And now?"

"We get by." She glanced at the clock again, as though the words were a reminder, and seemed only partially reassured by what she saw. "Hugo does what he can . . . well, why shouldn't he? And then there's Fran, if you get her off."

"Did you speak to her about it, when you heard of Mrs. Randall's death?"

"I never had the chance, they arrested her too quick. So that's why I thought I'd talk to you."

"I see." He got up as he spoke, and stood looking down at her. "Just one more thing, Miss Selkirk. It wasn't by any chance you who told Mrs. Randall—?"

"No, I didn't!" she said quickly.

"Are you sure of that?"

"Quite, quite sure. He'd already threatened—"

"What, Miss Selkirk?" he prompted as she hesitated.

"To stop supplies if . . . if I didn't do as he said." She paused again, and then added with a touch of defiance: "Keep quiet about it, I mean."

"I see." He didn't think it was any use persisting. "Have you known Hugo Randall long?"

"I was at school with Marian, a year ahead of her." She got up in her turn, and looked at him seriously. "I've got Jimmy to think of," she said. "You'll see Fran, won't you, and tell me what she says."

"I'll see her."

"I mean, I've done my best for you, haven't I? Even," she added, guessing shrewdly, "if it isn't what you wanted to hear."

"You said you'd like to help Fran," he said, on an impulse. "If I asked you to give evidence for the defense—"

"Don't try it! Not if you don't want me to deny every word." Her charm was dimmed again for a moment; for the first time he thought that perhaps she was afraid. But he was more puzzled by her reaction than disconcerted by it.

"Perjury, Miss Selkirk," he reminded her.

"You couldn't prove it," said Nancy, laughing again. But she showed some alacrity in following him to the door.

IV

The evening was well advanced by the time he had eaten, but some obscure sense of duty impelled him to telephone Tommy Davenant, and later—on being told that the solicitor was not at home that evening—Vera Langhorne. "There are things," he said when he got through to her, "that we ought to discuss."

"Would you like to come round here?"

"If I may." He was surprised to find that the suggestion pleased him. "Have you any Mozart?"

"Mozart? Oh, records! Yes, of course."

"Something soothing," he said. "I'm feeling battered."

She had not interpreted his request too literally, and one of the Horn Concertos greeted him when he arrived. "Exactly right," he told her gratefully.

"Want you to stay awake," she said.

The fire must have been made up after he telephoned, the flames were just beginning to struggle through the fresh coal. Again the chair she indicated to him was pulled hospitably close to the hearth; she pushed her own chair farther back as she sat down.

"You said, something to discuss," She was eying him in her earnest, intent way. "Glad you weren't hurt, last night," she added.

"It's about that," he said. "Well, it arises from that episode." He sat looking down at the fire, and thought perhaps he should have asked for something more harsh in the way of background music, something he didn't mind talking through. But the trouble was, of course, he didn't want to tell her. "Halford took a dim view," he said, postponing the moment.

"Not surprising, really."

"No . . . well . . . he offered to consider our application to have the trial transferred."

"What you wanted, isn't it?" she asked gruffly.

"I said so, didn't I?" Somehow he must explain his reluctance, as much to himself as to her. "It's all this damned gossip . . . no, more than that, the antagonism," he said.

"But that's why—"

"Yes, I know. I know what I said. And you told me in the beginning, 'she isn't getting a fair deal.' "

"Well, now's your chance. What's the matter?" she asked him impatiently.

The little room didn't provide much scope for prowling, but this time he yielded to his impulse to get up and move about. "I suppose I want to ram it down their throats," he said. "Prove she's innocent, and force them to believe her." He turned quickly, and found that she was following him, thoughtfully, with her eyes. "Don't you see?" he demanded. "Nothing else is really good enough."

"All very fine. Can you do it?"

"No . . . no!" Four paces from window to sideboard; he took them angrily. "At this stage I don't even see my way to an acquittal for lack of evidence."

"Know my view; what we ought to try for."

"But what sort of a life—?" He halted abruptly, and said with a change of tone: "I'm sorry. I didn't mean—"

"Know how you feel. All the same, change her name, go away somewhere."

"Oh, hell!" said Antony, with feeling, and strode back to the window again. Miss Langhorne pushed herself up out of her chair, and said as she did so:

"Get the coffee." She turned in the doorway to smile at him. "Give Mozart a chance," she recommended.

When she came back, Maitland had returned to his place by the fire and was staring moodily into the flames. She did not attempt to speak until the coffee was poured, and then she said, with an indirectness that was completely out of character: "Suppose you've been studying the evidence again."

"I've been doing more than that," he admitted. "First I went to Ravenscroft—"

"Without Tommy?" She didn't try to hide her disapproval.

"If you had rather an embarrassing disclosure to make, Miss Langhorne—supposing such a thing to be possible— would you rather talk to one person, or two?"

"See your point," she told him, after a moment. "Did it help?"

"That's the trouble, it didn't. In fact, I put in a very bad afternoon. Hugo Randall was by far the most promising suspect."

"Well?"

"He's been frank with me, up to a point. I don't see my way."

"You think he's innocent?"

"I don't know. I'd have to be sure of his guilt before I attacked him in court."

"I see," she said doubtfully.

"You ought to be g-glad," he snapped, suddenly irritable again. "We'll throw in our hand, and ask for a change of scene; and then we'll play for s-safety. Reasonable d-doubt!" he added violently. It sounded like an imprecation.

"Sorry you feel like that," said Vera mildly.

Antony picked up his cup. "I'm not behaving very well, am I?"

"Disappointed. Very understandable," she told him.

"I don't even know where I am with young Mark," he said discontentedly.

"You didn't talk to him as well!"

"Only about matters which I think can properly be regarded as my own concern," said Antony precisely. "He admits the first two anonymous messages, but not the green paint. And denies the shooting too."

"Not surprised."

"He could have done it. I think . . . oh, I think most likely he did. As for Hugo . . . how *can* I know whether the fellow's being honest, or extraordinarily subtle?" he demanded. And drank some of his coffee, and put down the cup with care.

"Would it help?"

"Yes, of course. I suppose I'd better tell you—" He gave her the gist of his talk with Hugo, and found her eying him thoughtfully when he finished. "So then," he said, "I went to see the girl."

"Unwise of you."

"Yes, wasn't it?" he agreed sourly.

"Have you told Tommy?"

"Not yet, he's out. I'll have to see Fran Gifford, of course."

"What will you tell her?"

"I don't know. We'd better make it Monday morning, I'll have to decide by then what to do about Halford's offer."

"I'll be free tomorrow," she told him, "any time you need me."

"Thank you. I ought to try to tell you, Miss Langhorne, how much I appreciate—"

"Have some more coffee?"

"—your generous attitude about all this."

"Want to do the best for the girl," she said, accepting his empty cup. "Don't know what that is, myself."

"Do you think I do?"

She didn't try to answer that. "One thing I ought to tell you . . . have you been doing any shopping while you've been in Chedcombe?"

"No. Nothing at all. I've had no need."

"Good thing, perhaps. Not a nice atmosphere. Hostile."

"You mean, you've been having difficulty?"

"Lack of cooperation. Can't mistake it. Makes things awkward."

"I can't tell you how sorry—"

"Doesn't matter. Only thought, anything else happens, could hardly refuse Halford's offer." She paused, looking at him questioningly. "Won't do to be disappointed," she told him. "At least . . . done your best."

"Don't you think that's worse than anything . . . to do your best, and fail?"

She seemed to be giving that serious thought. "Not really," she said at last.

"Well, I just wish I knew more about Alice Randall."

"What good would that do?"

"I've got a feeling that if I understood her I'd have the key to the whole affair." He looked up again to find her eyes fixed on him consideringly, and added with renewed irritation: "I'm not saying there's any logic about that."

"Don't see it, I'm afraid. I still think Hugo Randall—"

"I know you do, and I can't say you're wrong. What did you think of Byron's evidence?"

"What we expected . . . wasn't it?"

"Yes, of course. All according to proof. But what happened that day to upset Mrs. Randall, that's what I'd like to know?"

"Nice girl, Elsie Barber, but probably imagined it."

"I wonder." Both look and voice were vague, and she eyed him with growing exasperation.

"Don't suppose Fred Byron could tell you anyway. All there in his statement, he only saw her for a moment alone."

"So he did." He paused, and then said in an odd voice, "There's another question, you know; who told the old lady about Nancy Selkirk?"

"Can't see what good it would do us to know," said Vera flatly. "Probably Walter, don't you think?"

"He might have guessed where Hugo's money was going. I don't see how he could have known."

"If he was interested enough to make a few inquiries—"

"I suppose he might have found out. Miss Langhorne . . . what's his reputation?"

"A cautious man," said Vera slowly. "That's what they say."

"Would you agree with the estimate?"

"I'd say he was a frustrated gossip. Expect that means he has a careful disposition, doesn't it?"

"He inherits quite a considerable sum of money under his mother's will."

"So does your friend, Nell Randall," Vera pointed out, suddenly tart.

"That's very true," said Antony; and grinned at her. "You see, I was wondering, if neither Fran nor Hugo is guilty, why was the old lady killed just then?"

"What the jury must be wondering."

"I realize that. But does it occur to you that someone intended Hugo to be blamed, someone deliberately engineered his quarrel with his grandmother by telling her about Nancy Selkirk? It could have been someone who thought, if she went so far as to cut him out of her will, that they'd benefit."

"Then Fran Gifford—"

"That was just an accident. It couldn't have been foreseen that Alice would leave her all that money or ask her to Ravenscroft that night."

"I see." She was staring at him blankly. "*If* those two are innocent," she said.

The concerto was finished. He stayed until the coffee pot was empty and the other side of the record had been played, but neither of them referred again to Alice Randall's murder. Antony walked back to the George in a painful state of indecision, and found that Tommy Davenant had telephone twice in his absence.

It seemed a little late, by then, to return the call; but not too late, perhaps, to have a word with Jenny. He kicked off his shoes and stretched out comfortably on the bed while he waited for the connection, and wondered idly how his patient guardian was spending the night, and whether the management appreciated having a bobby on the premises. If he knew anything about it . . .

Jenny's greeting was drowned by the sound of hammering. "What on earth . . . I can't hear you," he said, raising his voice.

"I said . . . it *is* you, Antony? You're all right?"

"Yes, of course."

"There's no 'of course' about it. Just a minute." She must have turned her head, because he couldn't hear her next remark, but the hammering stopped abruptly. "There!" she said. Antony felt a sudden, quite disproportionate gratitude for the fact that she wasn't going to elaborate on her anxiety.

"Entertaining?" he inquired, with interest.

"Not exactly a party. Roger's here, and Meg's coming straight from the theater."

"Well, he doesn't have to break up the furniture, does he?"

"You ought to be grateful," said Jenny severely. And then, "I suppose Uncle Nick told you I was having a little difficulty."

"I don't think you were really trying, love. A little more, and Gibbs might have gone for good."

"It does seem a waste, doesn't it? But the shelves look marvelous now, darling . . . since Roger got at them," she added conscientiously. "Quite straight!"

"So I should hope."

"Well, it isn't really so easy. And he mended the vacuum cleaner."

"What was wrong with that?"

"It didn't seem to like wood shavings."

"Oh, lord!"

"You don't seem to appreciate—"

"Give him a medal," Antony advised. "And if any of the neighbors issue a summons for noise abatement—"

"Do you think they might?"

"Bound to, I should think. The fine will probably be enormous, and if you've spent all our money on the most expensive wood you could find—"

"Not quite all, Antony. And it won't need painting," she added, in an encouraging tone. "By the time you get home . . . when will that be?"

"It could be Monday. Jenny love, I hope it won't."

"Why not?"

"Because I don't like admitting defeat."

"Uncle Nick told me the case might be transferred, but surely—"

"And I don't like playing for safety. But I suppose I must." He sounded tired now; it didn't occur to him that he hadn't explained the nature of his problem. Jenny said:

"You must do what you think best," and there was a flatness in her tone that alerted him.

"No danger, love. Nothing's going to happen to me. I was thinking of my client . . . I hate lost causes," he said; and was grateful again that she settled herself to listen to his troubles without interruption, and without any attempt at reassurance.

V

When he got to bed he slept so deeply that it seemed no more than five minutes could have passed before he was awakened by the shrilling of the telephone. As he lifted the receiver he still wasn't quite sure where he was, and he couldn't place the woman's voice that greeted him, speaking far too fast and breathless with agitation.

"Mr. Maitland? I'm sorry . . . I'm sorry to wake you."

He groped for the light switch, blinked a little in the sudden illumination, and managed to focus on the dial of his watch. Ten to three . . . she might well apologize . . . "It doesn't matter," he said, not meaning it. "Who—?"

"Nell Randall. I wouldn't have disturbed you, only Hugo said I should tell you; and then I thought if I waited till morning, someone else might talk to you first."

He was wide awake now, but no less confused than he had been in the first moments of consciousness. He said, very slowly and distinctly, as though he were afraid she couldn't hear him: "Is Hugo there? Let me talk to him."

"But you can't! That's what I'm trying to tell you." Her voice rose on the words to something like a wail. "The police came and took him away with them. They say that girl . . . Nancy Selkirk . . . they say she's been murdered."

Sunday, 2nd February

THE THOUGHT went through his mind with startling irrelevance that he had been right in this, at least; Nell had known, or suspected, something of the liaison. The trouble was, he didn't want to accept what she was telling him, either the fact of Nancy's death or the consequences. He heard his own voice, sharper than he had intended:

"Do you mean he's been arrested?"

"Well, I suppose—" The question seemed to confuse her.

"Is his solicitor with him?"

"Oh, yes, I called Fred . . . Mr. Byron. He was going straight to the police station."

"And what about you? Is there someone—?"

"Tommy's here. We'll be all right."

He wondered briefly why Davenant hadn't done the telephoning. "Miss Randall, why did Hugo ask you to call me?" he asked.

"I really don't know." She was calmer now, but she sounded bewildered. "I think perhaps it was the—the murder he wanted you to know about, not what had happened to him."

"I see." That made a sort of sense, at least. "You mustn't upset yourself, you know."

"I can't," she said drearily. "There's so much to do. And I'm worried about the twins."

"If you'd just stop thinking of them as children."

"That's what Tommy says. He's here, Mr. Maitland; would you like a word with him?"

"Thank you." A moment later he heard Davenant's voice.

"This is a bad business, Maitland."

Antony agreed. He didn't envy the other man his role of family friend. "Have they made an arrest?" he asked.

"Not yet. Camden cautioned him, as far as I can make out from what Nell says."

"Do you know any details?"

"Only that she was strangled."

"I see."

"I don't understand anything," Davenant complained.

"Nor I. When can I see you?"

"This afternoon. Say, three o'clock. Shall I come to the hotel?"

"Yes, do. There's a good deal to talk about."

"I'm sorry we missed each other last night. I'd only gone round to the pub, but I forgot to tell my housekeeper where I'd be."

"It doesn't matter. Shall I get hold of Miss Langhorne, or will you?"

"Do you mind? I may be tied up here."

"How good are you at milking?"

Davenant laughed, a queer ghostly sound. "That's the least of my worries. You forget Nell was a landgirl." But he sounded faintly discontented as he added: "I'm sorry you've been disturbed, you know, but nothing would satisfy her—" His voice grew faint, as though he were looking over his shoulder, and then he added more strongly: "I can't imagine what interest Hugo thinks his amours are to you."

II

Detective Inspector Camden was waiting for him when he came out into the hall after breakfast, and Maitland took him upstairs with him. The bed was still unmade, and the room rather depressingly untidy, but at least they could be private here. He waved the Inspector to the armchair near the window, and dragged forward the stool from in front of the dressing table.

"If I may say so, sir, you don't seem very surprised to see me."

"I'm not, of course." It had taken him a minute or two downstairs to recognize the dark-haired, shortish man he had seen giving evidence; now he thought he should have done so straightaway, if only because of Camden's extreme impassivity. "Nothing stays secret in Chedcombe for long; and in any case your man will have told you I visited Nancy Selkirk yesterday."

"That, I suppose, would be why you didn't think of informing me."

"Precisely. I was sure you'd be here soon enough."

"Why did you visit her, sir?"

"You know why I'm in Chedcombe, Inspector. I hoped she might have some information that would help Frances Gifford's defense."

Camden frowned over this. "You meant to call her as a witness?"

"I believe there was no question of that."

To his surprise, the detective made no attempt to press him. "Let's see, then, we have the exact time of your visit. Did you go there by appointment?"

"No, I took a chance on finding her." He hesitated before he added: "She was in the kitchen, manicuring her nails."

"Was anyone else present?"

"Not in the room . . . not in the house, so far as I know. Except that she implied her baby was asleep upstairs."

"Would you say there was anything abnormal in her manner?"

"As a stranger, I'm hardly qualified to judge that. She seemed—" He paused, trying to remember precisely. "She seemed excited, perhaps a little apprehensive. And though she didn't mention the fact I concluded she had an appointment, because she kept looking at the clock."

"A date?"

"She left me for a while, to finish dressing. I should certainly say she was dressed for a date." He hesitated again; Camden's expression was not encouraging. "I was told she was strangled. Where was she found?"

"In the sitting room at her home, when her mother came in from the pictures at ten-thirty."

"Then she couldn't have been meaning to go out. Unless she had a baby-sitter."

"That seems a reasonable assumption, sir," said the Inspector unemotionally. "Now, you tell me there was some sort of connection between Nancy Selkirk and the Gifford case."

"I told you nothing of the kind."

"You thought there might be a connection," Camden corrected himself smoothly. "Do you know, Mr. Maitland, I find that very interesting."

"Is Hugo Randall under arrest?"

There was a blankness about the Inspector's gaze . . . a bovine look, that was a better description. "Can you think of any reason why I should answer your questions, Mr. Maitland?"

"I can't think of any reason for not telling me that. It'll be common knowledge soon enough."

"Perhaps you're right." Camden sighed. "He has been charged. And as a rider to that, I hope you'll agree with me that you stand in no further need of police protection."

"It wasn't my idea in the first place, Inspector."

"So I gathered," said Camden dryly. "Not that there won't be extra patrols in the town; there was another paint job done last night."

"Another? Where?"

"On the Shire Hall. The same green paint, Inspector Arkwright says. Would that be contempt of court, sir?" It was impossible to tell whether the question was intended humorously or not.

Antony said absently: "I shouldn't wonder." He was thinking that Mr. Justice Halford's sense of propriety was about to be still further outraged. "What did it say?"

" 'Whores hang,' " said Camden in a dead voice.

Antony blinked at him. "A singularly inaccurate statement, in view of the Homicide Act," he remarked, after a moment. "Look here, Inspector, will you tell me one other thing? It's important, really it is."

"Well, Mr. Maitland, it rather depends on your question."

"Did Mrs. Selkirk tell you Alice Randall had visited her daughter?"

"She did." There was a pause. "On Christmas Eve," he added, as though with reluctance. "Why do you ask?"

"Nancy told me the old lady went twice to Carlton Crescent. I had a feeling she wasn't telling me the truth."

"When was the second occasion?"

"The 27th December."

Camden took his time to think this out. "According to Mrs. Selkirk's statement, that's impossible. Nancy was in bed with a cold from Boxing Day to the following Sunday . . . the 29th. And as a consequence, her mother didn't go out at all."

"I see."

"Is it important?"

"I think it may be," said Antony. "Did you ever ask Miss Randall about the day she drove her mother into Chedcombe to keep her appointment with Byron?"

Camden's expression became even more wooden. "Yes, of course." He made the admission as cautiously as though it might incriminate him.

"I was wondering why she went to the Bank when she'd cashed a check on Market Day, as usual."

"You could have asked Miss Randall that in court."

"I could have done if I'd thought of it in time."

"Well, as far as I recall it was to collect a letter that had been addressed to her there; to the old lady, I mean. It didn't seem important enough to include in Miss Randall's statement, and in any case," the Inspector added shrewdly, "she was only there a moment . . . not long enough to have had a talk with Walter Randall, shall we say?"

"No, I see," said Antony, and sighed.

"If you've nothing else to ask me, Mr. Maitland—" Camden sounded dissatisfied, but he wasn't in any hurry to press his questions. It occurred to Antony that he must be very sure of his ground. "We'll have to have a formal statement, you know; and your fingerprints, of course, for comparison."

"Any time you like, Inspector."

"My shorthand writer's gone off duty. Will this afternoon suit you?"

"I've a conference at three o'clock."

"At two, then? At the police station." He stopped in the doorway and said, with a slight twitching of his lips that might have been meant for a smile: "It seems it won't take very long, Mr. Maitland. You can't expect me to be too pleased about that.''

It had been six o'clock before Antony fell asleep again after his talk with Nell Randall, but he couldn't say he felt much wiser for his cogitations. The only thing he was sure about was that he couldn't stay in his room now, alone with his thoughts; he was rummaging in the wardrobe for sweater and scarf when the telephone rang. This time it was a man's voice, deep, pleasant, vaguely familiar. ''Frederick Byron, Maitland. Could I see you?''

''Why, yes.'' It was ridiculous to feel startled, but it was the last thing he'd been expecting.

''It's about what happened last night. You've heard, of course?''

''An outline only.''

''Shall I come to the hotel?''

''If you like; but I expect the chambermaid's wishing me out of the way.''

''Then make it my office. In twenty minutes' time.'' A decisive man, thought Maitland, as the line went dead; in his own undecided mood he found this depressing.

He arrived at the office across the square just as a black Vauxhall drew up in the parking space on the cobbles. Frederick Byron was less formally dressed today, though still astonishingly neat. He said very little until they had walked up through the quiet desolation of the empty house to his office on the first floor; a big room overlooking the Market Square, with comfortable, shabby furnishings.

''I'm afraid this must seem rather odd to you.'' He was shrugging out of his overcoat as he spoke. ''Take the chair by the hearth, my dear fellow. I'll just put a match to the fire, then we can be comfortable.''

Maitland did as he was told. ''I'm hoping for enlightenment,'' he said.

''It might save time if you tell me what you've heard.'' Byron straightened himself and watched a little tongue of flame flicker up out of the nest of coal. Then he sat down and eyed his companion expectantly; but in spite of his easy manner, he did not look relaxed.

''A girl called Nancy Selkirk has been strangled; she was found dead at her home at ten-thirty last night. And Hugo

Randall has been charged with her murder,'' said Antony precisely.

"Yes." Byron drew out the word reluctantly, and seemed at a loss to know how to continue.

"Are you acting for him?"

"I am." The right question, it seemed; at least, there was to be no more hesitation. "And certain circumstances have arisen . . . it seemed wisest to waste no time in asking if you would be willing to accept the brief."

"I'm afraid that won't be possible." He had been staring down at the fire, but now he looked up quickly. "Was that Hugo Randall's suggestion?"

"In a way. He was very insistent that I should give you the facts." He shifted restlessly in his chair; there was no sign now of his earlier serenity. "So I thought, if it was consistent with your duty to Fran Gifford—"

"That isn't the trouble. These circumstances you spoke of—"

"I was present, of course, while the police questioned Hugo before the charge was made. From the trend of their questions it seems obvious that they connect this business in some way with Alice Randall's death. In fact, I should imagine that they suspect him of complicity in that."

"In association with my client?" As he spoke he knew the connection was obvious enough, he ought to have seen it before.

"So it would appear."

"Yes, I see." Maitland was frowning heavily, looking down at the fire. "Hugo Randall will plead 'not guilty'?"

"Those are my instructions." He added stiffly, as Maitland looked up at him quickly: "Whatever he's done, I'd like to do my best for him."

"What's their case?"

"You may have been told Mrs. Selkirk found her daughter." Byron's hesitation was so slight as to be almost unnoticeable. "She ran screaming to her neighbors, and the police were called. To them she made a statement: that Hugo was the father of Nancy's child, that he had been paying for its maintenance but recently had defaulted in the payments, that Nancy was pregnant again." He broke off, and passed a hand over his eyes; he might be as elegant as ever, but today he looked his age. "I must admit, all this was a shock to me. I'm fond of the boy, you know."

"The first two points Hugo confirmed to me yesterday . . . well, after a fashion," said Antony. "The third—"

"The police doctor says she was about three months pregnant. Mrs. Selkirk says Nancy was always secretive about her friends; she was certainly seeing Hugo . . . for instance, he always brought the money to the house. And while we're speaking of that, she says Nancy told her it was no use thinking she could shame Hugo into marriage, and he'd only pay her as long as she kept quiet about their relationship."

"She was only a girl," said Maitland slowly.

"I doubt if her mother had any influence over her, if that's what you're thinking."

"I suppose not. But Hugo denied to me that the *affaire* continued. Could there have been someone else?"

"As far as Mrs. Selkirk knows, nobody."

"There was a good deal of money going into the house," said Antony slowly. Byron sighed.

"The neighbors, of course, are in no doubt she had a lover—"

"And they'll be quick enough now to say they knew all along it was Hugo."

"Unfortunately, there's nothing to suggest they'd be wrong. Hugo, we know, went to the house on occasion; but when she went out she seems to have behaved more discreetly. The man must have had a car, because once or twice she mentioned having been to Northdean which is all of thirty miles away. But wherever he picked her up, it wasn't at the house."

"Did she ever stay away all night?"

"I think so, but so far Mrs. Selkirk hasn't admitted it. Perhaps she felt the fact would reflect on her in some way."

"You'll have to get someone on to that, you know. If she wasn't with Hugo—"

"I have the greatest fear—"

"Something you haven't told me yet," said Maitland, watching him.

"The neighbors saw and have described a man who was in Carlton Crescent at about nine o'clock last night. One of them saw him going down the path to the Selkirks' back door. Both identified Hugo from six other men this morning."

"The Randalls are well known in Chedcombe. Did they know him by sight?"

"They say not."

"I see. What has Hugo to say for himself?"

"Just that he didn't kill her."

"Does he admit being there?"

"No."

"But he hasn't an alibi?"

"He says he was out walking. He didn't get home till two in the morning; the police were waiting for him."

"Could he offer any confirmation?"

"No." He hesitated unhappily. "One of the farm workers, Kenneth Strange, who has a cottage near the drive, says he heard the van going out at about half past eight. He's quite sure about that because when he's off duty he expects to have the use of it."

"Is the van significant?"

"It was parked in Regent's Way, near the corner of Carlton Crescent, for an hour or two yesterday evening at the relevant time. The policeman on the beat noticed it because it wasn't the sort of vehicle people on the housing estate would own."

"Not quite the thing?"

"That's right. He rather wondered which of them had a visitor with so undistinguished a means of transport. Unfortunately he also made a note of the number."

"What do the doctors say about the time of death?"

"Probably between seven o'clock and ten. They may get that down a bit, I don't know."

Antony got up and went across to the window. A few people were drifting by, a decorous procession, on their way from St. Philip's Church at the other side of the square; it occurred to him to wonder how many of them would have a charitable word to say about the dead girl, even at this moment. And, almost as clearly as he had done last night, he heard Nancy Selkirk saying: "I'm damned, anyway, as far as Chedcombe is concerned." He said, without turning to look at Frederick Byron: "That's all very clear." And an echo in his mind added: too clear . . . too clear for comfort.

"Do you feel you could accept the case?"

"That isn't the point," Maitland told him; and turned and came back to the fire again. "I visited Miss Selkirk myself last night, so they're pretty well bound to want my evidence . . . don't you think?"

"I had no idea!"

"Of course you hadn't." Antony sounded impatient. "It's a pity, because I think you're right, you know; the two things should be dealt with together. But not by me."

"Are you going to apply for a change of venue?"

"I don't know. I don't know!" But he knew as he spoke that the decision had been taken out of his hands. "I'll have to see Hugo again," he added, as though he was speaking to himself; and looked up to find Byron's eyes fixed on him with an odd, almost calculating look. But then the solicitor smiled, and he thought perhaps he had been wrong about that.

"He'll be held at the police station until after the proceedings tomorrow. If you tell them you need his evidence," Byron suggested, "they can hardly object to that." And when Maitland did not answer, heaved himself out of his chair.

Antony was already on his feet. "Was it a complete surprise to you?" he asked. "Hugo's connection with Nancy Selkirk, I mean."

"Not altogether. After what Alice Randall told us—"

"But I thought—"

"She was by no means specific, and I admit I did not then understand her reference to a trust. But we shouldn't be discussing this, Mr. Maitland."

"Was this the day she signed the codicil?"

"It was." There was no mistaking the surprise in Byron's voice. He shut his lips firmly, as though afraid of being betrayed into further indiscretion.

III

Antony turned down North Street without thinking; probably because the other way would lead him past the hotel, and he didn't want to go there yet. The gossips would have material for more speculation than ever today, and he was surprised at his own reluctance to face the whispering, the sudden silences. And he wanted to think . . .

So he walked down North Street, and crossed Westgate, and saw Frost's Bank on the corner. It was another impulse that brought him to a halt at the side door and raised his hand to the bell. It seemed only too likely that Walter would be at Ravenscroft, but no harm in trying after all.

Again it was Mrs. Walter who came to the door; impossible to think of her as Wendy. She still had her hat on, and told him as she led the way up the stairs that she had just come in from church; he couldn't decide whether this was meant for a reproof, her tone was as flat as ever. She had shown no surprise at finding him on the doorstep, nor any reluctance when he asked to see her husband.

Upstairs, there was a heartening smell of roast beef. He wasn't surprised when she pushed open the sitting-room door, said, "It's that Mr. Maitland again, Walter," and departed without ceremony. He decided he had received a sufficient invitation, and went in.

Walter Randall was another one who looked his age today; more than his age, Maitland decided, after a brief calculation. He didn't get up or invite his visitor to be seated, but eyed him in an unfriendly way and said heavily: "I suppose you're wondering what you can make out of this to help that girl."

"I'm sorry," said Antony.

"I'll bet you are." Walter spoke with a sort of weak viciousness. There was a tumbler on the table beside him, and a bottle of Johnnie Walker; it didn't seem very likely that he had accompanied his wife to church. "It's a dreadful thing to have happened; a dreadful thing."

"It is indeed," Antony assented, feeling like a parrot. But he seemed to have found the right note; some of Randall's belligerence left him and he said quite cordially:

"I can't say I'm surprised, you know. Allan wasn't a steady chap, so what can you expect."

"Mr. Randall, did you know of your nephew's association with Nancy Selkirk?" No use trying to wrap his questions up; he didn't think Walter was in a state to understand anything but complete bluntness.

"All that money . . . there was bound to be a girl in it somewhere," said Walter, apparently pleased with his own acumen. He paused, considering. "I didn't think he had the gumption to make the grade with one like Nancy."

"Tell me about her," Maitland suggested.

"Bad lot," said Walter, looking at the door; perhaps it was his wife's opinion he was quoting.

"You know everything that happens in Chedcombe, don't you?"

"I didn't know about Hugo."

"Her other friends—"

"Lovers," said Walter. "Same thing, with a girl like that." He seemed completely mellowed now, and waved a hand invitingly toward the chair Antony had occupied on his previous visit.

"Her lovers, then."

"A crowd of youngsters, when she was still at school."

"Later," said Antony. "After her baby was born."

Walter laughed, and looked cunning. "A different story, wouldn't you say? They weren't so keen to start gossip then."

"Didn't she manage to amuse herself?"

"Not the same boys."

"She told me she liked older men."

"Oh?" There was sharp surprise in his tone, perhaps even displeasure; but then he seemed to forget what it was that startled him. "An older man would know how to be discreet."

"I suppose—"

"Hugo knew, for that matter." The words seemed to recall him to his grievance, and he sighed gustily. "Not that that's any help now."

"Did you know she was pregnant again?"

Perhaps the abruptness of the question had a sobering effect. "I can't say I'm surprised," said Walter carefully. And then: "Always said the boy was a fool."

"Suppose Hugo wasn't the father . . . of this second child, I mean."

"What's the use of supposing a silly thing like that?"

"It opens up a number of interesting possibilities. For instance, if Nancy's 'older' lover was someone with a financial interest in your mother's death—"

"Here!" said Walter indignantly.

"—it might have been to his advantage to see that it occurred . . . before she had time to change her will again, let us say." He started to move toward the door, but turned before he reached it. "In view of her known prejudices," he added gently.

Walter came halfway to his feet, and then thought better of it. "You've no right to say that. Libelous," he said viciously.

"Oh, I don't think—" Maitland was vague again. It was only when he was out in the street that he realized he had at last pinned down, to his own satisfaction, the connection between Alice Randall's character and the need for her death.

The only trouble was, he rather thought it was too late.

He continued his walk along Westgate; it was still fine, but a gray, sunless day. Perhaps that was why he felt so cold. When he reached the Nag's Head he went in; the place looked inviting, it would be warm inside, and no one would know him. He ordered Black Label and thought—with a momentary lifting of his depression—then even Willett might have sanctioned the indulgence on this occasion. As the barman slid his glass toward him, a voice was raised in the corner of the room, repeating the order and adding in an affected drawl: "That's what we drink in London." The imitation was clumsy, but there was no doubt at all of its intent.

There was a burst of laughter. Maitland's eyes met the bartender's for an instant before the man looked away; he didn't join in the merriment, his expression was half sly, half ingratiating. Antony picked up his glass and turned to survey the room.

A pleasant place, the bar at the Nag's Head, with paneled walls, a raftered ceiling, and a generous fire. Big enough to hold the present company with ease, about twenty persons in all.

It wasn't difficult to pick out the man who had spoken, a

slightly built, alert-looking fellow of about thirty who was standing with a group by the window. Where the others dropped their eyes for a moment and then raised them to watch covertly, his own gaze remained fixed and challenging. "You're the chap from London, aren't you?" he asked. (Did everyone in town know who he was?)

"I live there, certainly." He drank some of the Scotch. "When's the concert? If I'm still here—"

"What the 'ell do you mean?"

"Weren't you rehearsing? I thought—"

Someone laughed, and stifled it quickly. An old woman, nursing her glass by the fire, said admiringly: "There now, Sid. Good enough for the Palace, aren't you?" Antony looked down at her, and grinned as he met her eye.

"You keep out of this, Ma," said Sid. "We don't like murder in Chedcombe, nor we don't like immorality, and see what's come of your meddling."

"Big words he knows, and all, don't he?" said Ma confidentially to the room at large.

"Well, if you want to wake up one morning and find yourself strangled—"

"Not me, Sid. Not at my age."

"That's not the point," said a burly man near the window in an authoritative tone. "If them as does murder goes free, we're none of us safe."

"That's what you're after, isn't it?" asked Sid. There was an ugly look in his eye. "You and that woman."

"I can't discuss it with you, you know," Antony told him quietly.

"We don't want your sort here, interfering with what we could easy settle ourselves." And suddenly the whole group seemed to be talking at once. "First it was the old lady—"

"I always knew there was something between those two."

"A proper lady, she was—"

"What did the vicar say about her? Always ready with a helping hand—"

"And her wanting nothing but good to the girl."

"She was a quiet one, that Fran Gifford. You always know."

"Wonder how she'll feel when she knows she wasn't the only one he was messing about with."

And out of the pandemonium Sid's voice said clearly: "How much does it cost, mister, to get clear of a murder charge?" He came across the room until he was very close to Maitland, and thrust his face up at him. "Don't like that question, do you?" he jeered.

"If you want to know, I find it an impertinence," said Antony, nobly repressing the inclination to say instead, reprehensibly, "Shall I quote you rates?"

"Do you, then?" Sid seemed a little taken aback, but he was immediately reinforced by a thin woman with a cottage-loaf hat perched dead straight on top of her head. "And whose business is it what happens in Chedcombe, young man, if it isn't ours?"

"Then I'll leave you, madam, to the consideration of it." He turned a little to put down his glass on the bar, and felt Sid's hand on his arm.

"Oh, no you don't. Now you're here we've a thing or two to tell you." There was a murmur of assent from his supporters. "There'll be trouble, I'm warning you—" But Maitland's temper, hardly held, was lost without trace at the other man's touch.

"You b-bloody hypocrite," he said, and Sid recoiled before the blaze of anger in his eyes. "You're to p-play judge and jury, are you? You s-sanctimonious little viper." He went to the door and turned there, and saw their faces . . . angry . . . resentful . . . full of malice. Then he caught Ma's eye and she winked at him, and he spoke to her across the stillness of the room. "All this conscious virtue," he said. "I don't feel at all at home."

He thought he heard her laugh, but the conversation burst out again, loudly and indignantly, as he closed the door.

IV

It took a little time to persuade Inspector Camden that it would be interfering with the course of justice to deny him access to Hugo Randall. "The application should properly have come from Mr. Davenant," the detective told him.

"I shall be seeing him as soon as I leave here, but I

haven't time to stand on formality," said Maitland. Looking at him, Camden thought unhappily that, in spite of this, he had the look of one who was prepared to wait all day for what he wanted, and gave way with one of his expressive sighs. Antony said, "Thank you," briskly, and waited with unconcealed impatience while the necessary orders were given.

The room allotted for the interview was tiny; they faced each other across a narrow trestle table. Hugo greeted him calmly enough, but the sullen look was back on his face again. He said, as he seated himself: "I should thank you, I suppose—"

"Don't waste your breath. I can't act for you."

"I see." There was a languidness in his tone; as though, Maitland thought, he had gone beyond despair, to a point where there was nothing left to hope for.

"You don't see at all," Antony said sharply. "When I say 'I can't' that's exactly what I mean."

"Then why—?" But the sharpness seemed to have had the effect of arousing at least a spark of interest. "I hope you're not going to tell me I must be properly dressed when I appear in court," said Hugo, amused. He was still wearing jodhpurs and a gray pullover. "It's all Mr. Byron seems to be able to think about."

"I couldn't care less. Why did you want me to know what had happened to Nancy?"

"I thought it might help Fran." He paused, watching Maitland's expression. "Won't it?" he asked.

"It only makes everything about ten times worse."

"I don't believe it." He banged his fist down suddenly on the trestle in front of him, so that it swayed precariously. "It's got to help!" he said, with much more energy in his tone.

"Take my word for it, won't you?"

"I don't understand." And then, as though he couldn't keep his mind on any one aspect of the problem, he added in a worried voice: "What's going to happen tomorrow?"

Maitland didn't make the mistake of thinking he was referring to his own affairs. "We shall apply for a retrial . . . not on this assize."

"You mean, there won't be a verdict. Fran will still have to wait."

"It may be for the best," said Antony, not believing it. "It will give us time—"

"Time!" echoed Hugo, with something of his former violence; and was still again. "It's been a month for Fran, hasn't it? A month already." His hands were shaking; he clasped them together tightly on the table in front of him, and did not meet Maitland's eye.

"Never mind that now." Pity was an intolerable emotion; his voice roughened, denying it. "I still want to talk to you about her defense."

"I told you, anything—"

"You didn't tell me the truth."

"I admitted . . . enough, didn't I? And now, after what has happened—"

"Did you kill Nancy Selkirk?"

"No . . . no!"

"Did you go to her house?"

"There seems to be proof of that."

Maitland sat back. "I want the whole story of your dealings with Nancy," he said deliberately.

"I said I was willing—"

"The truth. Will you tell me that?"

"If it would help . . . it won't!" He spread his hands in a gesture that was strangely defenseless. "I might have told you yesterday. How can I . . . now?"

"For heaven's sake, Hugo, this isn't a decision *you* can make."

"I can. I must. If the story of—what did you say?—my dealings with Nancy will help, I'll tell it; in court, anywhere. The rest . . . will you believe me when I tell you my silence can't possibly harm anyone but myself?"

Maitland hesitated. "Fran's been hurt enough already."

"I know that, don't I?" said Hugo savagely.

"I wonder."

"You don't understand!"

"All right then, tell me. If you weren't Nancy's only lover—"

"I said I didn't kill her, but I was . . . responsible for her death. I can't deny that, even for Fran." In spite of its flatness, there was a finality in his tone. Antony, who knew when he was beaten, took his leave a few minutes later. It wasn't until he was walking away from the police station that it occurred to him to wonder just what he had expected from the interview. And the answer to that seemed to be that he hadn't expected anything at all . . . but until this moment he'd been hoping for a miracle.

He knew now there was nothing left to hope for. He'd done his best, and failed.

V

They had arranged to meet, after all, at Vera Langhorne's cottage, and he was a little late, but still the first to arrive. Davenant came at ten minutes past the hour, and replied shortly to questions about the family at Ravenscroft. "Byron seems to think the police are connecting the two murders," he said, glaring at Maitland as though he were in some way responsible.

"So it seems. I've a good deal to tell you, Davenant—"

"If you mean, about your visit to Nancy Selkirk, Byron told me that, too." His tone was stiff. "Did it help at all?"

"I can't say it did. I admit it was a mistake."

Tommy gave him a suspicious look, perhaps taken aback by this unexpected mildness. "What did she have to tell you?"

"Nothing beyond the fact of her affair with Hugo. She was expecting a visitor, if I know the signs."

"Hugo?"

"I don't know."

Tommy seemed to find this an added cause of depression. "Nell's half out of her mind," he said, very much in his usual manner. The little spurt of displeasure seemed to have worn itself out. "I can't see it myself, but she dotes on him, you know."

There was no music today, the little room seemed oddly silent; but Vera had cups on a tray, and a kettle singing on the hob. She was bending forward now to splash hot water into the teapot, and raised a flushed face from the task. "The thing we should decide is whether to make this application," she told them.

"Yes . . . well—" Davenant seemed uncertain. "How do you feel about it?" he asked, turning to Maitland.

"I'm afraid the decision has been made for us. We can't go on."

"That's all very well—" began Davenant. Miss Langhorne straightened her back, with a small grunt of protest at her stiffness, and said slowly:

"That means we've got no case."

"It means we've no longer any alternative but to apply for a change of venue."

"But you said—"

"I don't like it any better now. But too much has happened. When I got back to the hotel at lunchtime there was a message for me to get in touch with the Judge. I haven't done so, but I know what he's going to say."

"What?" said Tommy.

"That's he's prepared to discharge the jury and order a retrial himself, if we don't do something about it. Or he may put it more crudely, in terms of responsibility to our client. You see, I probably won't be in a position to act when the case comes on again; it could be said I wanted to continue now in order to keep the brief."

"Not true," said Vera, at her gruffest.

"No, but . . . that's why it was a mistake to go and see Nancy. You don't have to tell me. Not that it makes much difference to Halford's position, I'm afraid. Too much has happened to show the local prejudice. Too much is still happening."

"A lot of nonsense."

"Maybe. But Halford isn't going to like having rude comments painted on the walls of the court."

It was obvious that they had both heard already about the indignity the Shire Hall had suffered. Tommy shrugged his shoulders; Vera Langhorne said bracingly: "We'll have a better chance away from here." And then more hesitantly, watching Maitland's expression: "Or don't you think that's true?"

"No, I don't. Not now. The prosecution will have a smashingly heavier case when the trial comes on again."

"Do you mean, because of Nancy's death?" said Davenant. "I don't quite see—"

"Imagine for a moment that we're faced with a joint trial."

"Fran and Hugo?"

"Who else?" He accepted a cup of tea absent-mindedly from Vera, left it untasted on the table at his elbow, and got up to move restlessly about the room. "I'll bet anything you like it was Hugo she used to slip out at night to meet; everyone assumed they were 'going together' until she was arrested, when the assumption didn't seem to fit in any longer with the theory of her guilt. Now!" He looked from one of his companions to the other, daring them to interrupt. "Hugo is courting Fran; he's secretive about it because he doesn't feel he can ask her to join the household at Ravenscroft, and he can't get away from it himself until the twins are off his hands. Meanwhile, he seduces Nancy Selkirk . . . what better way could he find of passing the time? Grandmother finds out and disinherits him, but she doesn't know of his relationship with Fran."

"It seems to me—" said Davenant, but Antony swept on unheeding.

"So Fran stands to inherit, and Hugo has only to marry her to be just as happily placed as before. Even better, because he now has control of the cash originally intended for Mark and Marian as well."

"Whatever you think about *him,*" said Vera, "he's always done his best for those two."

"Would you care for the task of demonstrating that to a jury?"

"I suppose it wouldn't be easy," she agreed reluctantly. "But, knowing about Nancy, would Fran—?"

"She's in love with Hugo; don't you think she would have forgiven him?" He turned to give Davenant a black look, as though he suspected the solicitor of being about to challenge the statement. "And I'll tell you something else; if you put her in the witness box she'll give herself away on *that* point, just as she did when she talked to me."

"Take your word for it," said Miss Langhorne pacifically.

"All right then. Alice Randall is a healthy old lady, and if she discovers what's in the wind between Fran and Hugo she'll certainly change her will again; they're faced with the absolute necessity of concealing their attachment for an indefinite time. Do you think they would find that a satisfactory situation?''

"No, I don't," said Tommy, more positively than was his custom; and then looked at Vera in a deprecating way.

"But if Alice dies before she finds out, they're sitting pretty, aren't they? Nancy has no shred of proof of the old lady's intentions; at best she might get a court order for maintenance, probably no more than Hugo is paying already. So the obvious thing to do is to see that Mrs. Randall doesn't live too long.'' He paused, and looked from one of his companions to the other, a bright, impersonal glance that didn't encourage any further interruption. "Hugo tells Fran about the digitalis, Alice provides the opportunity by inviting her to Ravenscroft, and if Fran bungles her part of the business it's no more than anyone would expect. I imagine the prosecution will say that she meant to make it look like an accident; but any policeman will tell you that criminals are apt to make the most elementary mistakes. And she's an amateur, after all.''

Davenant drew a deep breath. "I don't like it," he announced.

"I can't say I'm enamored of the situation myself," said Maitland tartly. Vera Langhorne was looking at him in a troubled way.

"Should never have asked you to stay," she told him.

"I admit, I haven't been very successful." He smiled at her ruefully. "Or isn't that what you meant?''

"Not exactly.''

"I'm only giving you the case for the Crown, you know; the reason I think Hugo's name will be joined with Fran's in the indictment. I don't say I believe it.''

"Is there a defense?''

"Not one that would convince a jury. Not even one that would convince you and Davenant, if your expressions are anything to go by.''

"Not a laughing matter," she told him in an admonitory tone.

"No, indeed." He came back to his chair again and picked up the neglected cup of tea. "I happen to be rather concerned," he added mildly, "because I don't believe a word of it myself."

"Why not?" she demanded.

"No reason that could be put to the court."

"But you're going to tell us."

"What's the use? You've made up your minds, haven't you?" He glanced at Davenant. "Both of you," he said.

"We're still concerned in the defense."

"All right then!" He was as serious now as even Vera could have wished. "We know Fran lied when she said she didn't know about the new codicil until New Year's Eve, but we can make a pretty good guess at the reason. She didn't want to admit she'd told Hugo because she was afraid people would think he'd killed his grandmother for revenge; which they probably would have done if Fran herself hadn't been around with an even more comprehensible financial motive."

"If she thought Hugo'd done it—"

"I daresay she did. And he lied, in his turn, not knowing her reason, but wanting to back her up."

"In the circumstances," Tommy Davenant protested, "that is hardly a convincing argument for her innocence . . . or his."

"Perhaps you'll like my next point better. Why was Hugo so keen to keep the cause of the quarrel to himself? I decline to believe that he was motivated solely by embarrassment."

"For the same reason . . . to avoid suspicion."

"I don't believe that, either. But I'll give you that point if you like. So then we come to the question, who shot at me on Friday night?"

"Not Mark?" said Vera, raising her eyebrows at him.

"Perhaps. Perhaps not."

"Well, now, just a minute. You think he sent the first two messages; what about the others?" Davenant asked.

"I think they were just someone's idea of improving what Mark had started. But it doesn't really matter, there's plenty of other evidence of the town's ill-will, if that's what you're thinking."

"Yes, I suppose. But the shooting may just be part of the same thing."

"It argues an urgency—"

"Which may well exist in Mark's case." Tommy paused to consider this, and his eyes met Maitland's with rather a startled look. "If he's trying to protect Hugo—"

"I'm afraid that could be true."

"Look here, Maitland, do you still believe in Fran's innocence? I like the girl, I wish I believed her . . . but now you seem bent on whitewashing Hugo Randall too."

"Answer the rest of my questions then. What did Alice learn the day she signed the new codicil?" Davenant shook his head helplessly. "Why the digitalis? Its use argues either a member of the family or a spur-of-the-moment killing; is that necessarily true? Who told Alice of Hugo's dealings with Nancy Selkirk? Why—when these were already known—did Nancy have to die?"

"I can't answer any of those things," said Davenant; there was a trace of doggedness in his tone. "Can you?"

"I'm afraid the answer to the last may be that Nancy was killed because the attempt on my life failed. And I think now I ought to have foreseen the possibility, but I didn't."

"I don't see—"

"Never mind. I haven't mentioned the most important question of all: who told Nancy what the new codicil meant to her?"

"All this doesn't seem to take us very far, does it?"

"I t-told you I d-didn't like the s-situation," said Maitland, with sudden violence. "But do you think any s-solution can be the right one, that l-leaves so many things obscure?"

Vera Langhorne had been silent for some time, except for the normal heaviness of her breathing. She leaned forward now with an abrupt movement and picked up the teapot. "Beside the point, really. You say we must make application—"

"And, as you're about to remind me, once that's d-done the affair will be no c-concern of mine."

"Didn't say that. But what could you have done tomorrow, after all?"

"Nothing. Nothing!"

"You could have asked the jury those questions," she persisted.

"Oh, yes, I could have done that. I could even have given

them my version of the answers, without any facts at all to back it up.''

''You know what happened?''

''I think I know.'' He made a vague, dissatisfied gesture, but in some odd way the words seemed to have a finality, as though a door had been closed, cutting them off from all that had gone before. Then Davenant laughed, and gave Vera a sheepish look, and murmured something vaguely apologetic. Maitland drank the rest of his tea, and put down the cup with a clatter; he had again his intent look. ''There's the question of telling Fran,'' he said.

''Tomorrow morning—''

''I'd like to explain to her myself why I shan't have any further concern in the case,'' Antony told him with a sort of mild stubbornness. ''Can you arrange for them to bring her down to the court a little early, to give us time?''

''I can, of course. Do you want me to do it now?'' said Davenant, with a singular lack of enthusiasm.

''If you want to get back to Ravenscroft, I'm sorry. It needn't delay you long.''

''Oh, very well.''

''Use my phone,'' Vera told him, nodding helpfully in its direction. She sat in silence while Tommy put the call through and then added gruffly: ''Sorry it had to end like this.''

''I'm sorry, too.'' He smiled at her, with an instinctive need to hide his own distress. ''Do you know, in the circumstances . . . I just wish you'd have less faith in the evidence and more in your own judgment.''

She shook her head. ''Can't ignore the facts,'' she said sadly. ''Know now, shouldn't have tried.'' He realized then that, whatever he said, he wouldn't shake her opinion; which wouldn't have mattered so much if it hadn't been for the last, nagging doubt in his mind that it might, after all, be the right one.

VI

It was already dark when he left the cottage on the Causeway, and Tommy Davenant had departed for Ravenscroft ten minutes before. It was a relief to be alone for the moment, the night air was cold and sweet; he'd be able to think clearly now, away from the wrangling, the arguments . . .

But he could only think of Fran Gifford, now that he knew he couldn't save her; Fran coming from the court to their last interview with a blind look in her eyes, and taking her leave of him, later, with the odd, impersonal politeness of a child. And Hugo, who had admitted, at last, that he loved her; who understood only too well that a month in prison was an age of living . . . or of dying? How would either of them bear the long years that lay ahead?

What was it Hugo had said? *She never gave anyone a second chance.* Illogical to think of Alice Randall as though she were in some way responsible for what had happened. She was a victim, after all, and for Nancy Selkirk he felt nothing but compassion. But if only the old lady had been less uncompromising . . .

The hotel was quiet when he reached it; the receptionist saluted him guardedly as he went through the hall. He was aware suddenly, as he reached his room, that he was desperately tired . . . almost too tired to care any more. But then, as he fitted the key in the lock, he heard someone approaching and turned as the door swung open to see Mark Randall coming across the landing. He waited without speaking for a moment, and then said: "Well?"

"Can I talk to you?"

"If it's about your brother's case. Not about Fran Gifford." (But what would it matter, really, when he'd already given up?)

"It's about Hugo."

"Then you'd better come in." He pushed the door wider and waited for the boy to go past him into the room. "I hope you're not armed," he said.

"No," Mark told him stiffly.

Maitland shut the door and came across the room. "You mustn't mind my asking," he pointed out. "I couldn't concentrate if I was wondering all the time if you were going to pull a gun on me."

"If you think it's funny—" The stiffness had gone now. He sounded hurt; as if he'd asked for sympathy from someone he had a right to trust, and found his plea rejected.

"I'm sorry, really I am." Antony didn't stop to consider

the strangeness of Mark's reaction. He gave his sudden smile and added apologetically: "I'm worried, too."

"Nell said . . . I was mad with you, you know, after what happened in court . . . but she said she thought you cared about the truth."

"To be honest, Mark, there are times when I find it inconvenient." This time the boy returned his smile, though rather uncertainly. "Did your aunt send you here?"

"No. You see she thinks . . . she really thinks Hugo killed Nancy, though she won't admit it, of course."

"Of course not."

"I've been here since half past two," said Mark. "The hotel's quiet after lunch, so nobody saw me come in. I've been waiting in the bathroom down the hall."

"A long wait."

"Three hours, actually. It seemed like forever." He paused, trying to find words for his explanation. "I didn't know until quite late this morning what the police had against Hugo; and when I did I got in a bit of a panic. You see . . . always before he's been there to ask."

"Yes, I think I see."

"So I came to you instead. It didn't seem, somehow, as if I could tell Mr. Byron. And Tommy didn't seem to have time for anyone but Nell."

"We'll worry about that later, shall we? Don't you think we'd better sit down?"

"I think perhaps—" He broke off, and thrust both hands into his pockets; a gesture Maitland recognized, he had seen Hugo make it. But it wasn't just Mark's hands, his whole body was shaking. "It isn't very easy," he said.

"Start with the easy part, then. Why did you write those letters?" He sat down on the stool with his back to the dressing table, leaving the armchair for Mark, if he cared to take it.

"I didn't shoot at you," said Mark quickly.

"I'll take your word for that. What about the letters?"

"I heard some talk in the town. I didn't want you asking questions, finding things out. I thought you might try to—to pin something on Hugo. I suppose it wasn't a very good idea, but I really thought Fran had killed Granny, you know."

"All right, then. Do you still think that?"

"I . . . don't know. But I do know Hugo didn't—didn't do anything to Nancy."

"How do you know that?"

"They say he was seen, going to the house." He paused again, and then added in a rush: "It wasn't him, it was me."

"I see." Maitland's voice was carefully expressionless. "Why did you go there?"

"I wanted to ask her not to make more trouble; money was short, and she was being difficult. I thought perhaps if I promised . . . I couldn't do anything now, but later—"

"What happened? I want to know exactly, Mark."

"I took the van, I didn't know Ken would hear, and someone might have needed the car. I left it parked round the corner and walked to the house. Those people who identified Hugo . . . we're fairly alike, and they only saw me for a moment. I don't suppose they meant to—to mislead anyone."

"What happened when you got there?"

"Nothing. Nothing at all. I rang the bell for ages, and then came away."

"Was the house in darkness?"

"I don't seem to remember."

"Then think a little. Which door did you go to?"

"The back door. There wasn't a light in the kitchen," said Mark positively.

"But you came round from the front of the house. When you first looked up at it—"

"There was a light on the landing upstairs. And I'm pretty sure there was a faint glow through the sitting-room curtains; but some people do that when they go away. Leave a light on, I mean."

"Is that what you thought, that they'd gone away?"

"If they'd been at home there'd have had to be someone with Jimmy."

"So you went away again. Straight back to Ravenscroft?"

"Yes, I did. It's quite easy to get in and out of my room; I've done it often enough, and no one the wiser." He broke off there, looked quickly at Maitland and then away again. "That's the easy part," he said.

"Perhaps I can help you about the other. It isn't the first time it's happened."

"What do you mean?"

"Getting a girl into trouble. You're Jimmy's father, aren't you?"

"That wasn't the worst thing." Mark's chin went up. "I shouldn't have let Hugo persuade me into keeping quiet about it."

"You can't have been very old at the time."

Mark seemed to be considering this. "I was fifteen," he said at last. "I don't think that's any excuse. The thing is," he added, in a burst of confidence, "I get so fed up at home."

Antony's sense of the ridiculous, however oppressed, wasn't proof against this kind of thing. He allowed his expression to relax into a grin. "There are other ways of passing the time," he suggested.

It was touch and go for a moment whether Mark took offense again. "I thought you'd be shocked," he said in an injured tone.

"Oh, I am," Maitland assured him hurriedly. "Shocked *and* horrified." It was so obvious that disapproval would be preferable to amusement. But then Mark surprised him, as he had done in court, by grinning himself and saying:

"I thought you were going to tell me to take up a hobby."

"I might have done, if I'd thought of it," Antony admitted. "But to get back to what you were telling me, we've decided your conduct was inexcusable—"

"The thing was, you see, Hugo wanted me to finish my education. He said he'd help Nancy, and it wouldn't do any good if everyone knew. He said a good deal else besides. And Granny would certainly have been shocked, and—and furious, you know. So if I didn't manage a scholarship—" He broke off, and added miserably: "It meant a good deal to me . . . then."

"Doesn't it any longer?"

"Yes, I suppose." He sounded doubtful. "So Hugo came to an—an arrangement with Nancy; and he told her she'd never get another penny if she told anyone the truth. I never thought how it would look if anyone found out. But the dreadful thing is, once you've let a lie like that happen, you almost forget it is a lie.''

"When did you remember?"

"Not until . . . not really until Granny was dead. Even when Hugo had that row with her at Christmas I never knew what it was about; I never thought she might be blaming him. But afterward I guessed, when I heard she'd changed her will. So then I asked him.'' He broke off and looked at Maitland curiously. "How did you know?" he asked.

"I hadn't guessed it was you that called on Nancy last night. The other part wasn't really very difficult.''

"I see." Mark sounded uncertain. "But I *don't* see what Hugo's up to now. I mean, it was all very well before this happened . . . do you suppose he thinks I killed her?''

"He was already wondering whether you might not perhaps have poisoned your grandmother," Antony told him bluntly; and watched, without overt sympathy, while Mark struggled with a new idea.

"I suppose I've got to believe that," he said doubtfully after a moment. "But even so—"

"Don't ask me why he should feel himself responsible for you," said Maitland crossly. "It seems asinine to me, but perhaps it's the way he's made.''

"It isn't asinine at all," said Mark, flaring up immediately. He caught Antony's eye, and added with less assurance: "I suppose we have been in the habit of relying on him rather.''

"You and your sister. Don't you think it's about time you both realized you're responsible human beings, not children any longer?''

Mark's chin went up again; there was a gleam of resentment in his eye, but he answered steadily enough. "The thing is, how do I begin?''

Maitland's indignation collapsed on the instant. "I'm sorry, I shouldn't have said that.''

"I expect I deserved it.''

"No, because you've begun already . . . when you came here to wait for me this afternoon. But you'll have to tell Byron all this, after all; *and* the police.''

"I realize that, of course. But then . . . you'll help Hugo, won't you?''

The question brought Antony unpleasantly back to reality again. "There's no way I can help him," he said.

"You still think he's guilty!"

"I never thought that." It was true about Nancy's murder, at least. "The trouble is, I shall be a witness myself."

"That means you can't act for him?" He paused to think this out, and then added eagerly: "But you could find out what really happened. Everyone says—"

"If you've been listening to what everyone says in Chedcombe," said Maitland sourly, "you'll have got a totally distorted view."

"Not about you. I mean, now I've met you. You can't leave things like this, Mr. Maitland. Please."

"Will you answer one or two questions for me?" said Antony slowly.

"Anything. Of course."

"It doesn't matter really, but did you have anything to do with painting the town green?"

"I already . . . no, I didn't."

"Did you know Nancy was pregnant again?"

"Marian said she heard Mr. Byron say so to Nell. I didn't know if it was true."

"It was true. Were you responsible?"

"No, I wasn't."

"Is that the truth, Mark?" The boy looked back at him, frowning. "It's terribly important."

"I've told you I wasn't. You've got to believe me. I never wanted . . . afterward . . . I never wanted to see her again!"

"Did you kill her?"

"No." He was staring defiantly at Maitland, but then he turned away and went to the chair by the window and sat down with his hands between his knees. "Will they believe that?" he said. "It doesn't make any difference, but . . . will they?"

"I don't know." He spoke absently. "There's just one other thing, Mark. Were you there on New Year's Eve when your aunt said good night to Mrs. Randall?"

"Yes, I was." If he was surprised by the question, he didn't show it. "We were waiting for Marian to be ready."

"Something was said about Mr. Byron."

"She seemed to have a complete hate on him . . . Granny, I mean."

"Why do you say that?"

"Well, she said to Nell she was glad to know she was spending the evening in such—such unexceptionable company. That was Dr. Firmont and his wife, but she wasn't meaning a compliment to them, she was meaning to be nasty. Nell shouldn't have asked her why she said that, but she did, and Granny said: 'Lawyers! There's not one of them you can trust.' "

"Miss Randall thought—you weren't in court when she gave evidence; she thought your grandmother was still annoyed because Byron had tried to persuade her to cancel the new codicil to her will."

"Perhaps that was it, because when Nell protested Granny laughed and said: 'You be careful, my girl, and don't believe everything you're told.' She sounded angry."

"Yes, I see. Did your aunt ever mention a letter Mrs. Randall picked up at the Bank the day she came into Chedcombe to sign her will?"

"Well, yes, but . . . only afterwards." He hesitated, found Maitland's look encouraging, and went on. "It was just a plain foolscap envelope, and Granny opened it up right away and sat in the back of the car reading it before she went in to see Mr. Byron. Later, a bill came in for Granny, and Nell said: 'That must have been the people who wrote to her from Northdean.' Of course I didn't know what she meant, so then she told me. She said it was the same sort of envelope, only this time it was addressed to Ravenscroft."

"Mr. Byron would know the name of the firm then."

Mark looked at him for a moment; the statement seemed to make him uneasy. "I can tell you that," he said, "though I can't see why you should want to know. But Nell paid the account herself, for some reason, instead of passing it on to him with the rest."

"Well?"

"Beckhoff and Something. Nell could give you the full name, I expect."

"But what *are* they?"

"Professional services, that's all the account said."

A much overworked description nowadays. "Never mind

then. That's all," Antony said; and smiled to soften the abruptness of the statement.

"But what are we going to do?"

"You'll have to give me time." He got up with an abrupt movement and went to the window, and stood there looking out at the darkened square. Time . . . while for two young people freedom became only a memory . . . while the town that was their home became still more obsessed with malice . . . while the man he now suspected felt hourly more secure. "I don't see my way," he said.

"You mean about Fran, Mr. Maitland? I mean, Hugo'll be all right—won't he?—when I tell them—" He broke off as Antony turned to look down at him, and said again, "Won't he?" but this time in a frightened voice.

"You'll have to face it, Mark. I don't think they'll believe you."

"They'll think I killed Nancy. I realize that."

"That isn't what I meant." He hesitated, but it had to be said, after all. "They'll think you're trying to shield your brother, that the whole thing's an invention from beginning to end, that you never went near Nancy at all."

There was a silence. "You believe me, don't you?" Mark asked diffidently, after a while.

"Yes." The silence spread about them again. "I'm sorry," said Antony, "but you had to know."

"I must tell them just the same. The police?"

Maitland nodded. "It's only that I didn't want you to expect—"

"I won't expect anything. Should I see Mr. Byron first?"

"That would be the correct way to set about it." He added thoughtfully, almost to himself: "He's got to know." Mark got up in a purposeful way.

"I'll go and find him, then."

"Will you do something for me, Mark? Don't tell anyone you've talked to me about this."

"If you say not. But I'm *counting* on you, Mr. Maitland."

Antony stood staring at the door for a long time after it had closed behind Mark Randall. The thought was running foolishly through his mind that there was something wantonly cruel in the way things were falling out. He didn't want to give up, the action was being forced upon him. And if he tried to meddle after tomorrow . . .

When at last he moved it was to go across to the telephone; and by the time he had finished a rather one-sided conversation with Mr. Justice Halford he was in no doubt at all of what his lordship expected. But, then, he had known that already.

VII

With the Assize so nearly over there had been few members of the Bar Mess who stayed in Chedcombe after Thursday night, and the weekend had disbanded them completely. On the whole, this was a good thing, Antony thought. He dined in his room, had a long talk with Jenny, and a shorter one with Mark Randall, who told him gloomily: "They were so polite, I'm sure they didn't believe me." He then added: "I asked Nell about that account, but she said she couldn't remember it at all." That sent Antony to the phone book after he had rung off, but though he found a listing *Beckhoff & Manning,* with a Northdean address, there was no information concerning their activities. Nell might have forgotten the incident because she wanted to, or—more likely—because it was unimportant. It was just one other thing the defense should look into before the new trial, no concern of his any longer. After that he went to sleep rather early over a historical novel which he had bought on the strength of excellent reviews, but which proved on closer acquaintance to be of the "by my halidom" variety.

He was dreaming, uneasily, of spiders when he was aroused by the clamor of a fire bell and staggered across to the window, still only half awake, in time to see the engine disappearing into North Street. It was a while before it occurred to him that there were rather a lot of people about, some of them even running in the same direction. And then he realized that there was another sound to be heard, a roaring sound like the sea rushing into a narrow inlet; and that was a stupid thought, because Chedcombe must be at least forty miles from the coast.

A fire engine . . . people . . . the sound of many voices

. . . He gave it up and went back to pick up his watch from the bedside table. It was still only eleven-fifteen.

One thing was certain, he wouldn't get to sleep again in a hurry. He eyed the novel with disfavor, but at least it was better to be irritated by that than driven half frantic by his thoughts. And then the phone rang, and he picked it up and heard a thick, muffled voice that said urgently: "Miss Langhorne's house. She asked me to tell you—"

"What?" he asked. "What?" But the line was already dead.

He could ring back, of course, but he was seized with an illogical conviction that it would be a waste of time. He didn't take long dressing; slacks and pullover over his pajamas, and the pair of socks and walking shoes that he had thrust untidily under a chair. The main door of the hotel was open and the night clerk standing there looking in the direction the fire engine had taken. Maitland didn't stay to question him, but made off across the square.

The bell had stopped, presumably the firemen had reached their destination; but the roar of voices was very loud now, and quite unmistakable. Later he thought it strange that he had found no difficulty in crediting what had happened, for who would expect mob violence in a sleepy little town that prided itself on making its visitors welcome? Now he felt only that he should have anticipated this . . . "you and that woman" they'd said in the pub; and "there'll be trouble, I'm warning you," Sid had told him in his shrill voice. The police would be alert in the Market Square, where the previous incidents had taken place; so what better target than Vera Langhorne's cottage, in a quiet side street, with no one to interfere until the damage was done? She was one of their own, but she had called in an interloper and taken sides with him against the town.

Even in North Street people were milling and shouting; he began to push his way through, unremarkable where roughness was expected. Once a hand clutched his arm, a white face came close to his own, mouthing a question; even if he could have heard, but that was impossible in the uproar . . . he shook the man off and went on. He was conscious now of the acrid tang of burning, though nothing was yet to be seen of the blaze.

By the time he turned into the Causeway it was almost impossible to move at all, the narrow road was jammed with people. The flames were clearly visible now, though he couldn't see from which house they came. There must be some police about, to have made a way for the fire engine so quickly, but now the mob had closed in again. He used shoulder and elbow ruthlessly, but still it was slow going. The hoses weren't in play yet; he could hear the crackle of the fire, loud above the hostile voices.

And then he was near enough to see over the heads of the crowd. Firemen were working frantically to get the hoses coupled, but they were hampered in the confined space. It was Miss Langhorne's house all right, and No. 7 was burning too: a man and a girl stood looking up at it, and then at a word from a uniformed constable they turned away slowly and merged into the crowd; the policeman moved on to speak to Vera Langhorne, who wore her sack-like costume and looked no more disheveled than usual, with ner mammoth handbag clasped in her arms as though it was an animal that might escape again and run back into the burning building. As she in turn moved aside the crowd swayed forward, he could see that they were shouting; and it was like a nightmare, he couldn't move, he couldn't get any nearer. It never occurred to him that the constable was a better guarantee of her safety than he himself could be.

And then he found that he was moving again; not straight forward now, but toward the side of the street, toward the row of houses. Someone grabbed his right shoulder, but he hardly noticed the pain which in the ordinary way would have sickened him. He reached the narrow pavement and began to edge his way along. Past No. 3, there was an archway here, a narrow passage leading between the houses, the one place where the crowd, so far, had not congregated. As he passed the mouth of the arch he heard, and disregarded, a movement in the shadows; when the blow caught him he was completely unsuspecting, and went down into unconsciousness with only the briefest awareness of surprise and pain.

Monday, 3rd February

A VOICE said clearly in the darkness: "It's all a mistake really; I assure you, it's all a mistake." He wished the chap would shut up, for one thing there didn't seem to be any sense in what he was saying. For another, his head was aching intolerably, he needed a little peace . . . and quiet . . .

He pulled himself up on the verge of saying for the third time that there had been a mistake; and as he did so he remembered the noisy street, the crackle of the flames, the inhuman roar of the crowd. But here it was quiet, now that his own voice had stopped. Blissfully quiet. He opened his eyes and saw, rather mistily, Vera Langhorne's face hovering anxiously above him. "Now I know I'm in heaven," he said, and grinned at her.

Vera took this in her own way. "Feeling better," she assured him gruffly; but when he tried to sit up she pushed him back again. "Doctor left some muck for you," she said, and disappeared for a moment out of his line of vision. He recognized now the smaller of the two lounges at the George, but he hadn't the faintest idea how he had got there.

She saw his puzzled look as she came back to the sofa where he was lying. "Thought you wouldn't want a fuss," she told him. "Manager frantic, threw him out. And the others. Better drink this."

Antony obeyed her, there didn't seem to be anything else to do. Her hand behind his head was surprisingly gentle, but there was a look in her eye that reminded him irresistibly of a sergeant major he had once known and loved. The draught had obviously been concocted by someone who believed that nothing pleasant could be good for you. It had no noticeable effect on his headache, but when he had mastered his initial impulse to vomit he found his mind was clearer. "What happened?" he asked.

Miss Langhorne pulled up a chair and sat down with her hands on her knees. "Think someone hit you," she said.

"I know *that.*" Antony's hand went up to his head, and his eyes met hers rather anxiously as he felt the heavy bandage.

"Manager—fool of a man—wanted to send you to hospital. Doctor said no need," she reassured him. "Unless you think you'd be more comfortable. Bound to be bruised."

"Now you mention it," said Antony, "I am. But I meant, what happened to you?"

"Nothing to worry about."

"No, damn it all—" He sat up . . . an incautious move. When the room stopped spinning about him he looked at her reproachfully. "You'd better tell me," he said.

"Started with a gang of youths in the square, the constable tells me. There was an extra patrol on duty—all this painting business—and when they told the boys to move on they started kicking up a row. It was just after the pubs closed, so the noise attracted others, you see. They got to my place a little before eleven." It was the longest speech he had ever heard her make. Antony said in a worried way:

"I thought it was outside interference they disliked. I thought you'd be safe enough."

"Well, so I am."

"Yes, but the house—"

"Can't be helped. Sorrier for the youngsters next door, really, newly married, still care about *things*. My age, past all that," said Vera, at her most abrupt.

"How did it happen?"

"Stones through the windows, first. Finally, sort of a—a torch. Furniture old stuff, highly inflammable." She glanced at him sharply. "No loss," she said, daring him to sympathize.

He looked at her helplessly. "Can they stop it spreading?"

"Pretty well contained when I left. Police came quickly, got the fire engine through, held the crowd back as well as they could."

"Well, that's something to be thankful for." He wasn't

thinking as he spoke of her unknown neighbors, whose possessions were now presumably safe, but of the surge and sway of the crowd as he had seen it just before he was hit, the impression of uncontrolled menace. Perhaps Vera understood this, for she said more gruffly than ever:

"They kept me safe enough." And then, as he opened his mouth to reply: "Sorry you were hurt."

The hint that a change of subject would be welcome was broad enough to have convinced the most insensitive of men. Antony shifted his position a little and said obligingly: "A herd of elephants stampeding couldn't have done a better job."

"Lucky for you someone recognized you and raised a shout; took the crowd's attention. Police forced their way through just as they'd started to use their feet."

"Er—did you say lucky?"

"Might have been trampled to death, if no one had known you were there."

"I'm not at all sure yet that I haven't been," said Antony; and was glad to see that this time she returned his smile, though rather austerely.

"Nothing I could do there," she said. "More of a nuisance really. Got them to bring us both here. Chap in the crowd said you'd been hit by falling masonry; all nonsense, there wasn't any where you were."

"Did you ask someone to phone me?" She stared at him, and shook her head. "I thought not, but that's how I got on the scene."

"Someone taking advantage of the disturbance?"

"That's right. Well, it doesn't matter, after all. The police can sort it out, and tomorrow"— he paused— "tomorrow I throw in my hand."

She ignored the bitterness in his voice. "Well enough to go into court?"

"If Halford will hear me without my wig." He got up stiffly as he spoke; the pain in his head had subsided into a dull throbbing, but the dizziness had passed. As a consequence, of course, he was now more painfully conscious of his shoulder. "Have they fixed you up with a room?" he asked.

"Yes, all arranged." She went over to the table and

tucked her handbag under her arm. "Get what I need tomorrow," she told him; and opened the door and stood waiting until he got himself across the room to join her.

II

It took him all his time to get to the Shire Hall the following morning to see Fran Gifford before the court convened. There had been the police to see, and the doctor, and in the end he left both with ruffled feelings. But it wasn't surprising that he hadn't much time for their troubles, he was too preoccupied with his own, so that he was barely conscious of the difficulties of dressing, the ache in his arm and shoulder, the soreness of his head. Going out into the Market Square he noticed vaguely that there were more people than usual about, but he wasn't surprised that his appearance occasioned a few sidelong looks and didn't connect either with the reopening of the trial until he saw the crowd of would-be spectators milling around the side entrance where the public were admitted. It occurred to him then that there were also an unusual number of uniformed police in sight.

Miss Langhorne had reached the Shire Hall before him, and had already given Tommy Davenant an account of the night's events. Probably a sketchy one, thought Maitland as he came up to them and noted the rather dazed look in the solicitor's eye; but at least it meant that they could go to the interview room with the minimum of delay. Vera was ready for court; it was lucky she'd left her things in the robing room over the weekend. Antony had his gown over his arm, and Davenant insisted on helping him into it . . . an attention for which he should have been grateful, and wasn't.

The room was as cold and unfriendly as it had been on Thursday evening, and Fran came in with her usual composure, but it didn't take a second look to detect a new urgency in her manner. She greeted each one of them punctiliously before she turned to Davenant and demanded: "What's happened to Hugo?"

Tommy said weakly, "Oh, you've heard about that, have you?" and looked beseechingly from one of his colleagues to the other. Obviously he did not relish the task of explanation. Maitland said:

"He's under arrest for the murder of Nancy Selkirk," and then stepped forward and grabbed her arm and thrust her into the nearest chair. He said disjointedly: "I'm sorry, but if you've heard rumors . . . it's best to know." She looked up at him blankly, and in silence, and after a moment he added roughly: "Don't look like that. He didn't do it."

Davenant was making some sort of protest, but he hadn't attention for anything but the girl. The brown eyes were becoming aware again. She said, not much above a whisper: "Is that true?"

"It's what I believe."

"But . . . but—"

"Don't say anything now. Just listen. I've two things to tell you. The first is that I shall be making application this morning for a retrial . . . somewhere else, away from local prejudice. There are advantages and disadvantages to this, but Mr. Davenant will explain to you that we've thought it over very carefully. The second thing is that I may not be able to act for you when the case is reheard . . . he'll explain about that, too. So I want to tell you, don't try to hide anything; Hugo has told me why he quarreled with his grandmother, and that you told him about the new codicil the day before she was murdered. It may not help to tell the truth, but it will confuse matters terribly if you don't."

For a moment he wondered if she had heard him, then she said: "She was so bitter, so terribly bitter. I'm sorry I lied to you, but I couldn't have told you *that*. And I knew you'd think that Hugo . . . but now, with Nancy dead—"

"If you ever had any faith in him, Fran, hold on to it now."

"I'll do that, if you say I should. About . . . about the murders—"

"That isn't what I meant."

"No, but . . . do you think they don't matter, all the other things that have happened?" She paused, and then said carefully: "I might not mind, but it means, you see, that he doesn't care at all." She looked up and met Maitland's eye, and thought for an instant that he looked as if he hated her.

"If it helps at all," he said angrily, "you're wrong about that."

Fran shook her head disbelievingly. "She said he took after his father," she went on, in the same quiet voice. "And she said Nancy was pregnant again. She told me to see she was looked after; a matter of—of elementary justice, she said; and Ravenscroft was to be sold, she didn't want any Randalls there, when she'd gone."

"When did you see the draft codicil?"

"On the Monday morning, I was looking for the lease of the Vaughan property, it had to be engrossed." She glanced uncertainly at Davenant as she spoke, and he nodded reassuringly. Maitland said, with his intent look:

"Was there nothing in writing, no confirmation of the verbal instructions she gave you?"

"Nothing at all. Would it have helped?"

"Any confirmation—" Antony was vague again. "Well, I expect Miss Langhorne and Mr. Davenant will be talking to you after the court adjourns, but—"

"You meant what you said? You won't help me any more." She was staring down at her hands now, avoiding his eye, but when he did not reply at once she looked up at him and said in a surprised tone, "You've hurt your head," as though she had only just noticed the bandage.

"It's nothing. You'll be in very good hands, you know; you can rely on Miss Langhorne."

"Oh yes, I know that." He heard Vera clearing her throat in the background, a subtly admonitory sound. "It's just that I was hoping . . . I mean, you say I should trust Hugo, but do you trust him? And I've told you the truth now, really I have."

But they were interrupted there, to Maitland's relief. It was almost time for the prisoner to go into court. He thought he saw panic in her eyes as she gave him her hand for an instant and thanked him in her careful way; and when she had gone he stood staring after her for so long that Davenant, coming up behind him, asked urgently: "Are you feeling all right?"

"Perfectly."

"We ought to be getting into court ourselves."

"I'll be along in a minute. I want to look at my notes." After they had gone he pulled a handful of envelopes from his pocket and stared at them in a vague way, perhaps as some justification for the brief delay. The words he must use were written down there, but he knew them reluctantly by heart.

After a while he went out into the hall, and began to walk slowly across the flagged floor toward the courtroom. There was a uniformed attendant on duty, and a police constable near the main door, but apart from them the hall was deserted. He stopped and said on an impulse, "Do either of you happen to know a Northdean firm called Beckhoff and Manning? The phone book doesn't say what they do."

"Why, no, sir, it wouldn't." It was the constable who answered, turning his head from contemplation of the more animated scene beyond the open door. "Very reliable people, very discreet."

"Yes, but . . . what *are* they?"

"Private Inquiry Agents, sir, I think that's the term they use. Quite respectable. Why, even the Inspector—"

But Antony was no longer listening. The constable, happily launched on a tide of information, did not see his expression change: from indifference, to incredulity, to a blaze of excitement. What had Hugo said? *She started talking about the fact that I was responsible . . .* and Walter Randall, *we were at Ravenscroft on Sunday, as usual.* And when he himself had said to Vera that Byron's evidence was all according to proof she hadn't denied it. But always there had remained the puzzle of how Alice had known. "Bless you for those kind words," he said, interrupting, and swept into the court. The doorkeeper exchanged a significant look with the policeman, and sadly shook his head.

It was later than he had realized, but luckily Mr. Justice Halford had not yet put in an appearance. Glancing across the room he saw Walter Randall was seated among the spectators, his face heavy and expressionless. Frederick Byron, who must have been expecting to continue his evidence, was being directed to a seat at the side of the court. Maitland glanced inquiringly at Appleton, and received a nod in reply; well, it had been a foregone conclusion that the prosecution wouldn't object to an application that had the Judge's blessing. As far as Counsel for the Crown was concerned the hearing at Chedcombe was all over bar the shouting.

But Counsel for the Defense, concealing his excitement

well enough, was strolling across to have a word with the prisoner. The dock was raised only a little from the well of the court; he put his hand on the wide rail and wondered inconsequently how much longer it would be before the town council admitted that the woodworm had had the best of it and replaced the ancient timber. He said: "Fran, tell me quickly, did you tell Nancy Selkirk what Mrs. Randall meant you to do with the money?"

She leaned forward, frowning a little, trying to read what was in his mind. Something had changed him during the last few minutes, and though his voice had an urgency he looked at her in an almost impersonal way. "I didn't tell her," she said. "It all happened so quickly."

"Did you tell anyone? Anyone at all?"

"No," she said, and heard him catch his breath. For a moment he seemed almost afraid, she thought, and told herself that she was being fanciful. Then he looked at her and grinned.

"Hold your hat," he said. "There may be squalls." And was off to his own place.

Mr. Justice Halford was in a more complacent mood this morning. The unrest in the town had disturbed him, offending his sense of what was fitting; but that was all over now. Maitland had sounded subdued when he telephoned yesterday; whatever foolishness he had had in his head there was no doubt now he would make the desired application, and the case would be heard elsewhere. But Antony, on his feet and waiting to address him, had turned so that he could speak at once to Miss Langhorne and to Davenant, who was seated behind her. "Slight change of plan," he said. "Bear with me."

Vera said nothing, but gave him a look which seemed to indicate a dark suspicion of his motives. "We agreed—" said Tommy.

"Yes. Yes, I know. There isn't time—"

"What you think best," said Vera surprisingly. Davenant muttered something which Maitland chose to take as an agreement, but shook his head as though he still had some reservations. The Judge coughed, as he did each day when he had settled himself and his belongings to his own satisfaction. Antony turned to face him.

"There is something you wish to say, Mr. Maitland?" asked Halford, with an affectation of surprise.

"My lord, I must apologize—" The Judge cut him short at that; he'd heard all about the fracas the night before, and anyway it was manifestly impossible for Counsel to don his wig over the bandages.

"I quite appreciate your difficulty, Mr. Maitland," he said graciously.

"Thank you, my lord." He paused, and for a panic-stricken moment his mind was completely blank; afterward he thought that he must have been unnerved by so much judicial amiability.

"Yes, Mr. Maitland?" prompted Halford kindly.

"Your lordship is aware of the circumstances which have arisen—" This had all been written down and memorized, the words came smoothly. The Judge was nodding his approval. ". . . but there is one thing I must do before I reach the point of making this application. Your lordship may even agree that there is no need after all for a change of venue—"

"No need?" said Halford, not at all amiable now.

"I submit, my lord, that there is no case for my client to answer."

There was a moment of almost complete silence. The Judge's face reddened alarmingly; Appleton made a growling noise in his throat and bounced to his feet; Maitland—aware that he should be using the time to better advantage—glanced across the room. Here in the Shire Hall the witnesses who had already given evidence were accommodated on a bench near the wall, behind the press box. There was a full muster of reporters; he wondered briefly what sort of spread there'd be in the evening papers. If he succeeded in making his point . . . but he daren't stop to think about that now. Behind them he could see Nell Randall's profile, as she turned to say something to Frederick Byron. The solicitor shook his head without looking at her; he was staring straight across at counsel's table, a puzzled frown between his eyes. Beside him Mark seemed to have drawn himself as far into the corner as possible; he looked sullen and uninterested, as though what was going on was no concern of his.

There was no time for a further survey. Mr. Justice Halford cleared his throat again, directed an admonitory glance in Appleton's direction, and said in a displeased tone: "I must suppose you are serious in making this submission."

"Oh, yes, my lord."

The Judge inclined his head. "Then I will hear you, Mr. Maitland," he said grimly.

Up to that moment Antony hadn't stopped to think how he was to explain his ideas to anyone else. "I shall endeavor not to weary your lordship," he said, stalling; and bowed. He felt rather than heard that Appleton had subsided into his place again. Vera Langhorne was breathing heavily beside him. Perhaps it was just as well he couldn't see Tommy Davenant's expression.

"You have heard the case presented so ably by my learned friend for the prosecution, and I am sure you have the main facts in mind. Let me say at the outset that about many of these facts there is no dispute; it is the Crown's interpretation of them which is in question. I am going to tell you what really happened at Ravenscroft last New Year's Eve.

"But first I must go back a little. The deceased, Mrs. Alice Randall, wished to create a trust for a young lady, not a member of her family, and she wished to do this in a way that would give rise to as little comment as possible. In the event, things didn't turn out quite as she had expected; but she cannot have foreseen the manner of her own death.

"So, because she had confidence in her goddaughter, Frances Gifford—the girl who is now accused of poisoning her—she arranged to leave her a substantial sum of money. We are not concerned with Alice Randall's previous will, but only with her dispositions as they stood at the time of her death. She arranged to see Miss Gifford, to tell her of the legacy and give her instructions as to its disposal. The name of the girl who was to be benefited in this roundabout way was Nancy Selkirk."

The Judge's eyes were fixed watchfully on Counsel's face. He moved now, leaning forward as though he felt they might deceive him. "Mr. Maitland, I cannot permit you to bring before the court matters which have not been referred to in evidence."

"The point is susceptible of proof, my lord."

"That does not concern us," said Halford with finality.

"But your lordship will not forbid me to give my client's own account of events. And I am sure my friend will have no quarrel with my contention that the motive for Mrs. Randall's murder concerned this girl."

There was a little stir of interest in the silent room. Appleton was drumming his fingers on the table in front of him; his lips tightened a little as Maitland spoke, but he did not attempt to interrupt. Fran Gifford had made an abrupt gesture of protest at the first mention of Nancy's name; now she was staring at her Counsel with a kind of horrified fascination. Halford said brusquely: "You may refer to the prisoner's statement, Mr. Maitland. Otherwise you must confine yourself to the established facts."

"I am obliged to your lordship." The Judge may have suspected sarcasm, but Antony's gratitude was genuine enough. "From the prosecution we have learned something of the events which preceded Alice Randall's death. On Christmas Day she confiscated a quantity of digitoxin, a dangerous poison derived from the common foxglove, from her grandson, Mark Randall. She placed the test tube containing this substance in her workbox, which was kept in her own sitting room at Ravenscroft. On Friday, December 27th, she visited her solicitor, Mr. Frederick Byron, with instructions for the new codicil to her will; Mr. Byron, as you have been told, is the senior partner in the firm of Byron and Davenant, of this town. He has told us that he attempted to dissuade his client from her intended course of action, so far as it was proper for him to do so.

"On Monday, December 30th, the new codicil was already prepared, and was lying among other papers on Mr. Byron's desk. On the morning of that day Miss Gifford, who, as you know, was Mr. Davenant's clerk up to the time of her arrest, was looking for the draft of a lease which was ready for engrossment. She was glancing through a pile of documents, and looking more closely at any one which might have been what she needed; and so she came across the codicil, and saw her own name. Having no previous knowledge of Mrs. Randall's intentions, she was upset by what she saw; too upset to speak of the matter even to her

friend, Miss Elsie Barber, who was Mr. Byron's clerk. She
had had no expectation of being remembered in her godmother's will, except in a very small way." He was
improvising unashamedly, but Halford wasn't to know that.
And it didn't seem likely that Appleton would protest; there
seemed nothing here to help the defense.

"In the afternoon came Mrs. Randall, to sign the codicil.
We know several things about that visit: her intentions remained unaltered; she signed in the presence of Mr. Davenant and Miss Barber; before she left she spoke alone to
Miss Gifford in the main office, asking her to visit Ravenscroft the next evening.

"Now, remember that Miss Gifford already knew the
contents of the codicil; she guessed Mrs. Randall wished to
speak to her about this, and I think her curiosity, if nothing
else, would have prompted her to accept the invitation. But
she had another reason; like Mr. Byron, she wanted to ask
the old lady to change her mind."

"That may be true, my lord," said Appleton, on his feet
again. "We have no evidence of it."

Maitland was far too engrossed now to be put off his
stroke by the interruption. "My friend," he said, "has out-
lined a case which is purely circumstantial. I may surely be
permitted a similar latitude."

"I am not at all sure," said Halford, "that I see the force
of your argument." The reporters' pencils were racing; he
was uneasily aware of the interest that was being aroused.

"Your lordship has already indicated that I may refer to
Miss Gifford's statement."

Well, that was true enough. "You may continue for the
moment, Mr. Maitland; but I should advise you to be careful."

"Agag in person, my lord," said Counsel, and disconcerted the Judge by grinning at him. Then he paused, looking around deliberately, reclaiming the attention of the
court. "That brings us," he said, "to the day of the tragedy
itself."

"I suppose you would say we are progressing," said Halford sourly.

"Mrs. Randall was alone in her sitting room when Fran
Gifford came to Ravenscroft; after the housemaid, Sophie,

had left with her escort only the cook remained in the house, and she is deaf. Now, I think you will agree with me that, although my learned friend has described most graphically what happened that evening, he has not produced an eyewitness who saw Miss Gifford place the contents of the test tube into the hot toddy she prepared at her godmother's request. His case rests on motive, and his explanations are ingenious; but there is an alternative explanation. One which I think you will agree, when you have heard the facts, has an even greater plausibility.''

"The facts, Mr. Maitland?" said Halford, coming to life again and fixing him with a steely eye. "You are still speaking of the facts?"

"I meant of course—as your lordship is kind enough to point out—my interpretation of the facts," said Maitland. He was getting to the tricky part now, and he had a nasty feeling he was going to have to fight the Judge every inch of the way, not to mention the fact that it might dawn on Appleton at any moment that Fran's statement, as quoted, was not precisely as she had given it to the police. "As Miss Gifford expected, the old lady had asked her to Ravenscroft to tell her about the legacy, and to give her instructions as to what was to be done with the money." He hesitated, and looked across at Fran Gifford and smiled at her. "In effect, her inheritance was to be held in trust for Miss Nancy Selkirk—"

"Why?" said the Judge.

"My lord, this is a matter not entirely covered by my client's statement," said Counsel apologetically.

"Nevertheless, Mr. Maitland—"

"Miss Selkirk was the mother of an illegitimate child, my lord. This child was Mrs. Randall's great-grandson." He managed to sound as if this was the last thing he had wanted to say. There was a pause while Halford worked that out. "Was?" he asked. "Miss Selkirk is dead, my lord." Appleton coughed, and Counsel for the Defense turned to look down at him. "The fact does not form part of my client's statement," he admitted, "nor could it have been given in evidence. Nancy Selkirk was murdered—strangled—on Saturday evening last.''

Oddly, Halford issued no reproof; perhaps he felt

justified in recognizing a fact as well known to all present as the date of Christmas. He said slowly: "This statement you made about the child . . . surely, if it is true, the deceased lady would have told your client."

"She did, my lord, but she was herself misinformed. She told Miss Gifford that the father was Hugo Randall—"

"If I have understood the evidence, this Hugo Randall is her grandson."

"One of her grandsons, my lord."

"All this is very irregular, Mr. Maitland," said Halford plaintively. "Is it in any way relevant to your submission?"

"In two ways, my lord. It explains Miss Gifford's distress that evening . . . a matter which my friend has asked the jury to believe is indicative of her guilt. And it brings me to the motive for Mrs. Randall's murder."

"Does it?" said the Judge weakly.

"The prosecution has rightly laid great stress on the question of motive. I want to show you that there was a man who had more reason than my client to wish Alice Randall dead."

"What man?" asked Halford. His tone was pettish.

"If your lordship will assume for a moment the truth of my statement—"

"I will assume anything, Mr. Maitland, anything at all, if only you will come to the point."

"But, my lord—" said Appleton.

"A hypothesis only. You understand that this is to be taken as a hypothesis only, Mr. Maitland?"

"I am obliged to your lordship." (Why had he started this? He wasn't getting anywhere, he wasn't going to get anywhere.) "Let me tell you a few things about this man . . . this hypothetical murderer. He is acquainted with Alice Randall; well acquainted, we must assume, since he wishes her dead."

"If he exists, Mr. Maitland . . . if he exists." Halford sounded cross.

"As your lordship pleases. So far as it goes, I have no fault to find with the prosecution's account of the events of New Year's Eve. Miss Gifford went to Ravenscroft and spent about an hour with Mrs. Randall. She was told of the digitoxin; it sounds, indeed, as if the old lady was so indignant that she showed the test tube and made her complaint to everyone she saw. Before Miss Gifford left, she plugged in the electric kettle and mixed the toddy; then she waited until the kettle boiled and left in a hurry to catch her bus. Alice Randall didn't go upstairs immediately, she stayed by the fire in her sitting room, waiting for the toddy to be cool enough to drink. And while she sat there another visitor arrived.''

"My learned friend has a lively imagination," said Counsel for the Prosecution suddenly. Maitland bowed, accepting as a compliment a remark that had obviously a very different intent.

"You may think it was an odd time for a visit, that the visitor must have had a very good reason for coming to Ravenscroft at that hour. But he knew, you see—or thought he knew—that on that particular evening Alice Randall would be alone.''

"There was no evidence that anyone else had been there that night," Appleton protested.

"I doubt if he advertised his presence. The cook was deaf, and if he tapped on the window—''

"I thought I had made it clear, Mr. Maitland, that the court is interested only in facts.''

"Well, that's what *I*'d have done, my lord," said Counsel, suddenly abandoning formality. "My learned friend's statement," he added, recovering himself, "concerned matters which can only be regarded as conjectural." He heard Davenant mutter something behind him, and Vera Langhorne moved uneasily and her breathing became more labored.

"In that case—'' said Halford. He did not look quite happy with the explanation.

"This man knew Nancy Selkirk, and kept his knowledge secret. A man, then, of some local reputation . . . but we all know how easily a reputation can be lost in Chedcombe. We also know that Nancy was pregnant again. Mrs. Randall had visited her, and suspected her condition. She made it her business to discover who the father was. I suppose she felt it her duty.''

"Oh, dear!" said the Judge, looking anxious.

"At that time the girl was hardly a problem to him—a

lighthearted child, happy enough with what he gave her. But he knew the old lady too well to think she would keep silent, and in his desperation he could see one way only . . . murder. He was ready for this, no doubt he came prepared. Certainly he came in secret."

"Mr. Maitland, are you trying to tell us that Mrs. Randall was blackmailing this person?" said Halford, a little querulously.

"Nothing of the kind, my lord. I think she was willing to hear his explanation before making her knowledge public; but when she came to do so she would have been motivated purely by a sense of her obligations to society. From the first I have felt that if I could understand her character . . . and in a way it is true that she was responsible for her own death. There is a poem of Chesterton's—"

"Spare us the poetry," muttered Appleton, under his breath. Maitland ignored him; perhaps he did not hear.

"This poem expresses very well what I mean. Chesterton described a lady, in all other respects the antithesis of Mrs. Randall, and said, in effect, that everything might be forgiven her . . . everything except her righteousness."

"Her righteousness, Mr. Maitland?"

" 'But for the virtuous things you do . . . it shall not be forgiven you,' " said Counsel, suddenly apologetic.

"Oh," said Halford. And then, rallying: "Are you presenting this as another fact, Mr. Maitland?"

"If I may return to Ravenscroft, my lord, I think Mrs. Randall's visitor found that what he had feared was true: she knew of his association with Nancy Selkirk . . . and he had no good explanation to offer. And so she told him— virtuously—that it was not a matter she felt justified in keeping to herself. The digitoxin was still on the tray, and he took an opportunity of adding it to her drink."

"You are assuming, then, that he knew it would be ready to hand?"

"I think, at least, that he knew when he saw it what the test tube contained. He might well think it a better method than the one he had intended. Or perhaps I am wronging him and there was no premeditation, it was the sight of it that gave him the idea. But, however it may have been, he watched her drink her toddy, and now he knew he was safe, he knew she had taken the poison.''

''We seem to have strayed a long way from the facts, Mr. Maitland. How can you know this?''

''Because, my lord, of the statement Frederick Byron made concerning Mrs. Randall's visit to his office the day she signed the codicil.'' The court was very quiet now. ''I have here the copy which accompanied my brief; may I ask my friend to refer at the same time to the one in his possession?''

''If it is here,'' said Appleton, but his eyes were on Maitland's face. Finding the document with commendable speed, his junior put it silently into his hand, and he looked down at it obediently without voicing any further protest.

''There can be no objection to my quoting,'' said Maitland hopefully, but it was noticeable that he proceeded rather hastily with his reading. '' 'My partner, Mr. Davenant, and my clerk, Miss Barber, attended to witness her signature. In their presence I again endeavored to question her intentions—apart from my own feelings there could later have been raised the question of her competence—but she repeated that her decision was irrevocable. After the codicil was signed Miss Barber left my office, and Mr. Davenant left a few minutes later.' ''

''Just a moment.'' Counsel for the Prosecution looked up sharply. ''There's quite a lot more to come before that.''

''Then may I ask you to let us hear it?''

Halford's expression gave no clue to his thoughts, but at least he made no objection. Appleton read slowly: '' 'Mr. Davenant was about to leave when Mrs. Randall called him back. She then said that, on reflection, she would like to amplify her remarks about the bequest. In effect, it was a Trust; it was also the first step in putting right a wrong that had been done; a wrong that had led in its turn, as these things will, to further evil. And then she added that we both knew her well enough to realize she would always do her duty, whoever was involved. She said it as though challenging us to disagree with her. I have no idea what she meant.' ''

''As though challenging us,'' Maitland repeated. ''Don't you think it was a little odd, my lord, that so much of the statement was missing when it came to my learned junior's attention, and to mine?''

"But, Mr. Maitland—"

"Only one person could have had a motive for suppressing that information. It could have no relevance to the prosecution, who have presented so ably a case in which, I am sure, they had complete belief. To the defense it would have formed, at least, a cause for conjecture, a basis for cross-examination. It might well have led me earlier to the motive for the crime." He paused and looked round the court, and then raised his voice a little.

"Only one person had a motive for suppressing Mr. Byron's evidence," he said again slowly. "Only one person *could* have done so, so far as my colleague and I are concerned. I am speaking, of course, of the man on whose instructions the brief was prepared."

He heard Tommy Davenant's movement behind him, and was already turning when he felt the grip on his shoulder, twisting him round. "Damn you!" said Tommy unoriginally. "Damn you to hell!"

Oddly, there was still a hush in the room, the scene was being played in silence. Halford looked rather wildly from Counsel for the Defense to his instructing solicitor, and then at Appleton in a helpless way. Maitland said in a curiously flat tone: "In case you think I'm taking advantage of our position here, Davenant, I am quite willing to repeat my statement in another place, before any witness you like. I think you killed Alice Randall—"

"Just try and prove it!"

"Thank you, I shall." He shrugged away the restraining hand and turned to face the court again. He was so pale now that Halford suffered a moment's incongruous anxiety on his behalf. "In the meantime, my lord, if you will not consider my application as it stands, that the case be dismissed, I must put to you our request for a retrial with a change of venue. I must also ask the court to take the rather unusual step of making an order concerning alternative legal representation—"

At that point it became obvious that no one—least of all the Judge—was listening to what he had to say. After a brief hesitation he sat down and rested his head on his hand. He did not look again at Tommy Davenant.

III

Looking back afterward at leisure, the session that followed in the Judge's chambers had an unreal, not to say nightmarish, quality. There was no question now that his explanations would be heard, they were being demanded. Halford himself, more worried than ever, but more decisive too; Appleton, no longer openly skeptical, anxious to find the truth; Vera Langhorne . . . he couldn't tell what Vera was thinking; and Davenant, ready—but not too ready—with his answer. "A clerical error, I had no idea—" But Antony was to remember later the look on his face as he spoke.

When the solicitor had left them, Halford said soberly: "You realize this is a serious matter, Mr. Maitland."

"Only too well." He sounded tired now. "But as things are, how else could I have dealt with it?"

Beside him, Vera Langhorne came unexpectedly to life. "Only way. Instructing solicitor . . . no precedent," she said in a militant tone.

"Er—quite so, madam," said Halford unhappily.

"I could have gone to the police, I suppose, and they'd have found evidence of his motive—at least, I think they would—but that's not everything. I hoped if I could take him by surprise—"

"Slander," said Appleton succinctly.

"It may come to that," Antony agreed, without enthusiasm. "It may be the only way of dealing with the matter." And again Vera interrupted him:

"Couldn't risk his continuing to act for Fran Gifford, quite see that. Felt myself he was dragging his feet." She looked at Halford, noting his indecision. "Why I asked Maitland's help."

"You suspected Davenant—?"

"No. No, just thought he wasn't trying. Because he didn't believe the girl, you see. Didn't think I could handle it on my own."

"But if the accusation is false—" Halford began, and broke off when he met Maitland's eye. It was only too obvious that the consequences had been weighed and accepted before ever counsel began to speak. "You have done no more than indicate a motive," he said.

"I was hampered by your lordship's ruling. If I may now speak more freely—"

The Judge glanced at Appleton, irresolute again. Appleton said nothing, his eyes were on Maitland's face. "Very well," said Halford. "Very well."

"The two deaths must be considered together . . . Mrs. Randall's and Nancy Selkirk's." He looked at Appleton in his turn. "I believe the police would agree to that now."

"They put rather a different construction on the fact," said Appleton dryly; but his tone was not unfriendly.

"Yes, I guessed that. I'll have to start with a completely illogical statement: when I first talked to Fran Gifford I became convinced of her innocence. For a while I was pretty sure Hugo Randall was the guilty party, though even then I didn't think Fran would thank me for proving it. When Nancy Selkirk spoke to me outside the court on Friday evening, and Miss Langhorne told me something of her history, it seemed fairly clear why Hugo had quarreled with his grandmother. But there was one big question: who had told Mrs. Randall of his supposed liaison with Nancy?"

"Well, who?"

"I'm coming to that, Judge. The second time I saw him he took the wind out of my sails by offering to tell the whole story at the trial, if it would help matters; I didn't think it would do any good, but I was beginning to feel he was sincere. I was wondering about Walter Randall at that stage, of course, because of the financial motive; only it seemed such a coincidence, if he was going to poison his mother, that he should decide to do it just then. But that objection applied to almost anyone, except Fran and Hugo.

"So I was casting around for a way out of the difficulty, and after a while I began to wonder if the quarrel between Hugo and Alice Randall might not have been deliberately engineered with the idea of getting him blamed for her death when it occurred. The fact that she disinherited him might or might not have been foreseen; if she did, Walter and Nell would have been the obvious persons to benefit. Walter, with some knowledge of Hugo's financial affairs, was more likely to have been the mischiefmaker; but two other people who were closely connected with the family had to be considered too . . . Frederick Byron and Tommy Davenant both wanted to marry Nell.''

''And that's why you went alone to see Nancy Selkirk,'' said Vera; and glanced triumphantly at the Judge.

''Yes, that's why. And when I did all my ideas were turned upside down again. I only saw the kitchen, but it seemed as if there was more money going into the house than Hugo Randall could provide; Nancy told me she liked older men, and it was obvious she was expecting a visitor . . . someone with whom she was on familiar terms. And now I began to see that perhaps I could explain the coincidence that was bothering me. Hugo wasn't Nancy's only lover; if the other man was known to Alice Randall, and she had found out in some way . . . well, I went into that in court.''

''You didn't tell us—''

''She consulted what I am assured is a most reliable firm of private detectives.''

''That still sounds like guessing.''

''Yes, but if I'm right it must be susceptible of proof. Alice went to see Nancy on Christmas Eve, and on Christmas Day she made two very significant remarks to Hugo Randall. She asked him if his relationship with Nancy continued, and when he denied it she spoke about his responsibility for setting the girl on the downward path.''

''So then you think she consulted this firm—''

''Beckhoff and Manning. Yes, I do, and I think she expected them to confirm her own opinion that Hugo was lying, that the second child was his, too. It was probably for this reason that she arranged for their report to be delivered to her at her Bank; she received it and read it on the 30th December, just before her appointment with Byron.''

''You're saying they named Davenant?''

''No, I shouldn't think so. There couldn't have been time for a positive identification. If they'd found evidence from some hotel, for instance . . . 'Mr. Smith' might be anybody. But a description, say, and in particular the make of his car . . . there could easily have been enough in the report to make her suspect the truth.''

"And, as you say, if it is the truth the proof will be there to find."

"I think you're right in this, at least," said Appleton unexpectedly, "those rather cryptic remarks of hers in Byron's office would have been quite enough to worry a guilty man."

"Yes, but I wonder now if they really would have put ideas into my head if I'd read the complete statement at the proper time. Davenant wouldn't know where Mrs. Randall had got her information, of course, but once she was on to him there'd have been confirmation enough. I expect he still hoped he was mistaken when he went to Ravenscroft, but I don't imagine she left him in doubt for long."

"But when we digressed," said Appleton thoughtfully, "you'd only got as far as surmising there was someone else."

"Yes, but then Nancy said something that sounded as if she had known beforehand that I should be offered the brief; and a moment later she was displaying a rather unusual knowledge of the legal position concerning Alice Randall's will. That didn't sound as if her friend was Walter, it sounded like one of the lawyers. But the really interesting thing was that she obviously knew what Mrs. Randall had intended in leaving Fran her money. She said Mrs. Randall had told her, and invented a second visit to throw me off the track, but she wasn't a good liar; and later Inspector Camden confirmed that what she had said about a second visit from the old lady couldn't have been true.

"When I heard Nancy was dead I realized I ought to have expected it, the sequence of events was plain enough. She spoke to me on Friday evening, on the steps of the courthouse; that same evening there was an attempt on my life. It seemed rather drastic. Chedcombe hadn't worked up to violence at that stage. Well, I wasn't harmed, but you, Judge, insisted on police protection; if someone wanted to prevent Nancy's talking to me, it was she who was vulnerable, not I. But I didn't think of that at the time."

"It is difficult to see how you could have done so," said Halford seriously. "I'm puzzled, though. At that stage, why did you suspect Davenant rather than his partner?"

"Well, when I began to think about them both I realized

that my instructing solicitor, even while he protested that he wanted to do his best for Fran Gifford, was losing no opportunity of ramming her guilt down my throat. Not just the strength of the case against her, which it was his duty to show me; he wanted to convince me—"

"I see."

"Besides, I got the impression that Davenant might be more sensitive to public opinion than his partner, even though Byron was an older man." He paused, and added apologetically: "That's a bit vague, but the question of Byron's statement really clinched it. He's an extremely conscientious chap, and he wouldn't have mentioned it at all if he hadn't thought I already knew its contents. But I realized then there was something more than I knew about, he was so clearly surprised at my ignorance. And if a mistake *had* been made in preparing the brief, Davenant must have realized it in the course of our discussions. He'd had plenty of opportunity to put me right."

"Perhaps if you were to give us the sequence of events again, as you see it. Very briefly, Mr. Maitland."

Antony hesitated. He thought it must be imagination that there was more sympathy in the Judge's tone. Or perhaps, if it was there, it was merely regret at his wrongheadedness. "Well, then," he said, "I think Davenant told Mrs. Randall of Hugo's supposed association with Nancy—"

"Wait a bit," said Appleton suddenly. "Wasn't Hugo her lover?"

"No, that was Mark. He came to see me last night."

"Everyone's confidant!" But Appleton's tone was now more amused than sarcastic.

"He told me about it," Antony admitted. "Hugo wanted the affair hushed up, but I don't suppose he'd any intention of taking the blame himself. But when Alice took it for granted—Mark was so young, she never thought of him—he didn't want to give his brother away."

"This is all very confusing," said Halford, with a slight return of his querulous manner.

"I'm sorry about that. My point is that Davenant was now Nancy Selkirk's lover, and she told him about the payments Hugo made to her, but not the whole truth. He told Mrs. Randall; I was wrong when I thought the idea might have been to frame Hugo, but it wasn't completely purpose-less meddling. If the old lady changed her will, Nell ought to benefit somehow. Or he may have thought, if the quarrel was serious enough, it would result in the three young Randalls leaving Ravenscroft; in which case surely Nell wouldn't see any further impediment to their marriage.''

"I see," said the Judge, mystified.

"So Mrs. Randall went to see Nancy, who took a rather malicious delight in putting the blame on Hugo; after all, he'd threatened to cut off supplies if she told anyone Mark was the father. As a consequence, Alice told Hugo to marry the girl, Hugo said no (but didn't tell her the true state of affairs); so she changed her will, and went to Byron's office on December 30th to sign the new codicil. Byron said she spoke to 'us' afterwards; that could only have meant himself and his partner. If that was true, one of them could have passed the information on to Nancy. And I've already explained why I guessed it had been Davenant.''

"And what then, Mr. Maitland?"

"Alice was horrified at what she suspected and went away to think about it. She knew all about Davenant and Nell, remember. But he was already on his guard, and he went to Ravenscroft on New Year's Eve because he knew Nell was dining with the doctor, and the rest of the family would be at the dance. I don't think there's anything to add to the account I gave in court of the night of the murder. It's pretty obvious, isn't it, that if anybody offended against Alice's principles they'd be in for it. Hugo said himself: 'She never gave anyone a second chance.' Chedcombe society is censorious, Davenant had a position to keep up; and he meant to marry Nell.''

"I will grant you all this," said Halford judiciously, "as far as motive is concerned. But you haven't proved he was there.''

"I've been told there hasn't been a murder in Chedcombe for a long time. If he killed Nancy Selkirk, as I believe he did—''

"Very well, I take your point. You don't feel you can accept two quite independent murderers.''

"No, Judge, I can't. There's just one other thing. Most likely it was Davenant who got me out of the hotel last night by phoning me when the uproar started. In the crowd he couldn't have been sure an opportunity would present itself of taking a crack at me, but I expect he thought it was worth taking a chance."

"But the girl was dead, and could no longer give him away."

"I'm afraid I'd done my best to make his flesh creep when I saw him yesterday. I hoped he might see the red light and decide it was too dangerous to act for Fran any longer, and that would have been something gained."

"You've no proof of that, however."

"None at all. There's only one other small point: Davenant's wife died of cancer. It's possible he had morphine in his possession all this time, that he intended to use that to poison Alice Randall—" He left the sentence unfinished, and turned to look at Vera Langhorne with a question in his eyes. Halford had given instructions that no one should leave the Shire Hall, but he hadn't said that any particular precautions should be taken.

Before he could say anything else the Judge got up purposefully. "I can see only one way of dealing with the matter. I will dismiss the jury and order the transfer of the trial on your application, Mr Maitland," he said formally. "After that, the whole matter will be referred to the Director of Public Prosecutions."

Antony came to his feet. He hadn't, for the moment, the faintest idea whether he'd succeeded in convincing Halford or not. But there wasn't anything else he could do, and Vera, he thought with a touch of bitterness, would tell him he'd done his best. Then the Judge turned in the doorway and looked back at them, and for the first time his expression lightened.

"If the proof you mention is forthcoming, I don't think he'll have much difficulty making up his mind," he said. "And, strictly between ourselves, I found our friend's reaction a trifle excessive."

"Thank goodness for that, anyway!" said Maitland, in a tone of heartfelt relief. Some of the severity returned to Halford's face.

"I should not be commenting on a matter which may be

said to be *sub judice,*" he remarked. "But I, of course, shall not be trying the case."

Antony caught Appleton's eye, and exchanged a weary grin with him. "That would be most improper," he agreed.

But Counsel for the Prosecution, suddenly reverting to type, thought that the less his learned friend had to say about impropriety the better.

IV

The Director of Public Prosecutions was not, after all, put to any great trouble in the matter. Tommy Davenant was found dead ten minutes later in the cold little room that was used for interviews at the Shire Hall. His diary was in his hand and in it he had written:

Why face it? The last few days have
been hell. And once they start looking,
there'll be evidence.

I killed them both.

The doctors said he had died of morphine poisoning.

EPILOGUE

IT WAS the beginning of the Easter recess when Vera Lang-horne took herself to London on a shopping trip and made Jenny Maitland's acquaintance for the first time. "It seems a shame," said Jenny, "that you should have lost your home."

"Might be worse. Rebuilding," said Vera, but she smiled at her hostess. People nearly always did smile at Jenny.

"But all your furniture. Antony told me—"

"Insured. Tell you the truth," she added, in a burst of confidence, "not too sorry about that. One or two things I always wanted, couldn't afford."

Jenny waited hopefully for her to continue. Antony asked bluntly: "What, for instance?"

But Vera had the last word. "Always thought I'd like a chaise longue," she told him, silencing him completely.

Later, when they had finished tea, and it was nearly time for her to leave and catch her train, she asked in her abrupt way: "Coming to Chedcombe next week for the wedding?"

Jenny said: "Yes, we are. Shall we see you there?"

"You will."

"I'm glad, of course, but I don't see how they sorted that one out," said Antony.

"Why not?"

"Hugo Randall's not . . . not exactly a reasonable sort of chap. I told him myself not to be a fool; the old lady acted under a misapprehension when she cut him out—"

"Wrong way round. Gave him the girl's point of view. Saw he'd been selfish," said Vera. Antony gaped at her.

"You mean, you persuaded him—?"

"Not quite so easy. Saw my point in the end." She was looking round for her bulging handbag as she spoke. "No use two people being unhappy. Besides, there are the twins to consider. And the baby."

"For heaven's sake, not another baby!"

"Jimmy Selkirk. Both wanted to adopt him. Neither can, while they're single."

"I suppose not," said Antony faintly.

"As for Nell—" Now that it was time for her to leave, Vera seemed to be wound up at last to imparting her news.

"What about her? I always wondered how she felt . . . about Davenant, you know."

"Kindhearted creature," said Vera, as she had done once before. "But not—not passionate." She paused, apparently considering the word doubtfully. "Marry Byron, I shouldn't wonder, now she doesn't have to make up her mind between them."

"And they'll stay at Ravenscroft . . . Fran and Hugo, I mean?"

"Why not? Too happy to mind the gossip. Soon forgotten," said Vera, in her wisdom.

Thinking it over later, Antony decided she was most probably right.